THE
MASTER'S
INN

THE
MASTER'S
INN

Deb Gorman

Edited by Dori Harrell, Breakout Editing.
Cover design by Emilie Haney.
Author's photograph by Ric Brunstetter, RBIII Studios.
Formatting by Colleen Jones.

ISBN 978-0-9979587-6-8 (Paperback)
ISBN 978-0-9979587-7-5 (Digital)

Published by Deb Gorman
Debo Publishing
https://debggorman.com

Dedication

This novel is dedicated to **Pointman International Ministries**, an organization of veterans helping veterans.

Pointman International Ministries—Our Mission: To connect the hurting veteran as well as their families and friends with others who have already begun the transition home after war. With Jesus Christ as our focal point, our desire is to provide spiritual and emotional healing through our existing Outpost and Home Front system.

Readers can visit **Pointman International Ministries** at https://www.pmim.org.

Chapter 1

"**M**om! Where's my iPad?" Joanie bellowed.

Susan Brown, downstairs in her newly remodeled dining room in Sandpoint, Idaho, ignored the stomping overhead and her fourteen-year-old daughter's frantic voice. It sounded like she was on a rampage again.

Joanie's voice drifted down the stairs, every foul word in her teenage vocabulary just loud enough for Susan to hear. Something else to confront.

She rubbed a nervous tic on her right temple and reviewed the contents of her garment bag once again—no mistakes this time. Two other bags were packed and strapped by the front door. Her plan was to surprise Bill by being ready and on time tomorrow. He was such a stickler for schedules and sometimes lashed out at any little bump.

Scanning her list for the third time, she found it too long, as usual. After crossing off two items, she'd pared it down to two evening gowns and three mix-and-match day outfits.

She tucked everything into the bag, making sure the clothing was tightly strapped. It wouldn't do to arrive with wrinkled outfits—although the company convention hotel in Las Vegas offered full valet service. Nothing but the best for Bill.

Lining up the bags by the front door, she made sure the edges formed a neat, straight line. She stretched and looked at her watch. He would be home from his meeting soon.

Susan returned to the dining room, noticed a streak, grabbed a clean microfiber cloth, and wiped the table where she'd set her bag. He had such a critical eye.

She anticipated the long weekend with schoolgirl eagerness. It would be just her and Bill. One thing she didn't look forward to was his comparisons of her figure and clothes to the glamorous women on stage and in the restaurants. She'd never had any reason to question his loyalty, but she knew—after all these years—that she didn't measure up. She'd lost her petite girlish figure, and the glow had faded from her complexion.

Susan walked back out to the entry hall and stood in front of the elegant full-length mirror and didn't like who was staring back at her. Her clothes were nice—Bill always insisted she buy the best for herself—but it didn't hide the years piling up on her small frame. She tugged at her gray blouse and rolled up the long sleeves for a different look. Seeing her pudgy arms exposed made her unroll those sleeves.

The noise from upstairs reached a crescendo. She tried to ignore the blaring music and thrashing sounds coming from her daughter's room.

What could she be doing up there? I need a break.

"Mom!" Joanie yelled again. "Are you going to help me or what?"

Susan rubbed her eyes. Did other mothers of teenage girls sometimes hate the name *Mom*? Another reason to leave her behind.

They needed a game plan for dealing with her rebellious attitude—and she and Bill needed to play on the same team for once.

"Mom!" Joanie roared. "Why don't you answer me? What are you doing down there—nothing as usual, I guess!"

That's it!

Susan marched to the bottom of the stairs and saw the top of Joanie's head as she stood in the hallway outside her bedroom door.

"I'm packing." Susan kept her tone even. It wouldn't help to set her off even more. "Maybe if you'd stop yelling at me like some wild animal, I'd answer you." She moved to the bottom step and craned her neck. "What are you doing anyway? It sounds like you've got a wrecking ball up there!"

The answer came sweeping down the stairs like a tidal wave crashing against a rocky shore.

"I said, 'Where is my iPad!' I can't find it anywhere!" Joanie yelled. "There, did you hear me that time?" She turned and disappeared, swearing like a street kid in a bad movie.

Susan ran up the stairs and down the hall. She peeked in the doorway of her daughter's large bedroom. A heavy three-ring binder flew by, missing her nose by inches. After hitting the wall and rattling the blinds at the other end of the room, it landed on the dresser, scattering jewelry and knickknacks to the floor.

Susan stepped inside gingerly, not wanting to be brained by any other flying objects. "Joanie! For crying out loud, stop throwing things around. Calm down."

She looked around in dismay. Joanie's entire closet lay on the floor at her feet—sweatshirts, underwear, jeans, jewelry, and heavy outdoor clothing—jumbled in an impossible tangle. Susan glanced toward the dresser. A gouge dented the wall above it, where the heavy notebook had connected.

Bill had allowed Joanie to paint her room the way she wanted—black walls, purple trim, and one wall covered with posters of her favorite bands and fantasy movie heroes. Their garishly made-up eyes accused Susan, the intruder.

The gouge pierced the black paint, showing the primer like a beacon. There'd be another explanation to Bill, she was sure, and he'd want to know what had caused Joanie to throw it in the first place.

She felt his glare as she stooped and turned off the music.

Joanie barged out of her walk-in closet. Her long rust-brown hair was dyed black—courtesy of her friend down the street—with some of it sculpted into short bright-green spikes on top of her head, but dark green and purple where it hung over her shoulders. She glowered at her mother, nostrils—adorned with a nose ring, courtesy of Bill on Joanie's last birthday—flaring in anger.

Susan stared at Joanie's attire—flip-flops, ripped jeans, and a low-cut tank top covering her tall, lanky frame. Hardly proper clothing for the cold winter weather. Black glitter fingernails, plastic orange earrings hanging to her shoulders, heavy silver rings on every other finger, and a tattoo of her favorite graphic novel hero on her upper arm completed her ridiculous ensemble.

Susan looked away, choosing which issue to tackle first. She was saved from the decision when she saw what was on the nightstand. She knelt next to it and shoved aside two paperbacks and a locked journal.

"Mom! Why don't you help—"

"Umm, is this what you've been ransacking your room for?" She held out the iPad.

Joanie snatched it out of Susan's hands without a thank-you and turned to put it into her suitcase.

"Thank you to you too!" Susan admonished. "And you will clean up this mess you've made and make your bed, understand? I want every article of clothing that you're not taking hung up where it belongs and everything else put away before we leave tomorrow. You always seem to have time for everything else on your agenda—"

"I don't *have* an agenda unless you give it to me. Geez, Mom, I don't have a life!" She plunked her hands on her hips, drawing out the last words. "So will you please let me get on with it? I'm trying to remember everything you told me to pack, and you're not helping by ordering me around."

Susan closed her eyes and massaged her throbbing temples.

"Settle *down*. And I guess you haven't remembered that I told you *not* to take your iPad to Mrs. Brewster's. If you would be so kind as to unpack that item, I'll put it in the safe while we're gone."

"Mom, *why* can't I take it?" Joanie moaned and hugged the tablet to her chest.

"Really, Joanie?" When had her daughter become such a drama queen? Maybe she should audition for a part in a soap.

"I've already explained, but I'll be glad to go over it again. It's only four days, and there's no reason you can't leave it here and spend time with *her*. After all, she took care of you for years when you were little and I had to work."

She ignored Joanie's drawn-out groan with difficulty. "She's fond of you, and I expect you to behave yourself and give her some company. She's so looking forward to having you. It'll do you good to think of someone *else* for a change."

Joanie's response was typical, and Susan lost it, flinging her arms up in frustration.

"Stop rolling your eyes at me! I've had enough of your attitude—"

"Yeah, and I've had it with *you* controlling my whole life. When do I get to make my own decisions? All my friends do. Even my cousin can do whatever she wants. Ginny doesn't have to check in or out with anyone, and I'd rather stay here by myself than be stuck with that old bat Mrs. Brewster."

Susan tightened her fists. She wanted to slap Joanie, but she took a calming breath and leaned forward, wagging her finger in her daughter's face. "Listen, Joan—"

"Mom!" Joanie jerked her face away from her mother's finger. "It's not fair! You leave me out of the trip to Las Vegas—you and Dad never take me anywhere fun—"

"Oh—you mean like skiing at Schweitzer? Or Colorado? Seattle on a shopping trip? Boating on Oreille? Should I go on—all those *unfun* things?"

"—tell me I can't go to Ginny's. And then foist me off on Mrs.

Brewster. She's so . . . old. She smells funny and wears too much of that lavender crap to cover it up. She's like all old people—all they do is talk about the past. Who cares what happened a hundred years ago? And if it's not that, it'll be reruns of *Bonanza* or the one about some weird geek named Beaver. I can't take four days of that—"

"Joanie, stop this—"

"Please?" Joanie pleaded. "And I promise not to play with it every single second. I promise to talk to her. Can I take it? Please?"

Susan squared her shoulders.

"No." She held out her hand. "It'll be good for you to be without it for a few days and have some face-to-face time with a real live flesh-and-blood person instead of TikTok time. Now hand it over."

Redness crept up Joanie's neck to her cheeks. With her green-and-purple hair and orange earrings, she resembled a Roman candle about to explode. She stepped toward Susan and held out the tablet—her glittering, heavily made-up eyes never leaving her mother's.

Susan didn't know if Joanie was going to hand it over or hit her with it. Warily, she took it from her.

Heading toward the door, she heard Joanie mumble a rude expletive.

"Listen, I've had it with you and your attitude." Susan braced for another explosion.

Chapter 2

"Hi, girls! What's going on?" said a cheery voice behind Susan.

Joanie's eyes brightened.

Bill glided into the room, skirting Susan and the mess on the floor, heading directly for Joanie. Putting his arm around her shoulders, he kissed her cheek. His gaze roamed the room, seeing the mess on the floor, the bed, and inside the closet, and finally skimming his daughter from feet to face.

"You look nice, honey. Did you lose something?"

Joanie's face cleared. "Thank goodness. You're just in time. Mom won't let me take my iPad to Mrs. Brewster's. Please? You promised. Can you talk some sense into her?"

Joanie's little-girl wheedling tone, adopted for Bill alone, irritated Susan to no end.

"I don't see why you can't take it, honey." Bill took the iPad out of Susan's fingers and handed it to Joanie.

Susan recognized defeat. She'd fought this battle many times—Joanie and Bill lined up together, facing her—and she always lost.

The skirmishes had begun years ago, as soon as Joanie had started grade school. Susan eyed Bill, again trying to figure out what made him suck up to their daughter. What used to be a tenderhearted father-daughter relationship had become, over the last eight years, a manipulative alliance. And Susan was the target.

Even Bill's meticulously groomed appearance—trim and tan, thick black hair combed just so, expensive gray slacks, and casual open-necked shirt revealing the gold chain he'd treated himself to on the China trip last year—annoyed her. He spent as many hours at the gym as he could squeeze in. She used to enjoy his tall, muscular frame. But there was only one reason he spent so much time on his body. He was always a salesman, even at the gym—where he'd *network*, as he called it.

And here he was again, working the angles in his own home with his daughter, seeking to cuddle up to Joanie as if she were a client he had to impress.

And Susan, the lowest bidder, would never be an insider in his world.

"What's the problem, honey?"

The endearment rankled her further. His gaze raked over her through his round Matsuda wire frames—nothing but the best for him. Those frames cost sixteen hundred dollars, and that fact frequently made it into conversations with his clients and even their friends.

"We already talked about this. We agreed Joanie spends too much time with the thing anyway—those were *your* words—and that she should visit with Mrs. Brewster. You know, talk to her?"

Bill frowned, rubbing his forehead as if the conversation pained him. "I still think you're being picky. And anyway, yes, those were my words, but I just agreed with you to keep the peace. I saw you were spoiling for a fight over it." He shot a sympathetic glance at Joanie. "Frankly, I can't imagine what it'd be like to be fourteen and have to spend four whole days with an old woman you don't even know anymore. Why not let her take it?"

Susan simmered inside, shoulders tense.

"And then there's the matter of her attire—not appropriate for this time of year, or any time of year for that matter. That tank top is too revealing, and the rips in her jeans—they look trashy."

"Why are you so mean?" Joanie whined.

Bill put his arm around Joanie and gave Susan a withering glance. "I think she looks fine, Sue. She's a teenager—she's not supposed to dress like you." His critical scrutiny swept her form. "And by the way, that shirt's a bit tight on you, don't you think? Maybe you should wear a sweater over it—that new one you bought the other day," he added, his expression bland.

Susan felt the heat flaming her face. He never lost an opportunity to remind her she'd gained a bit of weight over the years and couldn't seem to remain as trim and fit as he did. She tugged the hem of the shirt over her hips.

Joanie snickered, then busied herself picking up the clothes.

Susan waited for the next onslaught to start, then watched in dismay as Bill's gaze traveled to the gouge in the wall. She saw Joanie out of the corner of her eye, a smirk on her face, clearly guessing what would come next. These skirmishes were almost scripted, each of them playing the same part.

"What in blazes happened here?" He walked to the dresser and ran a hand over the wall.

Susan rallied. "Maybe you should ask Joanie."

Bill glanced at Joanie, who stood up, laden down with clothes.

"Right, Mom. Blame me! You're the one who wouldn't help me. Dad, I'm sorry, but she made me lose my temper."

Bill put a finger in Susan's face. "You'll have to call someone when we get back. And it won't be cheap. You might have to forego some personal shopping."

"Can't you fix it?"

"Do I look like a drywaller or painter? Call someone!"

He stepped over to Joanie's side and reverted to their former conversation. "Maybe Joanie could use her iPad to teach Mrs. Brewster something about the new century."

"I don't think—"

"Yeah, Mom." Joanie picked up on Bill's cue. "I could show it to her and maybe teach her how to use the internet or play games. It might be fun. Come on, Mom. What about it? Huh?"

"No! And that's final." But Susan had lost the advantage. She'd been outmaneuvered again by a clever, successful man who finessed deals for a living—and Joanie became more like him every day.

"You're unbelievable. Let her take it." Bill patted Joanie's back, then pulled her close. She laid her head on his shoulder.

Another scripted maneuver. The knot in Susan's stomach twisted.

But she would not give up so easily this time. She reached the doorway, where she paused and rotated in time to see Joanie grin at Bill and tuck the iPad into the bottom of her suitcase. They high-fived each other.

Susan threw up her hands. The calm words she had planned to say fled in the wake of her anger and frustration.

"We're supposed to be a team," she challenged, her voice tinged with more anger than she'd intended. "When will we start playing by the same rules? It doesn't do her any good when you and I are always on opposite sides of the fence."

"You know where the gate is."

Susan stilled, hands clutching the hem of her shirt. Her mind cowered and retreated.

How dare he! And in front of Joanie . . .

Her knees almost buckled, and her heart raced as the jumbled thoughts in her head rearranged themselves into familiar hard-won discipline. She wouldn't . . . she couldn't risk it.

He picked up the heavy suitcase and strode for the door, shouldering Susan out of the way, Joanie close on his heels.

"I'll put this down by the front door, sweetie," he said to Joanie, giving her a peck on the cheek. "All you'll have to bring down in the morning is your backpack."

"Right, Dad. Thanks for helping me with it."

Bill glanced at Susan, still standing in the doorway. His expression of self-satisfaction told her that, as usual, he'd cleaned up her mess and kept the peace.

"Hey," he continued in his jovial salesman's voice, "anyone for a movie and hot chocolate with marshmallows? I'll make popcorn."

"That sounds great, Dad. I'm up for it." She slewed around in the hallway, her voice like thick, sweet maple syrup. "Coming, Mother?"

They left Susan staring down the hall after them. She heard them dump the bags in the entryway, their voices fading into the kitchen.

She stepped back into Joanie's room—still a mess. Susan sighed as she picked up clothes and jewelry, straightened up the dresser and the bed, and closed the closet door. She glanced around, satisfied everything was in its place.

If only life could be cleaned up so easily. If things out of place could be put back . . .

Stepping into the hallway, she heard Joanie's girlish giggle drift up from the kitchen, followed by Bill's deep chuckle, cups and saucers rattling, then the pellet-gun sound of the popcorn maker. All the while, Bill and Joanie talked and laughed like old friends, their high-spirited bantering hurled at her like darts. From her vantage point halfway down the hall, she heard every word.

Her shoulders drooped when she heard her name mentioned, then more laughter. She didn't want to hear any more. Susan was in grade school again, the last one picked for the team while the other kids snickered and whispered behind their hands, separating at the teacher's direction to let her stand, crimson faced, in their midst. She'd never been the athletic type and found any sport a challenge.

She was awkward, whether on the soccer field, the softball diamond, or the basketball court—and that failing had carried over to her adult life and even into her own home.

Susan entered Joanie's room again, closed the door, and sat on the bed covered by a quilt Bill had handpicked for Joanie—more expensive than the one on their own bed. She ran an unsteady hand over its black-and-tan silkiness.

She looked at the rest of the room—perfect in every way, posters notwithstanding—from the top-of-the-line paint on the walls, to the draperies, to the luxurious carpet. She stopped at the ruined wall and tried to picture it before Joanie threw the notebook, but couldn't conjure it up.

It was like their marriage—she couldn't remember it without the hole. She couldn't remember what it was like when she and Bill talked and laughed, when Joanie was a baby and they'd cuddle her together. She couldn't remember being that young and happy. When Bill's eyes lit up when she walked into the room. When he'd ask her opinion about everything. When he'd introduce her to his clients by her name, instead of "and this is my wife." Who could she call to fix that?

Susan stood, squeezed her eyes shut, then opened them. She stepped to the mirror suspended over Joanie's dresser, smoothed her hair, tugged at her shirt again, and used a tissue to wipe the streaks from her face.

Then she paced out of the room and down the stairs, hearing the sound of Joanie's favorite movie playing in the family room—on the brand-new seventy-five-inch Samsung Bill had brought home last month. She remembered Joanie's shriek of joy, as if an expensive TV made life worth living. Bill had kissed her on the cheek and said, "For you, sweetie."

Susan went to the kitchen and saw they'd poured some hot chocolate for her. She brought the cup to her lips. Cold.

After reheating it in the microwave, she forced herself into the family room to watch the movie. She sat down in her chair, placed next to the end of the sofa. Joanie and Bill were at the other end of the long sofa, squeezed together in his oversized leather recliner, like they'd done when she was a toddler.

The three of them used to sit close together when they watched movies.

Susan sipped her steaming cup of chocolate. She glanced at them. They were intent on the movie they'd watched so many times together—*The Hunger Games*. It wasn't Susan's favorite genre, but she'd always watched with them, if only to preserve the illusion of closeness. Her heart lifted a little.

Hope, indeed, was the only thing that could slay fear.

They would drop Joanie off tomorrow at Mrs. Brewster's and take off on their adventure. They'd reconnect, hold hands, and laugh together. They'd *agree* on how to handle Joanie's rebellion, and when they returned, they'd be a team. They'd love and respect each other again. They'd slay the enemies of their family—she was sure of it.

And come spring, when the weather was warmer, she'd work on losing weight. Maybe a different hairstyle.

And with these bright thoughts simmering in the back of her mind, Susan concentrated on the movie while the snow outside drifted from heaven to earth, blanketing the ground with white purity, hiding the dead brownness underneath.

Chapter 3

Morning dawned cloudy and cold. Susan went through her checklist one last time as Bill sorted through his small carry-on duffel. She zipped her bag, placing it on the ornate, high-backed entry hall bench she'd ordered last year from Perigold. Although the price tag had been outrageous, she loved the piece. Bill called it her "five-thousand-dollar chair," but she knew he liked it—it was an impressive sight for guests as they entered their home.

He picked up his bag. "Got everything?"

"Yeah, I think so." She frowned. "Did you remember to clean out the car yesterday?"

"I had it completely detailed. You'll be riding in style and comfort all the way to Spokane."

Susan glanced out the window at the gleaming silver Lexus LX—purchased last spring with Bill's bonus check.

"Didn't you already have it detailed? I thought you were only going to wash it and vacuum it."

"Yes, I did have it detailed—a month ago. Remember, I work for a living," he said smugly. "And that work involves selling software systems to not-so-easily-impressed corporations. Those VIPs from Atlanta had to be wined and dined in luxury, or I wouldn't have gotten the contract."

Susan unzipped her bag again, not listening to his answer. She'd heard it all before. Everything, even vacations, revolved around his important job—and impressing important clients.

"So do you have everything?" he asked again.

"Yes, I guess so. I don't want to forget anything." She stepped closer to the window and parted the curtain. "I'm worried about the weather."

"Hey, don't worry about it. The weather won't stop us, and if you forget something, we can buy it in Vegas, right?" He wore his best salesman's smile. "Do you know where Joanie is? Is she ready to go? We should get on the road if we're going to take her all the way across town to Mrs. Brewster's before heading out."

"She's probably sulking somewhere." Susan's frown deepened. "I have to admit, I'm worried about leaving her with Mrs. Brewster. I can see her throwing tantrums—like the one yesterday. Mrs. Brewster shouldn't have to deal with that."

She cringed as Bill's face took on an exasperated look—she half expected him to pull a Joanie and roll his eyes.

"It was your idea, Susan. I told you in the first place we should let her stay with your sister and Ginny. And that tantrum, by the way, was more your fault than hers. She's a kid—kids have tantrums. I don't know why you had to make such a federal case over that stupid iPad."

"I know, I know! But we'd talked about it and agreed . . . oh, never mind that now," she said, weary of the subject.

Bill lifted his shoulders. "Well? What then? Go ahead and take it away from her again."

"No. That's over and done with. But I still don't think Ginny's a good influence. All she ever talks about is boys this and boys that. And to be honest, my sister's not much better. Since Joe died,

Aimee's either working, glued to social media, or out on the town. You know how she is. Ginny gets almost no adult supervision. I'm not sure which is worse—making Mrs. Brewster put up with Joanie's attitude or letting her stay with Aimee and Ginny."

"You can't have it both ways. And stressing out over it now isn't helping. Besides, what young girl *isn't* boy crazy? I remember another one who was, although it wasn't with me." He laid one hand on her shoulder and playfully flicked his index finger under her chin.

She pulled away from him. "Bill, please. This isn't funny. And we don't have time for a walk down memory lane."

He dropped his hands. "Fine, but I think you're being too hard on your sister."

"Too hard on her? You don't remember the last time we let Joanie spend the weekend with Ginny? If I live to be a hundred, I won't forget seeing both of them at the police station or the smell of alcohol on my thirteen-year-old daughter's breath. And not being able to find Aimee anywhere. What a nightmare! It's a wonder Joanie had the presence of mind to call you, as drunk as she was. How can you stand there and—"

Bill held up both hands in surrender. "Okay, okay. You're right—we don't have time for this. Let's get these bags out to the car." He glanced at the gold Rolex on his arm. "I want to be on the road in ten minutes."

Susan nodded in defeat and picked up her bag, calling over her shoulder. "Joanie! We're ready to go. Get down here!" She heard heavy footsteps upstairs, then the slam of a door.

Susan's phone vibrated as Joanie huffed into the room. Pulling her new iPhone out of her pocket, she looked at the screen.

"Now what? It's Mrs. Brewster. Bill, can you take my bag while I answer this?"

Bill threw up his hands and grabbed her bag as she answered the call.

"Oh, Mrs. Brewster! Yeah, we're leaving now . . ." Susan's voice trailed off. "What? What do you mean, you're sick?" Her stricken eyes met Bill's.

He dropped the bags in the open doorway with a thud as Joanie groaned at the bottom of the stairs.

"I wish you'd called sooner. We're walking out the door right now."

Susan's face heated. "Oh, I'm sorry, Mrs. Brewster. I didn't mean to be rude, but—"

She listened to Mrs. Brewster's raspy voice as Bill and Joanie waited impatiently.

"Okay, I guess. Feel better," Susan said. "No, don't worry. We'll figure something out. You take care of yourself. I'll check on you when we get back home. Goodbye, Mrs. Brewster."

Susan shook her head as she slipped her phone into her purse.

Bill banged the front door shut. "Well?"

Susan dropped to the entry hall bench. "She started feeling ill this morning, and now she has a fever. Her daughter's coming to take her to the doctor. We can't take Joanie over there." She looked at Bill in desperation. "We need to get going! We can't miss our plane. And I've heard the weather reports—they expect it to get worse."

"Looks like I'm Vegas bound!" Joanie snickered with glee.

"No, Joanie, you are not going to—"

"It seems simple to me," Bill interrupted. "Call your sister. See if we can bring Joanie over there on short notice. I don't see any other option." He gave a sidelong glance at Joanie.

"To Newport? But that's thirty miles away—and not in the direction of Coeur D'Alene. I thought you said going through Coeur D'Alene to Spokane would be shorter. Won't that foul up your timetable?" She glanced at Joanie. "And anyway, I still don't want her to stay at Aimee's."

"Oh, Mom! You're such a dweeb—"

Bill waved her to silence. "Don't worry about my timetable—

it's not set in stone. Look, we'll take Highway 2 over to Newport, then it's a straight shot down to Spokane. The distance is within about three miles either way. It won't make that much difference," he said. "And again, you're worrying over nothing. We can check in every day with Aimee and Joanie and make sure everything's okay. What do you say?" He tapped his watch. "I need a decision. We need to get on the road—now."

Susan shrugged. "You win, I guess. Again. Let's get going, okay?" She picked up her purse and started toward the front door.

Bill stopped her with a hand on her arm. "Honey, aren't you going to call your sister?" he asked with exaggerated patience.

"Oh, right." As she pulled her phone out, she caught Joanie's smile of triumph. She knew that smile, the one that always left Susan out—like she was watching a stage production of her life from the nosebleed seats, so far away she'd never be part of the closeness they shared.

Why was she always on the outside looking in? "Oh, hi, Aimee! Yes, I'm fine, but say, we have a favor to ask of you . . ."

Chapter 4

The windshield wipers on Tom Masters's beat-up Chevy pick-up barely kept up with the heavy snow as he rumbled into the driveway of the bed and breakfast he and his wife, Barb, had owned for several years after selling their hardware store in Boise.

They'd only had the store for a year or so after he'd returned from 'Nam—the year he'd tried to kill the jungle in his mind. They'd moved after discovering Barb was pregnant with their first child. And after the hard part, they'd agreed they needed a change, and neither wanted to raise a child in the middle of a big town. It was the only thing they could agree on back then.

The B&B perched on a small bluff half a mile north of Highway 2, between Sandpoint and Newport, Washington. He'd inherited the property and a large rustic cabin from his grandparents. They'd worked hard together to make the Master's Inn popular and prosperous, remodeling it themselves.

Tom had made an early run for supplies to the mom-and-pop at the junction of the highway and the service road, and now, as he sat watching the driving snow, he wondered how much worse this storm would get. So far it'd been a mild winter, but the darkening sky over the mountains worried him. The reports had been for clear, cold weather this weekend with lots of sunshine.

Staring at the worsening weather, Tom slapped a broad hand against the steering wheel. If it got much worse, Bob, Gwen, and the boys—due for a visit this weekend for the first time in five years—would be holed up inside instead of hiking, skiing, and playing in the snow.

He climbed out of his truck—his powerfully built six-foot-four-inch frame unfolding slower than usual. While carrying wood yesterday, he'd hurt his back, and he grimaced as he grabbed the grocery bags. Tom hated to admit that he wasn't that young marine lieutenant anymore. He prided himself that, at almost seventy years old, he could still work twelve-hour days, ski, hunt, and chop his own wood.

He carried the grocery bags up the icy walk and opened the door to the enclosed back porch they'd turned into a cozy sitting room.

"Barb!" Tom stomped the snow off his boots on the back porch. He stepped in and yelled again. "Barb! I'm back! Where are you?"

No answer.

Why didn't she answer him? He carried the groceries through the sitting room and into the large farmhouse-style kitchen and set them on the counter.

He took off his belt and unholstered his .44 magnum revolver, laying it on the counter. His holster and sidearm were as much a part of him as his hands and arms, and he never went anywhere without them. Bears, mountain lions, and snakes still made their presence known on occasion.

Barb hadn't appeared, so he stowed the groceries away himself. He wasn't sure if he'd put everything where she wanted, but since she wasn't here to help, she'd have to deal with it.

He glanced around the spotless kitchen, searching for a crumb, a piece of lint, anything out of place on the shiny countertops. Barb and her tidiness—sometimes he wished she'd give it a rest.

He smelled fresh coffee, along with the tantalizing aroma of Barb's famous chocolate chip cookies. He reached for his favorite cup, but it wasn't there. That was odd. He'd left it next to the coffeemaker this morning, after his usual predawn hike.

Then he realized the dishwasher was running.

Darn it!

He jerked open the dishwasher. Steam rushed up and clouded his vision. Grabbing the cup, he yowled in pain.

"What's wrong, honey?" Barb said from close behind him.

He jumped, lost his hold on the cup, and dropped it on the polished hardwood floor. It shattered into a hundred pieces.

"For Pete's sake—I've told you not to sneak up behind me," he snapped.

"I'm sorry. And I wasn't sneaking." She backed up, pushed her long graying hair out of her eyes, and tucked it behind her ears. "I was coming in to see if the coffee had brewed, and I heard you scream. Is it your back again?" She reached for him.

"I didn't scream—screaming is for girls. Don't exaggerate. My back's fine—the cup was hot."

"What's wrong? Why are you in such a bad mood?"

"Wasn't until now. Look, I told you I'd be back from the store in an hour, and I come in and call you, and you ignore me."

"I was upstairs. I didn't hear you."

"And I left my cup right here." He slapped the counter with his palm. "And you put it in the dishwasher. I've told you over and over again not to put my cup in the dishwasher—it ruins the taste of the coffee. Why can't you remember that? Now it's in a thousand pieces—and it's not like we can buy another one."

She pushed one of the jagged shards with her toe. "I'm sorry—I know how much you loved that cup." Her eyes had the old sadness in them, but there was nothing he could ever do about that. And Lord knows, he'd tried.

Tom bent and picked up the biggest chunk, stroking it with his thumb. Katie's blue eyes peeped at him from the curve of the shard.

He placed the fragment on the wide windowsill, arranging it so Katie's eyes and part of her tiny nose were visible.

He heard Barb's footsteps retreating into the dining room, and he started to call her back but saw the stiffness in her posture as she disappeared through the kitchen doorway. He exhaled slowly. He'd hurt her again, just like he had all those years ago. It happened over and over. When he thought they were past it, that they'd never hurt each other again, he had to go and be so stupid. Hands on his hips, his gaze strayed back to the windowsill. Even Katie's eyes accused him. He brushed his hand over his head in frustration, feeling the stubble of his close-cropped iron-gray hair.

He'd best get this over with—a marine never shirked.

# Chapter 5

He ambled into the dining room and stopped. Barb stood in front of the window, eyes fixed on the snow-drenched landscape. Even from across the room—after forty-plus years together—he felt her anguish. She'd wrapped her arms around her middle, as if to insulate herself from the coldness of the last few minutes and the hardness of the last four decades.

He eased over to her side and wrapped his arm around her. She melted into him, her head barely reaching his chest. At a petite five foot one inch, he towered more than a foot over her.

She looked up at him. "I'm so sorry about the cup." Her words ended in a strangled whisper.

The sadness etched on her face transported him back to the nightmare they'd lived through decades ago. He brushed a stray hair from her cheek, always struck by the smooth glow of her unlined face. She never wore makeup, preferring to let people see "the real me," as she always said.

"No, *I'm* sorry. I shouldn't have gotten so mad. It's not like you did this on purpose. You didn't even do it at all—it was an accident. It's not like we're going to forget Katie because the cup broke. Right?"

"Of course not. Katie will always be part of us."

They stood in silence, each wrapped in their private grief, and gazed at the peaceful white landscape inches away, separated from it by the cold thickness of insulated glass.

"And, honey, I should never have tried to get you to—"

"No—"

"But I shouldn't have. I think about it now, and it's like it was someone else, not me—"

She laid a finger over his mouth. "We've been down that rutted road, and I'm not going there again. I can't. I can't." Her grip on his hand almost crushed it. "I forgave you for that a long time ago. I don't want to think about it. It . . . it might destroy us again."

He took her face in his hands and kissed her forehead.

"Okay, okay. I'm sorry I brought it up."

She backed away from him and searched his face. "Let's switch gears here. There's a mess in the kitchen that needs cleaning up, and then we have to get down to it. We have guests coming today—or did you forget? After you clean up the floor, come upstairs and see what I've been doing while you were out shopping. And I have a couple more chores you can do for me if you have the time." Then, in a severe tone tempered by a smirk, "And stay out of the cookies."

Tom saluted and returned to the kitchen. The camaraderie was gone—he could tell because of her businesslike voice. But at least they weren't fighting. That was something.

He grabbed the broom and dustpan, swept up the broken pieces, and dumped them into the trash. He'd left his revolver on the counter, so he replaced the weapon in the holster, then hung his belt and holster on a hook inside the closet in the living room, next to the front door.

Going back into the kitchen to grab some coffee in a different cup, his eyes sought Katie's again. Blowing her a kiss, he grabbed a cookie on his way out and went upstairs to find Barb.

"Where are you?" he called from the top of the stairs.

"In here," she said from the closest of the three guest rooms. Each large, comfortable bedroom had its own private bath, and they were arranged around a communal sitting room. The bedroom doors each had a small entryway. Tom had reinforced the bedroom walls with upgraded insulation for privacy, and they'd equipped the sitting room—or the "community room," as they called it—with plush beige carpet, a sixty-inch TV, a gaming station, shelves of books for adults and children, and a board-game closet. By far, most of their remodeling dollars were spent on this area. Over the years, it had become a favorite place for guests to relax with their families and get to know each other.

As he entered the yellow guest room—each upstairs bedroom was a different color—he saw Barb's backside bending over in the walk-in closet. Her arms were loaded with a thick comforter and pillows, still in the clear plastic packaging. They started to slip out of her arms as she straightened up and turned.

"Here, let me help." He reached out to catch them.

They laid them on the bed, and she unzipped one of the bags, shaking out a comforter. "What do you think? I got them on sale last time we were in Spokane, remember?"

He stared at it, trying to keep his expression noncommittal.

"You don't like it?"

"I guess I don't remember it being so . . . feminine," he said. "Our guests this weekend are a marine vet and his two boys, remember? Why not something with a moose or a bear?"

She rewarded him with a tight-lipped glare. "It isn't only for them—"

"I didn't mean to be so critical. I'm sorry."

"Forget it. Why would I think you'd like my choice?"

"Barb—"

"We're sure saying 'sorry' a lot today. Why do you think that is?" She flicked a cookie crumb from the front of his shirt.

Tom shrugged and studied the room, pristine under Barb's

meticulous cleaning. The antique white dresser—once used by his grandmother and then his mother—had a guest basket placed to one side, and the old-fashioned tilt mirror had been polished until it gleamed. Barb had insisted on not updating this piece, preferring the character of the distressed finish. He had to admit that it looked stunning against the sunny yellow paint—another of Barb's decorating ideas he'd been against. He preferred muted wall colors. But she'd insisted that not everyone had such boring ideas about paint. He had prevailed in the downstairs rooms, where they spent most of their personal time when not entertaining, but upstairs was all Barb. This room had twin beds—and the two nightstands also had guest baskets, one filled with packaged energy bars and two water bottles, the other with chocolates.

"What do you think? Did I miss anything?"

"You? Miss anything? Don't make me laugh! If you missed a detail, the world would stop spinning." He was trying to lighten the moment, but he guessed by her annoyed expression that his attempt fell flat.

"What did you need me to do?" he asked.

"Would you check that pipe under the bathroom sink in here and make sure it's not leaking again? And the closet door in the blue room is still sticking a bit."

"Will do. I can have that done in a jiffy. Anything to fix in the green room?"

She shook her head. "No, only those two things. I'm going to put the new bedding on the beds and set out the other guest baskets I've arranged. Then I think we'll be done."

When Barb finished thirty minutes later, Tom had arranged a small portable fountain in one corner of the upstairs sitting room. He turned it on, and the water tinkled over the small stones. Then he switched off the overhead light, and in the dimness the underwater lights glowed a peaceful amber.

Barb's face clouded. "It . . . it's perfect, Tom. I'd forgotten about that fountain moldering away in the attic. I'm amazed it still works." She walked over and touched the stone figure of an angel reclining on one of the larger rocks. Years ago they'd ordered wood-carved replicas of the angel and used them to cap the newel posts on the front steps.

"Remember how she used to—"

"Yeah, it's been up in the attic a long time, hasn't it? I thought it was time to resurrect it."

"I think you're right. It's time."

She gave the angel a last pat on the head. "Did you get the other things done?"

"The pipe is fine, and all the closet door needed was a little oiling. Everything on my end is shipshape. How about you?"

"Everything's perfect. I still have to give the rooms a final dusting, but I can do that later."

"If they're anything like this room, I think you're done. Sometimes you're a bit picky, you know?"

"So you've told me. But I'll still go over them again."

He glanced around the spotless sitting room, stopping on the built-in bookcase.

"And where in the world did you find all these books? The shelves are groaning. I thought we'd be hiking and playing in the snow with Bob and Gwen and the boys, not lazing around the house with books."

"They have to have something to read when they're not out with you—trying to be men." She straightened one, lining it up so the spine was even with the others. "I got them at the used bookstore in Newport—you know the one—it's called BookWurm. Old Mrs. Wurmbrand still owns it—can you believe it?"

"Yeah, I've seen it. That's more your thing than mine though." He grinned. "Give me a hunting or fishing magazine with lots of pictures, and I'll be happy. But I do plan to take Bob and the boys hiking if the weather straightens out—and you girls if you want to."

Tom opened the blinds covering the lower half of the high-arched paned window and watched the trees bend in the wind. The view overlooked the creek rushing along at the back of the inn—but the creek wasn't moving today. A thin layer of ice covered it, and snow covered the footbridge spanning the creek.

He had more shoveling to do. Maybe he could get the boys to help him.

He turned to Barb. "I'm not hopeful, though, with the way the weather is developing, so maybe the books are a good thing." He flicked off the fountain.

"What's next, Sarge?" he asked, using the nickname he'd given her when they were first married.

She tapped her watch with her forefinger. "We have time for a bite to eat. According to you, they should be here in two hours or so."

She led the way downstairs. At the bottom, she stopped and jabbed her finger at his chest.

"But no more cookies, sir. You've had quite enough."

"Oorah, ma'am!"

As soon as her back was turned, he pulled one from his pocket and stuffed it into his mouth.

 # Chapter 6

The storm had grown in intensity, the early afternoon sun hidden under darkening skies. Tom slid open the curtains of the large picture window in the living room and stared at the wild vista. The wind whistled in from the mountains, bending the large pines and driving the snow sideways. Snow drifting on the wide front veranda covered the porch swing and the other outdoor furniture, turning them into ghostlike apparitions. There had to be at least an inch of ice on the stretch of dirt road below and in front of the inn, and he figured the water in the ditch alongside would be frozen solid. Freak storms were not unusual on their mountain, and his gut told him this one would shut everything down.

"Barb!" he called, "I can't even see old man Henderson's fence across the road!" No answer from the kitchen.

Figured. She had one thing on her mind. She expected him to make everything right, even the weather.

His mood darkened. He couldn't fathom spending four days cooped up in the house with two active boys. They'd have no use for those books upstairs and would want to spend most of their time playing computer games. Not that he knew them all that well, but he'd wanted to enjoy the outdoors with his family, and especially some quality time with Bob, who was now stateside after two tours in Afghanistan. Bob's father, Jerry—Tom's own brother— had passed away a few weeks after Bob had mustered out, adding another layer of grief to his nephew's life. Tom shook his head. Sometimes it seemed like once things started going wrong, they kept on going wrong. Bob and Gwen's wayward teenage boys, Kyle and Kasey, added to their problems.

Maybe Bob's problems were more than Tom could help him with. He couldn't straighten them out—shoot, he couldn't straighten himself out. He and Barb . . . they weren't on the same page anymore. He remembered when they could finish each other's sentences. Now it was like they lived separate lives. He'd thought that was all over years ago, when he'd come back from—

Tom shut those thoughts down. It didn't do any good to dredge all that up again. Turning his back on the storm outside, he faced the closed kitchen door and wondered what was going on in there with all the pots and pans banging and cupboard doors slamming. He guessed he should see if she needed help, but he couldn't rouse himself enough to care. He plopped down into his recliner and put his head in his hands, praying for God to lift his foul mood and for him and Barb to stop fighting, at least long enough to have a good time this weekend.

The past always invaded as soon as things seemed positive, like having family visit.

They usually reserved this particular weekend to take some time off for themselves, but they'd made an exception when Bob had called to say they wanted to visit. But how could Tom and Barb try to help them when they could barely be civil to each other?

He knew why the tension was brewing now. It always crept in this time of year. Katie had left in a December so long ago, and December had never been the same. Some years were better than others. But this time, with his family coming, it seemed worse than ever. Tom was unaccustomed to helplessness, but he sure felt that way today.

Funny, he'd been able to get the boys in his squad to follow his lead no matter what the situation. He guessed being a soldier didn't always count in real life.

Tom stirred himself and poked his head into the kitchen—in time to see Barb take another batch of cookies out of the oven. As she set the baking sheet down on the counter, she caught sight of him leaning on the doorframe. He smirked.

"Now don't you start on me," she said. "I want to be sure we have—"

The phone jangled in the dining room. Tom went to answer it, leaving the swinging door open.

"Hello! Master's Inn. Tom Masters speaking," he said in the cheerful voice he reserved for guests.

"Oh, hi, Bob! You guys must be almost here—"

Barb came through the doorway, wiping her hands on a towel.

"What? You haven't left yet? But—"

Barb stopped two steps past the entryway, questions written all over her face.

"What do you mean you're not coming?" Tom shouted into the phone.

Chapter 7

Barb threw the towel on the kitchen counter and stood with her hands on her hips.

Tom barely controlled the edge in his voice. "All of them canceled? Aren't there any other options?"

"I guess we shouldn't be surprised—it's nasty here. Man, this is awful! We . . . we so looked forward to seeing you guys."

"Tom—" Barb interrupted but was stopped by Tom's index finger waving her to silence. She clamped her lips shut and dropped into a chair at the table.

"Okay, Bob. I do understand—and hey, forgive me for blowing up at you? I know it's not your fault. Maybe we can plan something for another time. Maybe . . . maybe we can travel your way or something. What do you think?"

He turned away from Barb. "Okay, maybe we can work that out. Hey, have a great time at Disneyland, even if you won't get to eat Barb's cooking! More for me, I guess—"

Tom forced his voice to sound cheerful. "Yeah . . . okay, you too. Bye!"

He slammed the phone down and shuffled to the table. Sitting down next to Barb, he stretched his arms out on the table and lowered his head.

"I don't believe this." He sat up and rubbed his eyes.

"What happened?"

"You heard, right?" he snapped. "You were sitting right here. Didn't you hear me say the part about the flight being canceled? Weren't you paying attention?"

Barb sat back in her chair, lips tight and arms crossed across her chest.

He blew air out through his teeth.

"I'm sorry. I shouldn't have bitten your head off. How could you know what happened?"

"Why aren't they coming?"

"All flights into and out of Spokane are grounded. They expect the weather to worsen over the next few hours. More snow and an ice storm, I guess. The plane can take off from California, but it can't land in Spokane. Dang weathermen—all that blather about clear weather the next few days. Can't count on their forecasts."

Her anger spilled over. "So our weekend got canceled. I guess God doesn't want them to come, right? After all the prayer and planning we've put into this. It's not fair."

Tom watched her gaze travel the room, replete with Masters' family traditions—old-fashioned photographs of Tom's parents and grandparents, heavy antique claw-footed furniture, and a grandfather clock from the turn of the century, still ticking away.

After more than four decades together, Tom read her mind. She was thinking of the rooms upstairs, readied for the ones they'd prayed over. He smelled the lingering sweetness of dozens of cookies, each one fashioned and baked with God's love in her heart. She thought of Gwen's sadness and inability to deal with Bob's problems since he'd come home—and of all the encouraging words, born of her own experience—she'd intended to say to her. Clearly, her anger and confusion were at the boiling point.

"I just can't figure God out. We've waited and waited for a chance to help Bob and Gwen. Now who's gonna do it?"

Tom laid his arm across her shoulders. Yes, he wanted to help his nephew, but he felt almost a sense of relief they weren't coming. Getting ready for their visit had brought some old wounds to the surface. Sometimes it was better to let the past stay buried, but he knew better than to say so to Barb.

He tried to comfort her. "I know. I don't understand it either. It doesn't make much sense. It seems like he doesn't care about our plans."

The set of her shoulders told him she didn't want to be comforted. She wanted to vent. Her next words confirmed it.

"Yeah, like he didn't care when Katie . . ."

Why, oh why did everything have to circle back to this?

Every disappointment fed their grief, keeping it alive and flourishing—like the day in late December 1976 was yesterday and not forty-four years ago.

Would it never stop?

"Honey—"

"Don't start on me, Tom. Maybe I should have done what you wanted. Maybe if we'd never . . . had her . . . maybe it wouldn't hurt so much now."

She'd buried the knife in his chest again, right up to the hilt, but her stricken face kept him from saying the words on his tongue. Words he'd held back for more than half his life.

They sat in quiet disappointment, staring out the window. Then Barb returned to the kitchen. The door into the back porch sitting room opened and then banged shut. He thought about following her, but what would it accomplish?

He might as well go out and check the roof for ice buildup. At least it was something to do—and the Lord knew, he was tired of chipping away at the ice in here.

He pulled his heavy coat and gloves out of the closet, put his high-topped rubber boots on, and marched out the front door. The storm smacked him in the face, stinging his eyes and taking his breath away. He pulled his gloves on and strapped his fur hat under his chin to keep it from flying off in the icy wind.

At least twenty to thirty miles an hour, gusting higher. But still better than the frigid air inside.

Tom headed for the shed where he kept his snow shovel, hoping to work off some of his frustration. He started on the pathway from the back door to the creek, attacking the ice like it was his nemesis, but wondering in the back of his head who the real enemy was.

# Chapter 8

Late that afternoon, Barb sat on the sofa flipping through magazines while Tom tried to get a signal on their TV. Barb had rallied and seemed to have recovered her good spirits. She'd made popcorn, and they planned to stream a movie, but the building storm outside interrupted the reception. The lights flickered off and on several times, and the woodstove fan went off with a loud clicking noise. Darkness descended.

Barb jerked up. "What happened?"

He rose to his feet and stood rigid, with his hand perched on his right hip, fingers fluttering as if trying to grasp something there. He looked down.

Where was it? Where did he leave it?

He put the other hand out in front of him, palm outward. Then he took one step backward and fell into his chair with a groan, his white-faced stare locked on the front door.

Barb grabbed a flashlight from a nearby drawer and turned it on his face. "Tom? What do we do now?"

Tom didn't answer. He wanted to answer—he heard Barb—but he couldn't get his mouth open to say anything. Then her voice faded away like the echo of a wolf howl on a distant mountain, and he was seven thousand six hundred and ninety miles away.

Barb knelt beside Tom's chair. She knew he wasn't there, that he'd gone where she couldn't follow—caused by the sudden darkness and the loud clicking of the woodstove.

And she knew she could do nothing but wait out the terror that had swamped him—beside him but not with him. Never with him.

His large hands clutched the chair arms, as if he hung on for dear life. His wide, glassy eyes stared straight ahead. Sweat leaked on his forehead. The skin on his face stretched tight. She braved a light brush of her fingers on his bicep. The muscles were bunched rock hard.

A moan escaped from his lips, then a raspy whisper. "Mack, get down!" His head turned in her direction, eyes focused right through her to some frightening scene behind her.

She resisted the urge to turn around, to try to see what he saw. She knew all she'd see was the front veranda through the partially opened drapes. She'd been through this before, too many times to count. But it'd been a long time since it'd been this bad. These days it lasted a moment or two, without the physical manifestations—sweat, body movements, and speech.

Barb sat down on the floor next to Tom's chair and waited for him to come back. Like she'd waited for him since he'd left for the jungle so long ago. He did come back, but *he* didn't return to her until years later. They'd spent the better part of ten years after the war trying to find a way for him to escape it. Every victory he'd had over those ten years was tainted, shrouded in some defeat she couldn't see. He'd told her a few stories, but she knew he was holding some things back from her, things he couldn't face. And things he said she shouldn't have to face.

Now she knew better than to force him back, like she'd done when they were younger and the flashbacks had frightened her. Once, during a bad one, she'd slapped his face to snap him out of it. He was wearing his sidearm at the time and reached for it. It was a good thing for her that he'd come out of it before he pulled it from his holster. The counselor told her never to do that again.

A groan caused her to stretch up and kneel beside him again, leaning in.

His black-ice stare shone in the flashlight beam. Then his mouth sprang open in a low scream. "My God, he can't be fifteen yet! What have I done?"

 # Chapter 9

"Tom! Snap out of it. Honey, please, come back." She stood next to him, leaning into his face, gripping the back of his chair.

Tom squeezed his eyes shut, then opened them, passing a hand over his dripping brow. As the jungle faded, folding and tucking itself back into the foxhole where he kept it in his mind, he saw Barb bending over him, worry stamped on her face.

"Sorry . . ." He stopped, puzzling over the disjointed memory. He never could remember everything in the correct sequence. It was like a nightmare coming to him in pieces, movie frames arising willy nilly with no rhyme or reason, and he was unable to put them in order.

"You don't have to apologize." She took his hand. "Do you want to talk about it?"

He jerked his hand out of her grasp. "Already have."

She straightened and backed up a pace.

"Okay, okay. It's always the same, isn't it? You have these flash-backs and won't tell me where you've been, and I must not try to help. I understand." Her voice was flat.

"Look, I've talked to counselors over and over. So give me a break, okay? They . . . they get less intense with each passing year. Remember how it was in the beginning? I couldn't function for a long time." He stared up at her. "You don't need to go where I've been, Barb. I won't have it. You don't belong there," he finished with a growl.

"Yeah, well, I've already been there, okay? You act like you're the only one who was there, but I was right there with you—still am. Maybe it's time—"

"It'll never be time, so just get over it. Now get off my back—"

Tom was chagrined at his frantic outburst, but it was always the same. He looked at the outline of Barb's face in the deepening darkness, knowing he'd hurt her but not knowing what to say.

She patted his shoulder. "Okay, honey." She moved back to the sofa. "Now, we're still in the dark here. What are we going to do?"

Tom stood on shaky legs, steadying himself against the recliner. He wiped his sleeve over his sweat-soaked face and took stock.

At least he could do this. At least he knew what to do about a power outage.

"Not to worry. I'll go flip the generator on," he replied in his best take-charge voice.

She handed him the flashlight, and he strode for the back door, stumbling over a box against the wall. He lost his balance and staggered against the wall.

"Oh, I'm sorry. Are you hurt?"

"Of course I'm not hurt—takes more than a box of quilts to hurt me—but why did you leave that there?" He rubbed his knee.

"I was going to ask you to take it upstairs for me earlier. I guess I forgot—"

He went out in the middle of her sentence.

Moments later, flashlight in hand, Tom stared in dismay at the generator housed in the shed behind the inn. He tried the switch again and heard it kick in, then out.

He groaned. Out of gas.

He picked up the gas can he kept nearby. He already knew nothing was in it, because he'd forgotten to take it with him to the minimarket earlier.

He slapped his forehead. Stupid. Now what?

He searched desperately for an answer but came up empty, like the generator. The storm outside grew in fury. Tom knew he'd be unable to drive even the three miles to the gas station, and there'd probably be no one there anyway.

What a brainless thing to do. He berated himself as he stomped back to the main house through the snow, over a foot deep on the path he'd already cleared once today. Time to get the shovel out again.

Barb still sat where he'd left her. "What's the verdict? Why aren't the lights back on?"

"I hate to admit it, but I forgot to get gas for the generator."

He waited for her anger—worse because it never came.

She drew a breath. "You can't drive in this, so what are you going to do?"

"We. What are *we* going to do—"

"What? We? You did this—"

"Candles."

She threw up her hands and headed to the kitchen, where they kept a supply of assorted candles and matches. Right behind her, Tom kicked the box of quilts out of his way, causing it to crash into the antique hutch along the wall. A picture frame toppled facedown on the hutch.

"Tom, be careful, would you please?"

"Sorry."

They busied themselves placing the candles, ten in all, around the living room and dining room. Tom lit them. They cast a cozy, suffused glow.

"Honey, I'm sorry I forgot the gas can earlier. But isn't this kind of nice?"

"Yeah, I guess so. Except for no stove, no refrigerator, no hot water, no movie. Very cozy. I hope you can get gas tomorrow or the power comes back on soon."

Tom stepped to the window and opened the drapes wider, leaving the white sheers closed.

"We used to like watching the storm instead of TV." He sat down in his chair, Barb taking her usual place in the corner of the sofa. The minutes ticked by as they sat in the flickering candlelight, punctuated by the wind and the sound of branches scraping the roof. Barb tucked in her feet and pulled a crocheted blanket over her.

"I wonder how long it will be this time," Tom said. "Remember, a few years back it was three days before power was restored. Maybe it's a good thing we *don't* have guests this weekend."

Barb's face appeared chiseled in stone. She clutched the blanket closer around herself, pulling it up to her chin.

"You're not going to convince me of that. God caused the storm, remember? And canceled our plans. He's not getting off that easy with me," she retorted. The candlelight caught the gleam of anger in her eyes.

Tom agreed, his face glum. He didn't care for her bitter tone, but didn't feel the need to comment. The candlelight sputtered and dipped, casting dancing shadows on the walls. The storm raging outside matched the building tension inside. Tom wished he could say something that would bring them back where they used to be—a loving couple whose purpose at the inn was to serve stressed-out people seeking a getaway.

Now they were the stressed-out people needing to get away.

"I guess I should get off the complaint train." Her soft voice floated across the room, a smile lifting the corners of her mouth. "Maybe God has better plans for us this weekend. Anyway, that's what Pastor Dan would say, right? Not that we've been to church much recently, but I think that's what he'd say."

Her attitude shift surprised him. "Yeah, maybe. Can't think what those other plans would be though. I'd have thought helping my family was the best plan."

Barb giggled. "Me too, I guess. Is this one of those plan B times you're always talking about?"

Her giggle was music to Tom's ears.

"Yep, guess so. But—"

"I wonder what—" Barb said at the same time.

A furious pounding on the front door drowned out their words. Tom sat rooted to his seat, hearing muffled shouts on the porch. Shadowy figures moved outside the window.

He counted four, two tall and two shorter, and his analytical mind raced, honed by leading young soldiers during three tours in Vietnam.

A couple with two kids—maybe not a threat, but couldn't be too careful. How had he not heard them come up on the porch?

He started for the door, but Barb leaped up and grabbed his arm. "Tom, it's after five o'clock and dark out there. We never get company this late—and the storm. Why are they here?"

She clutched his arm tighter.

"Barb—"

"Remember what happened to that family in Priest River last year? Those poor people—and the children. They didn't have a chance—"

Tom shook her by the shoulder. "Calm down. There's only one way to find out who it is. And in this storm, maybe they need help."

At the door, he hesitated, then stepped aside and reached into the hall closet, lifting his twelve-gauge shotgun off the rack. He checked to make sure it was loaded.

Tom put his ear to the door and heard several people yelling at once.

Barb had followed close behind him, clutching the back of his shirt.

He grabbed her hand and motioned her back a few paces.

She stepped back, eyes fearful, hands to her throat.

He checked the gun again, then put his hand on the knob and took a deep breath. The shouting continued, and now he could distinguish the words.

"Let us in!"

"Is there anybody home?"

"It's freezing out here—"

He opened the door a crack, shotgun at the ready.

 # Chapter 10

Peering out, Tom hastily put the shotgun behind the door, leaning it against the wall.

A young couple with two kids huddled on the porch, wet and miserable, as if they'd walked for hours in the storm.

Galvanized into action, Tom ushered them into the candlelit living room. Snow swirled around as they stumbled in. Tom managed to get the door closed and locked against the gale-force wind.

Barb hovered like a mother hen, helping the children out of their wet coats. The wide-eyed woman was tall and willowy, blond curls escaping under her hat. The kids were as alike as two matching bookends, both blond like their mother. Tom guessed they were about five and seven. He noticed the man eyeing the shotgun still leaning against the wall, so he eased over, picked it up, and stowed it away on the rack in the closet.

"All right, then," Barb said, "who do we have here?"

"Hi. I'm Steven Elliott. My friends call me Steve." He stepped forward and held out his hand to Tom, removing his stocking cap. Steve's bushy blond hair stuck up all over his head. His height matched Tom's, but he was lankier.

Tom sized him up and nodded at Barb. "We're Tom and Barb Masters. Welcome to the Master's Inn," he said, shaking Steve's hand.

"This is my wife, Sally, and these two munchkins are Samantha and Stevie," Steve said, gesturing to his family huddled together in the middle of the room.

"Please come and sit down," Barb said. "Tom, why don't you put another log in the woodstove and get it a little warmer in here, okay?"

Barb led the Elliott family to the two overstuffed sofas in the living room. Sally sank down with Samantha and Stevie and drew them close. Steve removed his coat and spread it over them.

Sally jerked it off and laid it down, letting it slip to the floor. "Your coat's soaked."

He plucked it from the floor and shook it. "I'm sorry—"

Barb lifted a heavy quilt out of the box Tom had tripped over earlier and helped Sally spread it over the two children. Giving an impish smile to Tom, Barb said, "Now I know why I forgot to bring this box upstairs."

"Oh, that's lovely. Thank you."

"You're quite welcome, Mrs. Elliott."

"Please call me Sally. And I'm sorry. I . . . I shouldn't have spoken like that, but sometimes he—"

"Sorry to barge in on you like this," Steve interrupted. He hung up his coat on a hook by the door. "We were headed to Newport to visit Sally's mother. She's not feeling well."

"Not feeling well?" Sally said, eyes like twin daggers, pointed in Steve's direction. "They said she could die. Or did you forget?"

"Of course I didn't forget. But do we have to spill everything? To strangers?"

Tom straightened up from the woodstove and glanced at the two of them.

What was going on?

"Sounds like you've had a rough time of it. Hope Barb and I can help a little. Is she in the hospital in Newport?"

"Yes. They want to move her to Spokane, but I want to see her first. They said she had a stroke—I guess not a massive one—but they don't have the facilities to care for her in Newport. She's still relatively young, but I'm nervous."

"Will you stop worrying? I'm sure we can get going soon."

"Mommy, I'm hungry. Can we eat?" Stevie whined from the shelter of Sally's arms.

"Of course, honey. In a little bit. We have to work some things out." She'd switched to her mommy voice, low and pleasant, which soothed the little boy. He settled back and put his thumb in his mouth.

"No thumb—" Steve started.

Sally shook her head. "Let it go this time, okay?"

Steve's lips clamped shut. He turned away from her.

Sally ran her hand over the fine stitching on the quilt and looked at Barb. "It's beautiful. Did you make it?"

"My mother did. I've got more of her handiwork. Maybe I'll have time to show you while you're here."

"Oh—your mother. Is she still living?" She flicked her gaze at Steve.

Instead of answering Sally, Barb backed toward the kitchen. "I'll go see about some snacks." She disappeared through the swinging door.

Tom scratched his head. "Okay then—we heard a news report earlier that they might be closing the highway down. Have they already done that?"

"Yeah," Steve said, "that's why we pulled in here—or rather, slid in. Our rig's in the ditch on the other side of the road. The highway's closed about two miles ahead and closed behind us too. We saw the sign and the arrow pointing up here and decided to see if we could stay a few hours until the roads open again. Then we'll be on our way."

"We've had a power outage," Barb said, coming back with paper plates and napkins. "That's the reason for the candles. I'm sure you already figured that out though."

"And I messed up and didn't get gas for the emergency generator when I went to town earlier," Tom added. "I'll have to try later when the weather breaks."

Steve glanced at the woodstove, now roaring. "You must have a battery-powered fan, right?"

Tom nodded. "Can't be too careful living up in this neck of the woods. Except for forgetting to put gas in my cans, that is." He grinned.

Steve grinned back. "I guess even a marine makes mistakes, huh?"

Tom stared. "How did you know?"

Steve pointed at the dining table a few feet away, where Tom's favorite marine corps hat lay. "Unless that's only for show . . ."

Tom's fists tightened at his sides. "Certainly not. Did three tours in Vietnam."

Steve stepped forward and stuck out his hand again. "Thank you for your service, sir. If I remember correctly, you guys didn't get much gratitude when you came home."

Tom glared. "We didn't want gratitude from anyone. Just a little respect."

In his periphery, he saw Barb rise from her chair, and he forced himself to relax.

Steve spread his hands wide. "You have mine. My father and grandfather were both in the army. I have nothing but respect and admiration for both of them. By the time I was old enough, they'd done away with the draft as it was, and I went to college. So I never had the honor of serving."

"Glad you didn't have to," Tom replied. He noticed Barb had

returned to her chair. "What about those snacks for our guests? Or are we eating the paper plates and napkins?"

Barb shot a look at him. "Very funny." To Sally, she said, "How about some . . . oh, I was going to say coffee and hot chocolate, but we have no power—"

Tom waved at the woodstove. "Can you heat up water and milk on the stove?"

Barb's forehead wrinkled. "That might take a while."

"Don't we have two full gas cans in the Jeep, Steve?"

"Hey, good idea, Sal. Mr. Masters, what about it? We could use that for your generator and fill my cans later. How big is your generator?"

"It's big—holds about seven gallons. If we filled it, being conservative, it should get us through until the power's back on. And none of this 'Mr. Masters' stuff—please call me Tom. It's the least I can do if you're going to supply the gas to run this outfit."

"We'd certainly like to pitch in if we have to stay until tomorrow. Do you want to give it a try? As I said, we have nowhere else to go—although we do hate to interrupt your weekend."

Tom smirked at Barb across the room. "Oh, we didn't have any *real* plans for this weekend, did we, Barb?"

She giggled. "Now, Tom, don't—"

Steve's brow furrowed. "Uh, did we miss something?"

Tom straightened up his face. "No, we didn't mean . . . it was . . . oh, I can't explain. It's a private joke. We weren't laughing at you. Honest."

"While you're trying to take your foot out of your mouth," Barb said, "how about you men go put some gas in the generator? Then I'll put on that pot of coffee. Kids, would you like some hot cocoa?"

"Yay—hot chocolate!" Stevie crowed.

Steve put his finger to his lips. "Not so loud, son," he said, tousling the small boy's hair.

"Yay—hot chocolate," Stevie whispered.

Steve threw back his head and laughed. "You little smarty pants."

"Folks, really," Tom went on, "the inn is empty this weekend, and you're more than welcome to stay as long as you need to. But is your rig okay?"

"Yeah, I think it is. We walked the short distance across the road and up your long driveway, but that was enough to convince me we're not going anywhere tonight. I managed to straighten it out, and it's off the road, but it'll be safer in your driveway. And we'll be glad to pay you when we leave. Please make sure you give us a bill. Right, Sally?"

"Yes, of course we will."

Tom pursed his lips. "We'll see about that. I'm not the bookkeeper, but we can talk about that later. The important thing is to get you warmed up after your ordeal."

Barb gestured toward the kitchen. "Yes, let's get you all comfortable and fed. You guys get going. We'll wait until the lights come on, then get started in the kitchen."

Within twenty minutes, the lights blinked on. Tom and Steve stomped back into the house, high-fiving each other.

"Okay, let's get this party started." Barb headed for the kitchen, followed by Sally.

Chapter 11

"This is so kind of you, Barb—" Sally stopped in the doorway, staring. "What a beautiful kitchen. I feel like I've been transported to the past, but with all the modern conveniences." Sally cast an appreciative downward gaze at the hardwood plank floor while running a hand over the blue-gray granite countertop to her right. "Did you and Tom do this yourselves?"

"Yes, I think we worked the hardest on this space—probably because we knew we'd spend a lot of time in here, with or without guests. I've always thought of the kitchen as the soul of a home."

Sally nodded, clearly enjoying the modern slate appliances juxtaposed with old-fashioned wainscoted walls and paned windows reaching the ceiling. A high shelf encircled the entire kitchen. Antique flour and sugar cans and appliances from the forties and fifties graced the shelf, interspersed with black-and-white photos of stern-faced folks posed stiffly in front of small cabins. Across the kitchen, the windowed door had a distressed finish and sheer white curtains partially covering the glass.

Sally went to the door and peered out. "Oh! This is a surprise—I thought I'd see your backyard. Is it okay if I go in?"

"Of course. It's Tom's favorite room in the house. It'll be icy in there though. We turn the heat off to that room while we're on the generator. If we spend any time in there, we can always fire up the second woodstove Tom installed."

She turned the vintage crystal doorknob and ushered Sally down two steps into the sitting room.

The room was dark, illuminated only by the glow of the kitchen light behind them.

The two women picked their way around the furniture to stand side by side in front of the windows.

Sally touched the glass. "You're right. It's cold in here."

Barb flipped on the porch light and opened the sheer curtains wider.

The back porch held an impressive stack of firewood Tom had cut and split during the summer and fall. The outline of a large shed—built by Tom—was just visible in the driving storm. The pine trees behind the shed bent in the wind.

"It's so . . . so wild looking. But inside, it's so cozy."

"We took an old falling-down screened porch and turned it into this sitting room. The door over there"—Barb pointed left—"leads out back. And if you look that way"—she motioned to her right, out the window—"you'll see the bridge Tom built over the creek for easy access to the hiking trails up the mountain to the north of us. Before he built the bridge, we had to walk down the road about a quarter of a mile to get across."

Sally put her face to the glass and peered at the bridge through the snow. "It looks quaint. Did he use recycled wood?"

"Yes, he used reclaimed wood from the house when we remodeled. Most of it came from the old flooring we stripped out of the kitchen and from walls we removed when we added our bedroom and sitting room, which are sort of hidden, down a short hallway from the dining room."

"What's the story of the old bell over there, on this side of the bridge?"

"It was Tom's grandmother's. It used to be mounted on the front steps to call everyone to dinner. Tom didn't want to part with it."

"I can see why." Sally turned her gaze back into the dimness of the room. "Some things from the past *should* be brought into the present," she added, "to tell us who we are."

Barb looked away, fists curled at her sides.

Sally glanced at her. "I'm sorry. Steve says I think too much. And he doesn't understand the urgency to leave and go see . . . oh, never mind that. I won't burden you with our problems."

Barb relaxed her hands, then offered, "Your comment about the past being part of our present is actually profound. And I bet you're not only talking about bells, are you?"

"No, I guess I'm not. Sometimes we tend to run away from the past like it's our enemy. Steve and I have done that, and it brought us to grief. We hide from it, or we try to box it in and tuck it away somewhere, like old clothes. But the past, no matter whether good or bad, is what tethers us to the present. Without the past, we're like anchorless ships." Sally stopped and looked at Barb's face. "Sorry. Didn't mean to get all serious like that."

"It's okay, Sally. And anyway, I think you're right."

Barb turned the outside light off and the room lights on. Instead of harsh overhead bulbs, small canned ceiling fixtures and several lamps glowed softly around the room. Three groupings of sofas and recliners, enclosed by mute gray-blue walls trimmed in white, created an intimate atmosphere.

Sally squealed in pleasure and walked to the middle of the room.

Barb loved this part—experiencing this favorite room through the eyes and emotions of her guests. She watched as Sally's gaze traveled over the dozens of family photographs and paintings on one wall, then to the small woodstove in the corner. She ran a hand over the chocolate-brown leather of Tom's favorite chair, then bent over the antique coffee table to look at the stacks of books and magazines.

Sally straightened, arms hugging herself, and turned to face Barb, soft freckles framing a wide smile.

"I'm so jealous. I've tried to get Steve to do some remodeling on our house. But he doesn't want to spend the money—or the time. I think of it as an investment, but he thinks of it as a big expense—one we can't afford right now. I'd like a room like this—a retreat from reality, so to speak."

"That it is—sometimes. Reality's overrated."

Sally giggled. "Agreed. You've done a great job. If I lived here, I'd never want to leave."

"I don't," Barb said softly. "Ever want to leave. We've poured our hearts into this place. And we love sharing it with others. Maybe someday you and Steve can have your dream house."

"Maybe—"

"Memories are tucked in every room, every floorboard, every corner of this inn. Some good, some not. But they're ours, the fabric of our life together."

Barb closed the draperies, then faced Sally again. "Some days I'd like to forget some of those memories. But you were right before—they made us who we are today."

She made her way back to the kitchen door. "Hey, we'd better get busy in the kitchen before your hungry kids storm the door."

Sally slowly sidestepped along the wall, leaning close to each picture. "I don't see any children in these pictures. You and Tom don't have any?"

"No." Barb steadied herself with a deep breath. "Let's go back in, Sally. *Yours* are still waiting for their hot chocolate. And anyway, I'm frozen."

She opened the door and stood aside to let Sally by, then turned off the lights to the sitting room.

"Thank you for showing me around," Sally murmured. "You and Tom must be so proud of what you've done here."

"Yes, well . . . I'm just glad to hear the refrigerator running again."

Sally chuckled. "There is that. How long do you suppose you'll be on the generator?"

"I have no idea. That's Tom's problem."

Barb busied herself putting the coffee on and pouring milk into two small mugs. She put the mugs into the microwave, setting the timer for one minute, then perched on a tall stool at the generous center island, gesturing Sally to the other stool.

"It's homey, peaceful . . . nothing can touch you here, like you're being guarded by all the other folks who've lived here before," Sally commented, clearly admiring the easy mix of past and present.

"We've had our moments." Barb's gaze strayed to the windowsill, to the curve of Katie's soft cheek on the cup fragment. Her blue eye winked in the glow of the light over the sink.

Sally's glance followed her own.

Barb rose and went to the sink—blocking Sally's view—and turned on the water, pretending to wash her hands.

"Do you like chocolate chip cookies?" she asked, desperate to deflect the conversation.

"Oh yeah—the children for sure, although Steve could outeat them if I let him," Sally said.

"Would you mind getting a platter down from that cupboard over the refrigerator?" Barb asked without turning from the sink. "I'm so short, I'd have to get a stool. You can arrange the cookies on it—they're in the tin on the counter next to the refrigerator."

"Of course."

As Sally opened the cupboard, Barb set the cup fragment inside a small bowl on the windowsill, facedown.

Sally brought the plate of cookies to the counter. "I'm sorry if I made you uncomfortable before. Sometimes I—"

The microwave chimed. Barb grabbed the coffee carafe and

gathered cups, spoons, sugar, and cream. Sally set the plate of cookies down and added chocolate syrup to the two mugs of steaming milk. They gathered everything on a rolling cart and wheeled it to the dining room.

# Chapter 12

As they entered, the children clapped their hands. "Cookies!"

"Chocolate chip—our favorite," Steve added.

Tom, placing another small log in the woodstove, stood and grinned as Barb set the platter on the table. "Oh, we have cookies? When did you make those?"

Barb shot him a glare. "Now don't start on me. You know very well when I made them—and it's lucky we have any to share after all you've filched."

Tom noticed the startled stares from Steve and Sally—and the kids frozen in their reach for the cookies—and thought maybe they'd gone too far.

Barb laughed. "Oh, don't mind us . . . Tom's teasing me. Let me explain. We *did* have a plan for this weekend, but it fell through. We'd planned to have Tom's nephew and his family for a long weekend, but with the weather and all, their flight from California was canceled."

Tom took up the story. "Yeah, and we've been working our backsides off for the last week or two getting ready for them. It's been better than five years since we've seen them. They're having some difficulties, and we . . . we wanted to try to help." He glanced at Barb.

She took the cue. "Sorry to unload on you like that, but we're a bit disappointed in not getting to see them."

"No, that's okay," Steve said. "Sorry you're stuck with us."

Barb waved her hand in dismissal. "Don't be sorry—we'd like to have company this weekend . . . and the good thing is, we're prepared."

"Yeah, I agree." Tom put his arm around Barb. "Have a cookie, Steve."

"We're only too happy to help, right kids?" Steve reached for one.

Tom sat down and gestured for Steve to take a seat. "Barb and I were sitting here in the candlelight—before you arrived, trying to figure out what God . . . well, why this storm had to happen *this* weekend, the canceled flight, and then the electricity going off. At first we were . . . to be honest, we were angry. Why *this* weekend, after all the plans we'd made?"

Tom heard nothing but munching and slurping after his mild rant.

Sally broke the silence. "You mentioned God. Do you blame him for the storm and your plans falling through?

"Who else would they blame?" Steve asked, flicking his finger up at the ceiling. Clearly, his attempt at humor fell a bit short. "Sorry. I didn't mean that the way it sounded."

Barb shrugged. "It's not that we're *blaming* God. He must have a good reason for it, but we'd sure like it if he'd share it with us."

"Are you folks churchgoers? Christians?" Tom asked.

Samantha beat her parents to the punch. "Yeah—we go every Sunday, don't we, Mommy?"

Sally laughed. "Most Sundays. I know what you mean, though, about wishing God would share his plans with you. I've been there.

In fact, I'm there right now. I'm not sure if I'll get to see Mom . . . while she's still . . ."

Steve patted her shoulder. "Now don't make it more serious than it is. Lots of people have strokes and recover. You have to be positive."

"While Gramma's still what?" Samantha asked, patting a staccato beat on Sally's elbow. "Still what?"

"Never mind. I guess I'm disappointed we're here instead of with her." She wiped her eyes and leaned down and kissed the tip of Samantha's nose. "But we must make the best of it."

Steve grunted. "Sal, let's be positive, okay?" He jerked his head at Samantha. "For them?"

"How about some more coffee?" Barb picked up the carafe and refilled their cups.

Sally sipped her coffee. "Oh, that tastes good, Barb." She leaned back in her chair. "I don't mean to complain. I *am* glad we have a place to stay."

Tom waved her off. "No, no, it's fine. I guess we have to go with what's happened, one way or another. I'm sure you'll be able to leave soon."

Steve cleared his throat. "Well, that's—"

"Mommy, can I *please* have another cookie?" Stevie asked, clearly bored by the conversation.

"Yes, you may, and thank you for asking instead of just grabbing." Sally leaned closer to her son. "Stevie, you've got chocolate on your nose," she said, wiping it with a napkin.

"Hey, I was saving that for later," he quipped, causing chuckles from the adults.

Tom picked up the plate of cookies, taking two for himself, and started it around the table again.

Sally took the plate from Barb. "You know, if we have to be here for a day or two, maybe I could help you in the kitchen—"

A hammering pounded the front door.

Stevie dropped his cup, splashing cocoa on Samantha, who let out an ear-piercing shriek.

Sally hushed Samantha while Steve rushed into the kitchen with Barb, returning with towels to clean up the mess.

"Hey! Anybody home?"

Tom started for the closet to get his shotgun.

"Let us in. We're freezing—"

"Come on. Open the door!" yelled a female voice, louder than the others.

At the sound of the girl's voice, Tom veered away from the closet and headed toward the door.

Hand on the knob, he said over his shoulder to Barb, "Where have I heard *this* before?"

# Chapter 13

*D*éjà vu.

This time a shivering trio stood on his porch—a man, a woman, and a teenage girl.

The teen—Tom thought about fifteen—pushed the woman aside to stand in front of Tom.

"Dude! It's about darned time—it's cold out here. Are you gonna let us in or what?"

Tom bristled at her rude glare, and he wasn't impressed with the multicolored hair straggling under her hat, nor the black fingernails and nose ring.

Samantha's head popped out from behind Tom, eyes glued to the spectacle.

"Can I help you?" the teenager demanded. "Stare somewhere else, ya little—"

Samantha scampered away in obvious fright, landing in a chair at the table next to Sally.

"Joanie," the woman said. "Don't be rude." She grabbed the girl's elbow.

"Ow—that hurt, Mom."

The mother's grip tightened. "There's more where that came from. Behave yourself."

Anger buzzed between them like an electrical current.

Who were these people?

Tom quelled the hesitation in his mind and stepped aside to let them in.

The man brushed snow off his coat onto the floor. "Hi. The name's Bill Brown," he boomed through a pasted-on smile showing rows of gleaming white teeth.

"And this is my wife and our daughter, Joanie—that would be the one rolling her eyes. We're from Sandpoint, trying to get to Newport to drop Joanie off so we can catch a plane in Spokane. Going to Las Vegas for the weekend—big company convention," he bragged.

He reminded Tom of an irritating tool salesman who'd called on his hardware store years ago.

The man's wife stepped forward. "Susan. Pleased to meet you."

Barb dipped her head. "Likewise."

Tom stuck out his hand to Bill, who shook it heartily. "I'm Tom Masters, and this is my wife, Barb."

He then offered his hand to Joanie. "Pleased to meet you . . . uh, Joanie, is it?"

She looked away and put her hands behind her, leaving Tom's dangling in midair.

He slid his hand into his pocket, trying to make it seem like a natural gesture—and failing miserably, judging by the awkward silence that followed. The snow from Bill's coat puddled on the hardwood floor.

"I'm sure you're all very tired and cold," Barb said, a shade too loud. "Won't you come in and join us for some coffee or hot chocolate, and cookies? It's warmer over there by the stove, Joanie." She gestured across the room.

Shoving past Barb, Joanie muttered, "Yeah." Jerking her wet coat and hat off, she dropped them onto Tom's leather recliner, grabbed a cookie on her way across the room, and stood in front of the woodstove, her disgruntled glare raking the room.

Barb retrieved the coat and hat and spread them on the bench closest to the woodstove. Grabbing a napkin, she wiped the moisture from the chair with jerky movements.

With a shake of her head in Joanie's direction, Susan said, "We hate to intrude, but the highway's a mess and we couldn't go any farther. Thank you for letting us come in for a little while and get warm and dry." She removed her coat and scarf, took Bill's jacket from him, and hung them on hooks next to the front door.

The Elliott family had watched the drama from their seats at the table, but now they stood and stepped into the living room.

Steve came forward and shook Bill's hand. "I'm afraid it's going to be for more than a little while. We heard the roads might be closed for a couple of days. And by the way, we're practically neighbors—just south from you, in Sagle. My name's Steve Elliott, and this is my wife, Sally. And those two"—he aimed a finger toward the children—"are Samantha and Stevie."

"A couple of days?" Bill exclaimed, ignoring the introductions. "That's no good. Are you sure?"

Susan put a hand on his arm. "Maybe it will clear up sooner than we think."

He shook her hand off. "So you're a weatherman now?"

"No, of course not, but maybe—"

Tom shook his head. "Not likely, I'm afraid. This has the makings of a major blizzard. Roads in these parts don't close unless they expect the worst. But you being from Sandpoint and all, I'd guess you know that."

Bill's face reddened. "Of course I know that. But the weather reports said nothing about a blizzard. Why can't those guys ever get anything right?"

Joanie's voice cut in above them. "What? You mean we have to stay *here?*"

"Joan—" Susan stepped away from Bill.

Joanie let her backpack thud to the floor. "That's great. We should've kept on going instead of heading up here. Way to go, Dad."

"Now calm down," Bill said, his voice tight. "I'll have to get busy on my laptop and change our reservations, that's all." He looked at Susan. "We can call your sister in Newport and tell her we'll drop Joanie off as soon as the weather clears." He took his phone out of his pocket.

Tom cleared his throat. "Umm, there's just one tiny problem with that. Our internet connection's down. You won't be able to change your flight on your computer. And we've lost cell service."

"Oh, I'll have to use your landline then. No problem. Can I use that phone?" He pointed to a side table against the wall.

"It's down too. But let me try again." Tom picked it up and, hearing nothing, put it down again. "Sorry. Guess you're stuck with us for a while."

Bill's face tinged red. One hand on his hip, he gestured vaguely to the room. "What in the world are we gonna do here—"

Susan stepped to his side and laid a hand on his arm. "I'm sure everything will work out."

Tom's internal radar activated. Susan had done this before, he was sure of it.

Susan glanced sideways at Tom and Barb. "It was to be a short vacation for us, a few days without . . . a few days alone."

"Yeah, leaving me behind, as usual," Joanie muttered from her perch by the fire.

Susan raised her index finger in Joanie's direction. "Stop—"

Joanie gripped the bench with both hands. "Mom, you always—"

"Joanie, please keep your rude comments to yourself."

"Oh, right, you can be rude, but I don't even have a say—"

Bill cut in. "It *was* going to be a great weekend. You know—the shows, the casinos and restaurants, the whole nine yards. And the suite I booked is fabulous—minibar, jacuzzi, big-screen TV. Guess that's not happening now." He rubbed the back of his neck.

"That's too bad," Steve said. "I'm sure you were both looking forward to time away."

"And *we* were on our way to see my mother," Sally explained. "She lives outside Newport in an apartment building. But right now, she's in the hospital in Newport. She's only fifty-six, but she had a small stroke, and they want to move her to—"

Joanie's voice filled the room. "Geez! Who cares about all this?"

"That's rude. Apologize at once, young lady," her mother insisted.

"Joanie—" Bill started.

"We've got four-wheel drive, Dad. Can't we leave now?"

"I said, apologize—now. This isn't all about you." Susan's voice raised a notch.

"Why should I? This place is stupid—no Wi-Fi, no TV, no phones, no fun." Joanie faced her dad. "Tell me we can leave, that we don't have to stay here."

Bill grimaced at Tom. "Maybe we should go to the local motel and get out of your hair."

"I'm afraid we're it for about ten miles in either direction." Tom tried to keep the regret out of his voice. "And, Joanie, I'm sure you'll be quite comfortable here. We have lots of food, rooms upstairs, and we do have some board games you kids can play—"

Joanie sneered. "Do I look like I wanna play board games with those two little brats—"

"I'm sure we'll be quite comfortable. How many bedrooms do you have?" Susan asked.

Barb answered with a twinge of pride in her voice. "We have plenty of room. There's our room downstairs and three good-sized rooms upstairs, each with its own bathroom."

"Only three? There's seven of us. Someone will have to share," Susan replied.

"Come on—tell me I'm not sleeping in the same room with these . . . these—"

Susan interrupted, her voice weary. "I'm sure everything will work out fine, Joanie. We'll have to adjust for a few days, that's all. I'm sure you can manage until we can get on the road. Try thinking of others for a change."

Joanie crossed her arms in front of her, clearly not giving an inch. "Dad, do something. Maybe I can bunk here on the sofa or something—"

Bill locked eyes with Susan. Her mute expression screamed at him not to give in.

What is it with these three? Tom thought. *A whole weekend of this?*

"I'm sorry, sweetheart," Bill said gently, taking Joanie's hand, "but I'm afraid you're going to have to make the best of it, like everyone else. We'll make it up to you. I promise."

She groaned. "Stuck with a bunch of idiots—I think I've died and this sure isn't heaven!"

Chapter 14

"**C**an you believe that dinner? I mean, the meal was fine—but that brat, Joanie. What's up with her?" Tom said as he helped Barb clear the table after a later dinner than usual.

"Shh, Tom. Keep your voice down."

"Geez, if she were my daughter, I'd give her a serious attitude adjustment," he added, carrying a load of plates to the kitchen. "And I'm sure the Elliotts were uncomfortable. They're probably afraid to come out of their room." He set the plates on the counter.

"I know." Barb slid the dishes into a tub full of hot, soapy water. "Sure wish I could use the dishwasher—"

"I know. Just a couple of days. Do you need some help with that?"

"No, but thanks."

Tom poured himself a cup of coffee and stared out the window.

Barb rinsed the plates and grabbed a towel. "The tension between Bill and Susan feels like a rubber band ready to snap. And Joanie plays one parent off the other like a virtuoso. Don't you think there's something unnatural about the way Joanie and Bill

talk to each other? It's as if he's sucking up to her or something."
She shrugged. "I don't get it. I'm glad dinner's over and they're all
upstairs."

"Hmm, never heard you say anything like that about our guests
before."

"You don't know what I've thought though," she responded.
"And I hadn't met the teenager from down under yet."

"The family dynamics are skewed, that's for sure," Tom replied.
"I wonder what happened?"

Their conversation was interrupted by a crash overhead and
raised voices. Tom started for the kitchen door, but Barb stopped
him.

"It's none of our business. It sounds like Joanie's demanding
attention again. We should let her parents handle it and pretend we
didn't hear anything," Barb insisted.

"*Pretend* we didn't hear?" Tom yanked his arm away. "I bet the
whole valley heard. And what in tarnation do you mean 'none of
our business'? This is *our* home, and I want to know what the trouble is—and what got broken up there." He leaned down into her
face. "And I'm dang certain after what we saw at dinner, they're not
going to 'handle it.'"

"Please don't—"

"Don't be a sissy. I'm gonna listen from the bottom of the stairs.
You can come or not."

He stalked to the door. As he opened it, he heard the argument
gaining in strength. He walked to the foot of the stairs and stood
with one foot on the first step, his ear cocked, now able to hear the
conversation.

Barb tiptoed behind him and stood by the dining table with a
death grip on the back of a chair.

The quarrel reached a crescendo when Bill's voice roared above
the others. "Joanie, I will not have this attitude anymore. This is
not our home, those are not your books, and I will not tolerate you

throwing things. You'd best get a handle on that temper of yours before you find yourself out on the front porch in a sleeping bag—do you hear? Now pick up those books and put them back on the shelf where you found them—"

Tom gave a thumbs-up to Barb. "I guess he is handling it," he whispered.

"I don't care. Put me out on the porch if you want to. I'm not going to be saddled with that little twerp, d'ya hear? Why can't she bunk with her brother?" Joanie yelled.

Tom grimaced. "I guess she's not—"

"Joanie, for Pete's sake—I think you can put up with it for a few days." Bill lowered his voice a notch. "We may even be able to leave as soon as tomorrow. Now, apologize to Samantha and to your mother. Now."

Tom heard nothing but an exaggerated snort from Joanie.

"Joanie, honey," Susan began in a measured tone. "She's a little girl, and she's trying to be friendly. Why do you make it so difficult? Can you please try to get along? We know it's hard. We would rather be on our way to Las Vegas right now, but this has happened, and we all must try to make the best of it. What do you say, huh? Can you try?"

Tom shook his head. "Mothers. I hate that wheedling tone."

"I wouldn't know, now would I?" Barb shot back. Her hands flew to her mouth. "Tom, I'm sorry. I didn't mean . . ."

They stared at each other in silence, the past lying between them like the shattered cup this morning.

"Barb, I didn't mean to hurt—"

"I know. Me either. Maybe her 'wheedling tone' will do the job."

Joanie's tirade heated up, pulling them back to the present.

"Fine. But she'd better stay out of my stuff and away from me. She's always asking stupid questions. She's never even used a cell phone—can you believe that? She thought mine was a toy. She. Is. Stupid."

"As I said, she's a little girl. Not every child is raised with all the whistles and bells the way you were."

"Yeah, Sue, make this about me," Bill sneered. "Like you always do. Everything's always my fault." Then in a coddling voice, "Joanie, I'm glad you'll try to get along. I appreciate it. Do your best to get through the next few days, and I'll buy you that sound bar you want for your computer. But you must try hard to be kind and considerate no matter how annoying anyone is. How about it? Deal?"

Tom raised his eyes to the ceiling. "Oh brother. Sure, bait the kid."

"Deal."

Susan exploded. "Why must she always get a reward? We're only asking her to behave. You don't always have to bribe her."

"It's not a bribe, Susan. It's a reward for good behavior," Bill countered.

"It's a bribe if the good behavior hasn't happened yet. Can't you see what she's doing?"

"Yeah, she's trying. And she knows a good deal when she hears it."

"And you know all about good deals, don't you, Mr. Salesman of the Year?"

Barb moved to Tom's side and drew him away from the stairs. "They're making it an argument between themselves instead of about Joanie's behavior," she whispered.

"And that's exactly what Joanie wants. They should be standing shoulder to shoulder instead of turning on each other. That young lady has divide and conquer down to a science. Man, what I wouldn't have given to have her tactical expertise on the battlefield—"

"Always a soldier. But this isn't the battlefield, Tom. It's our home, and these people need help."

Tom backpedaled. "Of course. I know that. I was only trying to lighten up."

She gave his hand a squeeze. "It seems much calmer, anyway. Maybe we should finish clearing the table now."

Tom nodded. "Yeah, okay, but they'd better knock off the shenanigans," he said, not moving.

"I'm going downstairs now," Sue said. "I'm sure Tom and Barb are wondering what in the world is going on up here. Joanie, make sure you finish picking up those books. Then come downstairs and try to be pleasant, young lady."

"Whatever, Mom—" Then a door slammed and it was quiet again.

Tom and Barb beat a hasty retreat to the table, picking up the last of the dinner dishes and carrying them into the kitchen. When they tiptoed out, Susan stood in the dining room with her back to them, head bowed, hands covering her face.

A floorboard creaked under Tom's shoe, giving them away.

Susan whipped around, pushing her hair back from her face, not meeting their eyes.

"Is everything all right up there?" Tom said.

"I guess you heard part of that? Some books . . . umm . . . fell off the bookcase in the playroom. Joanie's putting them back."

Fell off, my backside. Why do they cover for her? Tom couldn't think of anything pleasant to say, so he said nothing.

Barb jumped in. "I'm sure she will. There's no harm done. We want everyone to be comfortable. We know this isn't easy for you or the Elliotts, especially the children, to miss out on your vacation plans. And Sally's mother—I hope they can leave soon. Maybe this bad weather won't last as long as predicted and you can be on your way again."

Susan stole a look at them, then down at the floor. "Joanie's a little high strung," she murmured. "She has quite a well-developed knack for making a mountain out of a molehill. You . . . you know how teenaged girls can be."

High strung? Right. Tom headed for the sanctuary of his

recliner a few feet away, hoping for no more drama.

"Susan, would you like a cup of herbal tea? I always have one after dinner, and you're welcome to join me," Barb asked.

"That . . . that would be lovely. I'd like that."

"Why don't you come into the kitchen and choose your flavor. I have several varieties."

Susan nodded and followed Barb into the kitchen.

Tom sat down in his chair and picked up the latest issue of *Bed & Breakfast, American Style.* He'd flipped several pages and skimmed two articles when an angry bellow sounded from overhead.

Tom let out a groan. According to the grandfather clock, tranquility had lasted exactly seven and a half minutes.

 # Chapter 15

A stampede sounded on the stairs. Then a tornado roiled into the living room, pursued by a smaller one.

Joanie stalked across the room, a tablet under her arm, and dropped into a corner of the sofa, a scowl on her face. She opened the tablet, ignoring Samantha, who'd followed and stood next to her, spilling words a mile a minute.

Her high voice reminded Tom of baby birds in the spring pine trees, squeaking and calling for their mamas to bring dinner.

He lowered his magazine half an inch to watch the second act of this drama—*The Joanie and Samantha Show*. Joanie had changed into dry clothes before dinner, and Tom was not impressed with her choices. Ripped jeans, white tank top picturing a spiky-haired musician in heavy eye makeup holding a broken guitar above his head. Heavy black plastic jewelry climbed both arms to her elbows. Hair spiked even more—like bright-green icepicks pointed at the ceiling. Long purple tresses tied up into pigtails above each ear. The result was like something out of a horror movie, and it was anything but appealing.

"Joanie, what's that?" Samantha chirped. "Is that an iPad? I never saw one for real. Can I hold it? What does it do? Do you have games on it? Can I play with it? I promise not to break it." Samantha's excited chatter showed no signs of letting up as Joanie's face reddened.

Tom watched—over the top edge of the page—ready to intervene if necessary. His biceps tensed. He itched to back Joanie into a corner and teach her a lesson she wouldn't forget.

The moment came sooner than Tom anticipated.

Joanie launched herself from the sofa, clutching the tablet behind her in one hand, and shouted. "Get out of my face, you little—"

Tom thought her voice could've awakened his long-dead grandfather. "Hey, you—"

He stopped when he heard thumping on the stairs. Steve appeared at the bottom, and Tom pointed at the drama between the two girls just in time to see the escalation of the war.

Joanie pushed Samantha, catching her on the breastbone and causing her to step backward. She tripped over the edge of the claw-footed coffee table and fell to her seat. "Ow, Joanie! That hurt!" She held her foot up and rubbed her ankle, then scooted out of Joanie's reach.

Tom sprang out of his chair, waiting for Joanie to cross another line. He held up a finger at Steve, staying him where he was. Steve, clearly eager to intervene, instead moved to stand at the back of the sofa.

Joanie bent and pointed her finger in Samantha's face. "Get out of here and keep your grubby little hands off my stuff or I'll hurt you again." She glared at Samantha, clearly daring her to say something. Then she hunkered down on the sofa again and put her feet up on the coffee table, using her heels to move magazines aside. They fell with a crash to the floor.

Tom moved fast. He darted to Samantha's side, stepping over Joanie's legs, then shoved them off the coffee table.

"Hey—"

He pivoted, pointing his finger. "Don't—not another word. That's *my* table. Those are *my* magazines. And keep your feet on the floor," he said in a low, measured tone. He towered over her. "I've had enough of you. This is my home, and I won't tolerate your behavior anymore, do you hear? And I won't be making any deals with you for sound bars or any other toys you want. It's up to you to behave or not, but I guarantee you, if you choose unwisely, it won't go well for you—I'll see to it."

Joanie's eyes widened like twin moons.

"This isn't an idle threat—it's a clear promise. Do you understand me?"

She glared at him with narrowed eyes, like firing slits in her face.

"I asked you a question. Answer it—a simple 'yes, sir' will be sufficient."

"Yes . . . *sir.*"

Tom stepped over to Samantha and helped her to her feet, then steered her toward Steve. He turned on Joanie, ready to give her another dose of his pent-up frustration.

But he didn't have to say a word. Susan and Barb had come in behind him, and they'd obviously heard at least part of what he'd said.

Her mother had better get that girl in hand, or Tom would do it for her. If this went on much longer, he'd be arrested for murder.

Susan set the cups and saucers on the table, then strode to the end of the sofa.

"Now listen—no more of that. I heard you yelling like a banshee—"

"And she pushed Samantha down and hurt her," Steve added.

Joanie's scowl deepened.

Sally had entered the room from upstairs and moved to stand with Steve. She gave her small daughter a hug and rubbed her shoulders.

Steve put his arm around her. "Where's Stevie?"

"I left him playing a game on my phone. What's going on?"

"Shh. I'll fill you in later."

Sally nodded and took Samantha over to the table and sat her down near Barb.

Barb patted Samantha's hand, then turned toward the living room. "Joanie, I can see you're upset. Is there anything we can do to make you more comfortable?"

Tom shot a glare in Barb's direction. In his book, it wasn't pampering the kid needed.

"Yeah, sure," Joanie yelled at Barb. "You can keep this little monster away from me. I don't know why she has to be in my room."

"Joanie, apologize. We're guests here—" Susan yelled back.

"Right. When hell freezes over."

"Will you both stop yelling please?" Sally's voice rose above the din. "And stop swearing like that—there are children present."

"Oh, and I suppose you guys never swear. Right."

"No, we don't. So please stop."

"Ha! Then I guess you're just too good for me."

Tight-lipped, Sally turned her attention to Samantha.

Susan glanced at Tom. "Sorry, but I can't let this go."

Tom waved his hand in Joanie's direction. "Don't apologize. By all means, proceed."

He picked up his magazine again. He knew this wasn't his battle, as much as he wanted it to be. But he kept his magazine low enough to be able to keep one eye on the domestic skirmish playing out in his living room.

Susan marched over to Joanie, leaned down, and gripped Joanie's chin, forcing her head up.

Joanie grimaced in pain. "That hurts, Mom." She struggled to escape from Susan's iron clasp. "And anyway, where's Dad?"

"I don't know and I don't care. And that's not all that's going to hurt if you don't straighten up. I will have no more of this. Apologize—now."

Joanie sat unmoving, arms crossed, eyes focused across the room at the window. Susan leaned forward and pinched Joanie's earlobe with one hand, grasping her shoulder with the other and raising the teenager to her feet.

"Apologize now or you'll never see that iPad again."

"Mom, come on. I—"

Bill's voice boomed over the tension-filled room. "Apologize for what?" he asked, hands on his hips, surveying the scene.

"Wow . . . I take a short walk out by the creek and come back to my wife manhandling my daughter—"

Startled, Tom lowered his magazine to his lap.

Bill's eyes glittered at Susan. "What's up? Why does she have to apologize?"

Susan whirled around. "She's at fault, Bill. And I wasn't manhandling her. I won't stand her rudeness a moment longer—you know how she can be."

"What'd she do?"

"Steve said she pushed little Samantha down and hurt her for no reason, that's what. Now, either you discipline her—which'd be a miracle—or I will."

Joanie's lips curled in contempt. "Oh, right, Mom. Take the twerp's side." To her father in a buttery tone, "Dad, she tried to take my iPad. I was trying to tell her she can't play with it unless I let her."

"Hey, I didn't try to take it. I was only—"

Sally shushed the child. "Sammie, be quiet."

"Joanie, that's not what you said and that's not what you did. And you shouldn't have brought it anyway." Susan turned an accusing eye on Bill. "I told you so. I knew it would cause problems. You never listen to me—you always have to have your way, and you teach Joanie to behave the same."

Tom stifled the urge to intervene. He didn't think he could take much more of it. They didn't care about anyone else in the room—his living room.

Bill edged toward Joanie and put his arm around her. "I guess she has a right to do what she wants with her own stuff. And the little tw—uh, girl—shouldn't be touching her tablet anyway."

Susan jabbed a finger in his direction. "You weren't even in the room—you didn't see what happened. You're taking her word for it and I'm the bad guy again, as usual."

He let go of Joanie and advanced to within a foot of her. "Now *you're* whining. Grow up, why don't you? Always complaining, always pitting everyone against each other—"

"Me? It's you who does that—"

Tom threw his magazine on the side table and stood. He strode to the kitchen doorway, motioning to Barb as he passed her.

Steve and Sally followed suit, ushering Samantha out of the room and up the stairs.

As the kitchen door swung shut behind them, Tom heard Joanie whine again.

He pressed his thumbs to his temples and rubbed. If Bill didn't nip this nonsense in the bud, he would have no problem doing it for him.

Chapter 16

Bill watched until the kitchen door stopped its swing, then turned on Susan.

She braced for the onslaught.

"Way to go. As usual, you're making a federal case out of things. And you can stop with the victim mentality. It's getting old. If you feel like I'm making you the bad guy all the time, maybe it's because you are. Own it, why don't you."

"How can you say that to me? I want Joanie to behave, to obey what we ask of her. Why can't you see that?"

He leaned toward her and jabbed his index finger. "You mean what *you* ask of her."

She marched up to him and shook him by the shoulder. "What *we* ask of her," she said, straining to modulate her voice. "We need to present a united front. Don't you see how she manipulates us, always using every advantage to drive a wedge between us?"

She kept her eyes on Bill and jerked her thumb backward at Joanie, confident of her daughter's expression. "See? She's enjoying this—watching us at each other's throats. Please—we must put a stop to it before we fall apart—"

Bill slapped her hand from his shoulder and pushed her away. She watched his expression go from angry to conciliatory as he stepped back to Joanie's side.

Susan knew what would come next. This scene had replayed in their home over and over since Joanie was in grade school.

"And you call Joanie a drama queen?" He beckoned to his daughter. "Come on, princess," he cajoled. "Let's go somewhere where we're not always wrong. Maybe we can watch a movie or something—"

"Sure, do what you always do. Bribes always work for you, don't they? Maybe it's okay with clients, but your daughter isn't—"

Bill turned his back on her and enveloped Joanie in a bear hug. "We can use our room—it's bigger than yours and has its own TV. I saw some DVDs on the shelf up there, and Samantha won't be in there to bug you."

Still hugging her, he swung her around so they faced Susan. "Is that okay with you?" Sarcasm dripped in every syllable.

She knew she'd lost, but refused to give in. "We need to talk about this—"

It wouldn't work. It never worked. Bill never wanted to talk about anything unless it involved his own agenda.

Joanie tucked her iPad under her arm and took Bill's hand. As they edged past Susan to the stairway, she turned a condescending grin on her mother.

"Excuse me, Mother."

Susan stepped back to let them pass.

As they reached the stairway, Bill leaned over and whispered something to her, peering at Susan out of the corner of his eye. Their giggles followed them up the stairs.

Susan's heart thudded to her gut. She was the defeated enemy again. She rubbed her temples. One of her headaches threatened

. . . the headache that demanded why she'd ever married him. She hated going there, but she always did when they argued. In her mind's eye she saw Bill and Joanie raising the weapon of their close relationship and pointing it at her chest, challenging her to raise her weapon. She had none. She was helpless and always would be.

She might as well get used to it. She'd done this to herself. The bullet took flight and pierced her flesh, entered, and chipped off another piece of her heart.

Her fists tightened as hot tears formed in her eyes. She sat down at the far end of the dining table and lowered her head into her hands.

She faced the hard truth again. Bill and Joanie's relationship left no room for her. Susan felt like a stranger to her own husband and daughter. She remembered his veiled threat from last night. That could never happen.

Gradually her tears dried up, but she tramped the same ground again, littered with rocks and landmines. What happened? When Bill had returned from Iraq and had come to see her, she'd felt over that weeklong visit that her world had righted itself again after her devastating loss.

And when Joanie was born, Bill had stepped up admirably. They'd enjoyed several years caring for Joanie together, with close ties to family and church friends. When had it unraveled? When had Bill become so consumed with financial status? In the beginning, they'd struggled, but they were happy. When had the rot set in?

Susan's thoughts circled back to Bill and Joanie disappearing together, arm in arm, giggling and whispering—leaving her on the outside looking in.

She couldn't take this anymore. She was a third wheel in her own family . . . unwanted and unneeded.

But I need them—and there's the infernal misery of it.

 # Chapter 17

Susan started at the touch on her arm. She looked up to see Barb hovering over her, holding two steaming teacups.

Barb set the cups down. "I refilled them with fresh hot water." She hesitated, then plunged in. "Do you want to talk? Sometimes it's easier to confide in a stranger than in someone you know."

Susan shut her down. "There's nothing you can do. Nothing anyone can do. I know you're trying to be kind, but I don't want to talk about it."

Barb looked down at her hands, not sure what to say, not sure if she wanted this conversation. She was tired and still drained by the earlier conflicts with Tom.

She glanced at Susan, who had her chin in her hands, looking out the window. Then Susan lowered her forehead with a groan and pinched her eyes shut.

Compassion welled up in Barb's chest, pushing her fatigue aside.

She patted Susan's shoulder, then took the chair next to her and relaxed against the back.

She wanted to help her, but maybe she couldn't. Maybe she should just try to keep the peace between these people so Tom wouldn't . . . come unglued, like he did sometimes.

Susan finally raised her head, smoothing her short curls away from her face and straightening her collar. "I guess I should get this over with. Talk, I mean." She hunched over again, wrapping her arms around herself.

"You don't have to if you don't want to. But maybe it'll help. Lord knows, I need someone to talk to, even though sometimes I don't want to either. It's hard."

Susan frowned. "I don't know. You and Tom seem like the perfect couple and . . . I don't think you want to hear about our problems. Bill and I, we've made some colossal—unmendable—mistakes, and . . ." Susan trailed off, clearly surprised at the smirk on Barb's face.

"You're amused?"

"No, of course not. But somehow we have you completely fooled. We're not perfect by any means. I'm not sure I'm qualified to help you, but I have been known to be a good listener. Perhaps we can help each other."

Susan took a deep breath and sat back in her chair. Her hands fluttered, brushing nonexistent crumbs off the polished antique table. "After that scene tonight . . . is Tom angry?" She sniffed and dabbed at her nose with a tissue. "I'd hate that."

"He'll get over it. We're not strangers to arguments, you know. It's a universal human problem."

"But probably not among your guests."

"You'd be surprised. Remember, we cater to stressed-out people—like you and Bill—who're searching for a peaceful vacation surrounded by nature. We try to provide that, and some companionship if it's wanted. Believe me—we've heard some sharp words from time to time."

Susan frowned, obviously unconvinced. "Maybe we can all

leave tomorrow. I'm sure you and Tom have better things to do than—"

"Susan, we *are* a bed and breakfast." She grinned. "If it helps, I'll send you a bill with a separate line item for drama."

"Very funny."

Susan clasped her hands together, pushing the words out through clenched teeth. "What we've done can't be undone—by us or anyone." Her face darkened a shade, lips clamped in a thin line.

"What's going through your mind right now?"

"I know what's happening up there in *our* room," Susan blurted out. "Joanie and Bill aren't watching a movie. They're talking about *me*, laughing at *me*, sharing something between them I don't have anymore. I know. I've heard it all before."

Barb thought her heart would split in two—she was familiar with Susan's anguish, the loss of hope—but couldn't think of any words to dispel the heartbreak.

"I do love Bill, you know. I know it doesn't seem like it, but I do. He came into my life when I was down, and he *has* been a good husband to me and a great father to Joanie. I . . . I . . . don't know where we went wrong." Her eyes pleaded with Barb's. "Some of this is so hard to say out loud. I think I don't want to, because if I do, then it's real."

"I know what you mean. As long as it's tucked away in your mind, it never happened, right?" Barb dragged the words from the secret bower in her heart, where she'd hidden them long ago. "As soon as you say the words out loud, you have to confront what happened."

"Yes, that's it." She put her hands in her lap, clutching her pant legs.

"Susan, if you don't want to—"

"I was married before . . . before Joanie was born. His name was Michael." Her face softened as she whispered the name, as if savoring the taste of it on her tongue.

"Oh—"

Susan glanced at Barb. "Yeah, Bill's my second husband."

She drew out the next words like she was picking her way through boulders. "In fact, Bill's not . . . he's not Joanie's real father." She covered her face. "There. Now you know our dirty little secret."

Chapter 18

Barb leaned back in her chair, searching for words. "This is a surprise. We took it for granted that . . . but I guess we had no way of knowing. And really, it's none of our business—"

A slight scraping sound from the direction of the stairs distracted Barb for a moment. She swiveled in her chair but didn't see anything.

"No, it's not your business, but it's out there now. I've kept some things buried for a long time. I guess I have to dig them up to be free of them, right?"

"Will you be needing a bigger shovel, Susan? I have my own out in the tool shed," Barb suggested with a weak grin.

"Maybe . . ." Susan's mouth lifted at the corners, then flattened. "Michael was killed in Iraq by a roadside bomb. It blew him right out of the truck," she said in a hollow, dreamy voice. "We'd been married less than six months when he shipped out. It was almost fifteen years ago, but it was yesterday."

The crushing weight of her own secret sorrow coiled around Barb's heart again. She didn't think she could do this after all.

She loosened the grip on her chair and opened her eyes.

"I . . . I'm so sorry. It must have been very hard," she murmured. "What did you do?" The question sounded lame even to her own ears. She knew what Susan did—the same thing she herself did all those years ago—cried and died, then bucked up and started living again with her heart draped over a gravestone.

"I didn't know what I was going to do. For days I sat and cried. My mother had also died that year, and friends brought food and did all those things people do when someone dies, but nothing helped. I appreciated their kindness, but . . . Michael was gone and he wasn't coming back. I prayed God would tell me it wasn't true, but . . ."

Susan took a shuddering breath. "For weeks I pestered the State Department for proof he was dead. There'd been a funeral with a casket, but I never saw his . . . saw his . . . They told me what was left of him was pretty messed up. I made dozens of calls, pounded on so many doors. I . . . I made a real idiot of myself."

"I'm sure they see that all the time. They must be used to it." The words wound around the lump in Barb's throat. She remembered hours and hours of pounding on heaven's door for answers about Katie. Alone, though, since Tom had rediscovered his solutions in a bottle again.

"Probably. I . . . I couldn't believe Michael wasn't coming home. He died without knowing I was pregnant, and . . . and that hurt so much. We both wanted lots of children. He would have been a good dad."

Barb searched for comforting words through the crushing morass of her own heartache. She seized on one thought.

"I believe God allows him to see Joanie every day. And I bet he's worn a knee groove at the foot of the throne for her. Do you believe that?"

"I guess so. I never thought about it like that." Susan hesitated. "But having a husband in heaven is not the same as having a flesh-and-blood one on earth."

I know, I know! Having a child in heaven is not the same as having a flesh-and-blood one on earth. Why, God? Decades later, I can't get past it, can't leave her in the ground . . . can't leave her with you.

"It's been fifteen years, and I still can't leave him in the ground," Susan said. "And I don't want to hear 'God gives and God takes away, blessed be the name of the Lord,' okay? I've heard enough of those empty platitudes to last me a lifetime."

Barb breathed hard and came back to the present, hearing her own words echoed in Susan's.

"I've never lost a husband on a faraway battlefield, so I would never presume to know your pain. But I do know this. If my Tom had been killed, I'd beat on God's chest with the same fists, yelling the same words in his face."

"Thank you for that. Once a 'friend' told me it was like I'd crawled into Michael's grave with him. That hurt. I didn't want to answer my door or my phone for a long time."

"I know what you mean. People don't know what to say. But God does, and he waits for you to lay your broken heart at his feet."

"I want to know why—it would help to know why. Yes, I have Joanie, and I have Bill, and he takes care of us even though he's not her real father, but—"

She brought her hands down on the heavy table hard enough to shake it, rattling the cups and saucers. "Why doesn't God explain himself? He sits in heaven like some glorified chess master, moving us around like pawns. Maybe that sounds rebellious, but at least it's honest—" She twisted around in her chair.

Barb followed her gaze. "What?"

"I guess it's nothing. I thought I heard someone on the stairs, that's all."

Her shoulders slumped. "Look, I'm sure you have things you need to do, and I'm keeping you from it. I guess I'm not a very good guest, huh?"

"No, everything's done for today. In a little while, we'll have some pie—store bought, sorry—and ice cream. So what do you say? My ears are all yours."

Susan warmed her hands on her teacup, clearly trying to decide what to say.

"I was pregnant, no job, no husband. I'm . . . I was angry at God. But I kept reminding myself that my story has been repeated hundreds of times in other families of fallen soldiers. I'm not the only one—"

"But at the time, it felt like you were. Am I right?"

"Yes. I felt alone, forgotten, even in a crowd of people."

"I can relate to that part of your story. Tom and I lost . . . well, we're not inexperienced with loss."

Susan's face slackened, her voice a monotone. "Bill was with Michael when he died. They were best friends."

Barb closed her eyes.

"After Michael's death, Bill came to see me. He told me it was his fault Michael died. Something about an argument and trading places in the truck. I . . . I don't remember much of what he said. I think he still feels guilty, but he hasn't talked to me about it since."

"Susan, I—"

"When Bill came to see me, I was bitter toward him. I guess because he was alive and Michael wasn't. But he was so kind to me. He came over almost every day and helped me around the house. He even went to medical appointments with me. I . . . I fell in love with him. I needed him . . . I needed someone. Was that wrong?"

"I think it was only natural. Maybe I would have done the same thing."

"I still wonder sometimes if it was love or desperation on my part."

Susan leaned back in her chair, eyes glassy and unfocused, hands gripping her hair. "I've got to stop this—"

"Hey, calm down—"

Susan leaned forward again, arms stretched out on the table.

"This happened a lifetime ago. Why does it matter now? What matters right now is that Bill and I are falling apart and we're taking Joanie with us . . ." She lowered her face and wailed into her hands. "All those things they try to tell you when someone dies, they never work in the muck of real life."

"I know." Barb put her arm around Susan's stiff shoulders and again felt the ache of her empty lap, where Katie had drawn her last breath. She let go and picked up her teacup.

"There's more, Barb." Susan took a deep breath. "We never told Joanie about her real father."

Barb's fingers lost their grip on her cup, and it crashed to the table. They grabbed napkins and cleaned up the mess.

Susan caught Barb's shocked stare. "I know. I know what you're thinking. It seems stupid now, but we could never find the right moment. Bill hasn't even . . . hasn't even adopted her. We've kept the whole thing secret," she finished miserably.

"How in the world did you do that? Your families must have known."

"No, they didn't," Susan insisted. "We always let everyone believe Joanie was Bill's child, even my sister. She's always so wrapped up in herself anyway. It seemed easiest that way—now stop looking at me like that. We had to consider Joanie. We didn't want her to grow up knowing her real father was killed and that Bill . . . Bill—"

"—was her stepfather? That's not much of a stigma anymore, Susan."

"Don't you judge me—"

Barb backed off. She remembered when people had tried to give her advice—without listening to her first.

"I wasn't judging—I'm sorry. I didn't mean to. But consider this. You've been living this lie for how long? Fourteen, fifteen years? What will happen when Joanie does find out? She will, you know."

Susan cried, voice shaking with desperation. "I don't know. We wanted a normal family, not one all tangled up with another father in the picture."

"So now you have a snarled-up family built on lies and deceit. I'm sorry if that sounds harsh, but isn't it the truth? How much longer will you live this lie? Will Joanie *never* know about the father who fought for his country to keep her safe and who gave his life for it? Doesn't she deserve to know about Michael? Doesn't she *need* to know about him?"

Susan stood quickly, the chair crashing to the floor behind her. Not bothering to right it, she marched to the foot of the stairs, then jerked around. "Look, I appreciate you trying to help, but I'm not going to Joanie, or God for that matter, with my hat in my hands. Not now—"

She spun and ran up the stairs. Another slammed door.

Barb picked up the chair, pushed it in, and straightened the table runner. She gathered the teacups and headed for the kitchen, pausing in front of the window. The storm still howled. She looked up at the ceiling, thinking about the storm on the other side of it.

So much for pie and ice cream. What an epic fail.

# Chapter 19

Barb deposited the dishes in the kitchen, then headed for the back porch sitting room. Peeking through the windowed door, she saw Tom sitting in his chair.

She opened the door a crack. "Care for some company?"

He turned and motioned for her to come over. "Don't turn the lights on, okay? It's kind of nice right now, sitting in the dark, away from all that—"

"—drama?"

"Yeah, something like that."

She sat in her chair next to him, hands in her lap. There didn't seem to be much to say.

After a few minutes, Tom reached and took her hand. "Not what we expected, huh?"

"That's for sure. Susan unloaded on me. She told me some things—things I don't feel I can repeat."

"Oh?"

"They've got bigger issues than Joanie. In fact, after what Susan told me, I think they're responsible for the way she is."

"Sometimes parents are. Sad but true."

"I wonder how we would have—" She bit off her question.

She withdrew her hand and let herself sag against the back of her chair.

"I don't know if we can help them. It's all so complicated. I think we should just try to get through tomorrow and hope the roads open. She . . . she brought up some stuff that reminded me of . . . of . . ."

"What? Reminded you of what?"

She caught Tom in her peripheral vision staring at her, fingers drumming on the chair arm.

"She's so . . . I don't know . . . distraught over things that happened so long ago. And there's no way for them to go back and make things right. I think if they tried, it would drive the last nail in the coffin. Of their marriage, I mean." She stopped and eyed Tom's face.

"I've said too much. The bottom line is, there's too much murky water under their bridge. They need to figure out their own issues and deal with them. I don't want to." She crossed her arms over her chest and pressed her lips together.

Tom didn't say anything for a minute. Then he stood and pulled her to her feet, giving her a hug.

"Let's go to bed. Breakfast comes early, and maybe things won't seem so hopeless in the morning."

"All right." Relief washed over her like warm water. "I need to grab some bacon and sausage and put them in the sink to thaw. You go ahead. I'll be in soon."

Tom leaned over and gave her a peck on the cheek, then went out.

Chapter 20

As Barb made her way to the kitchen door, she flipped the sitting room light on and leaned down, inspecting the family photos Sally had examined earlier. She brushed a speck of dust from the picture of herself and her older sister, Maggie, who'd died in a tragic skiing accident years ago.

The photo had been taken when she and her sister were five and seven. Her father took it with their first family camera, what he'd called "one of those new-fangled" ones. The picture was black and white—framed in darkened silver—and creased with age, but it was still her favorite. Her mother stood nearby, on the edge of the picture, wearing the pink-and-green flowered apron now hanging on a hook in Barb's kitchen. She'd been telling Barb and her sister where and how to stand and harping at Daddy to hurry up and snap the darned thing.

A week later, they'd gathered around to look at the pictures. She still heard Mama's sarcastic voice criticizing Daddy.

"I told you so," Mama said. "Look—your shadow covers the girls. I told you to stand to the side. You can hardly see their faces."

"Fine. Next time you take the picture and we'll see if you do any better." Then he'd jammed his favorite marine cap on his head and tramped out to tend to some weeding.

In Barb's little-girl mind, Mama should've worshiped the ground he walked on—a soldier, a strong man who led with gentleness, with never a cross word for anyone.

The grown-up Barb now brushed her index finger over Daddy's shadow. Maybe that's how Mama had liked him best—a shadow—unneeded.

She put the picture down carefully and thought of Tom. The familiar burn rose in her chest.

Was she like her mother? Always criticizing, always pushing Tom away?

Barb turned the light off and made her way to the kitchen. She put the frozen food in the sink to thaw, then reached and touched Katie's plump cheek, feeling the smoothness of the cup—just like Katie's skin. Bowing her head, she gripped the edge of the counter.

There ought to be more of her than this broken cup. And there was, there was—all those pictures stored away. *But I can't . . .*

She turned off the kitchen light and left Katie in the dark. Stopping at the staircase, she stood, her hand clutching the stair rail, listening to the bubbling fountain upstairs and visualizing the water flowing around the stone angel, her head worn smooth by mommy and baby hands.

She knew what came next, smelled it—felt their approach—and stiffened.

Memories crept in on baby feet, tiny pink toes smelling of talcum powder.

She let them come. Like a troupe of actors entering one by one on a stage, the images paraded through her mind.

A small hand reaching, stroking the head of the stone angel. She felt those chubby fingers intertwined with her own, heard her coo and chortle, felt the weight of her wee body in her lap, breathed in the fragrance of her freshly shampooed hair.

Her first step. Her first tooth. Her first haircut, golden curls scattered on the kitchen floor like so many autumn leaves.

Tom, throwing her high in the air and catching her in his strong arms, then dropping to the ground and rolling in the grass with her.

Her first Christmas, surrounded by stuffed animals. Later, eating dessert with her fat baby fingers, feeding it to her new stuffed bear.

Her second—and last—Christmas, weak from chemo, held securely in Tom's arms as she gazed wide eyed at the winking red and green lights on the tree.

Birthdays—only two—sitting in her high chair surrounded by friends and family and torn wrapping paper, cake and pink frosting smeared on her face.

Barb didn't want it to end—she wanted to escape and live forever in these memories. This other dimension. The one where Katie lived and loved and had beautiful blond hair and not just wisps clinging to the back of her neck. The one without the doctor speaking incomprehensible words about therapies with unpronounceable names. Grim-faced nurses walking on hushed feet. The world without the tubes sticking out of her thinning body. Without the death rattle on that last day as she lay sheltered in her mother's lap.

Lost in the moment, Barb desperately hung on to the first year, pushing away the second.

As usual, the moment fled too soon. One by one the impressions faded, and her fingers relaxed their grip on the rail. Once again she was left with empty hands, empty ears, and unshed tears.

She tiptoed down the hallway to their suite, hearing Tom's snore over the wind whistling through the pines. Barb was glad he was asleep—she didn't feel like snuggling or talking.

She got ready for bed and slid in next to him. He reached for her, but she scooted away. Curled up tight, thick covers up to her neck, she closed her eyes.

But the past wasn't done with her yet. The worst memory of all clawed at the door of her heart with strong bony fingers stinking of death, wrenched it open, and forced its way in.

"Tom, I went to the doctor today."

"You did?"

"Yes. And . . . and we're going to have a baby. Can you believe it?"

"What? You are?"

"No, we *are, silly. Why are you looking like that? Aren't you happy? We're finally going to be three instead of two."*

Me, watching his darkening face, sweat popping out on his forehead. Gun hand snaking to his empty hip.

Him, turning away, standing rigid in the middle of the hardware store at closing time. Rubbing the back of his neck with jerky motions, forearm muscles bulging with marine tattoos from another lifetime. Then, facing me—the look in his eyes mirroring the dread in my gut.

"We can't, Barb . . . we can't be parents right now. We have no money. You have to work. I . . . I'm too messed up. We can't."

"You mean you *can't. It's a bit late now, isn't it? We aren't going to be parents. We* are *parents."*

She heard again the words from Tom's lips—words that still gnawed her soul in two and left it to rot until even four decades later she still whiffed the decay from time to time under the facade of normal life they tried to live.

"Can't you . . . can't you do something about it?"

The feeling of blood draining to my feet and into the floor, leaving me breathless.

"Do . . . do something? Wh . . . what do you mean?"

The casual shrug of his shoulders as he dismissed the tiny life within me like he would swat an annoying insect.

My heart snuffed out and lying in embers in my chest.

The slap—hard—across his face.

The front door of the hardware store closing, leaving me standing alone, cradling my middle in my work apron. Leaving me to wonder who this man was I'd married—the one who'd told me to kill our child.

Barb shifted on her pillow. A sob escaped. She put her fist in her mouth to stifle it.

God, why must I remember it so vividly? What purpose is there to remember that day, every word, over and over again . . . that day when we broke ourselves in two, when the stranger I married told me to pay someone to kill our baby?

She waited. Like every time before, there was no answer. She watched behind her eyelids as the clawed hand retreated—finger by bony finger—and closed the door to her heart, out of sight and mind until the next time.

She knew there'd be a next time.

 # Chapter 21

The next morning dawned clear and cold. Barb rose early to start breakfast for their guests. She felt hopeful in spite of the dismal end to yesterday. The memories that had plagued her were locked away again in their caskets in her mind, where they belonged.

Tom joined her in the kitchen. "Do you need help with anything? I'm going out to check things."

"When you come back in, could you bring in some more eggs and bread?"

Tom pulled his boots on, grabbed his hat, and went out to the back porch, where they kept a second refrigerator.

Barb cracked her last two eggs into a heavy yellow bowl, chipped and scarred with age, inherited from her grandmother. She cocked an ear and heard signs of life upstairs. She hoped the morning would progress without theatrics.

Tom came back in with the bread and eggs. "The sky looks like we *could* get more—black clouds moving in again over the mountain. But maybe not. We've already got about three and a half feet, more in the drifts."

Barb took the bread from Tom and put it on the cutting board. "I guess there's no snowplows working yet, right?" She jerked her head toward the ceiling. "So they can get on their way?"

"It's too early. I'll call the weather line in a bit, if I can get service. If there's more predicted, the county may not start plowing yet."

Barb opened another egg carton. "Umm, Tom," she said with a frown. "The phones are still out. I tried calling the weather line a few minutes ago. No go."

He laid a hand on her shoulder. "I guess there's nothing to be done then. I wonder how we can keep them entertained with—as Joanie so eloquently reminded us last night—no TV, no internet, no phone service, no Xbox?"

"And no fun, as I recall. I've got a bulletin for her—*she's* not my idea of fun."

He edged away from her, then smirked. "We're the zookeepers. We can always feed them—"

Barb threw an eggshell at him, catching him in the face. The laughter between them felt good. They were still laughing when Susan appeared in the doorway.

"Good morning, you two. Having a food fight or something?" She eyed Tom's chin.

He wiped eggshell off his face. "Hey, good morning yourself. Did you sleep okay?"

"Oh, for sure. Your rooms are so comfortable, almost like home. We so appreciate you putting us up. Did I already say that? Anyway, I slept fine, and I think Bill and Joanie did too." Susan's words, delivered machine-gun style, finally stopped long enough for Tom to answer.

"That's good. We—"

"Is there anything I can do to help?"

Tom excused himself, saying he "had things to attend to."

"Don't forget to check the generator," Barb called as the door swung shut. She shrugged.

"I hope I didn't run him out," Susan said with a worried expression.

Barb shook her head. "No, of course not. And yes, you can help by setting the table. In that cupboard, the one over there on the right, you'll find plates. The silverware is in the drawer right under that cupboard. And you'll find a cleaning cloth in the third drawer down."

"Okay." But she made no move to help.

Barb turned the heat off the bacon as Susan drifted around the kitchen, fingering knickknacks and pictures, then came to a stop on the opposite side of the island.

Barb put the last of the bacon on a platter. "Is there something else?"

"I don't know how to thank you for last night. I feel like I've dumped my whole life's baggage on you—and here we are strangers. And . . . and I'm sorry I ran out on you like that. I couldn't take any more."

"It's all good, my friend. You needed to talk, and I've been known to listen to others' heartaches a time or two. I guess I have big ears and big shoulders." She grinned. "But I can promise you I don't have a big mouth. And I do believe God brought us together for that talk. He never wastes time, his or ours."

Susan leaned forward. "I think you're right. This morning I woke up more peaceful than I've felt in a long time. Cleaner, too. After I went upstairs last night, I kept thinking about some things you said. I . . . I talked to God for a little while—although I don't know how he could possibly hear me over Bill's snoring."

She looked up, then down, clearly too shy to hold Barb's gaze. "It's hard for me to admit this, but it was a conversation I should have started a long time ago."

Barb wiped her hands on a towel and came around the island and hugged Susan tight. "I couldn't be happier for you." She drew back. "Now, about setting the table—"

"Yes, of course. I'll get right on it."

She gathered everything she needed, and a few minutes later she bustled away to the dining room.

As the swinging door opened, Barb saw their guests had begun to gather.

She piled the breakfast food on the rolling cart and prepared to play hostess again. She hoped it would be a normal meal—no drama, no sarcasm—and if not, that at least Tom would keep his temper in check. She paused in the doorway and took a deep breath.

Hostess smile plastered on her face, Barb walked in.

Chapter 22

Tom swung around as Barb brought the cart through the kitchen door. "Here we are," he said. "Honey, that smells great. Steve, after you." Tom followed Steve to the table, where Barb arranged steaming dishes on hot pads.

Noting the question in Barb's eyes, Tom nodded. "Yes, I refilled it. We have enough gas to fill it once more, I think. We'll be fine."

Bill came down the stairs alone and shuffled over to an empty chair across from Susan.

"Where's Joanie?"

Uh-oh. Susan's challenging tone set off alarm bells in Tom's mind.

"She's not coming down. She says she doesn't 'fit in' with . . . with us, I guess."

Susan pushed her chair back and stood up, face reddening. "And you're going to let her. Never mind. I'll go get her."

"Now don't make a federal case out of it. She's only being herself."

"This 'being herself' stuff has got to stop. We can't allow her to be rude. If I have to, I'll drag her down by her ear—unless you want the honors."

Bill shrugged his shoulders in defeat. "Go for it. Let me know how that works out for you. We might be sorry if she does come down."

Tom fought the urge to agree with Bill out loud as Susan, her eyes sparking anger and frustration, charged up the stairs. Several loud knocks sounded, then silence.

Tom drummed his fingers on the table. "Wonder how long we should wait."

"Mommy, why are they always so mad at each other?" Stevie's innocent question fell out of nowhere. "Are they gonna stop being married, like Aaron's mommy and daddy?"

Sally's face reddened as she hushed him. "Shhh, honey. It's grown-up stuff." She leaned over and tucked his napkin in under his chin.

Steve shrugged at Bill. "Kids. They do say the darndest things, right?"

"Yeah, guess so," Bill said through tight lips. He stood, threw his napkin on the table, and strode to the foot of the stairs.

"Susan? You coming or what? The food's getting cold." He stepped back to the table. "Guess we may as well start, Tom. No telling when they'll be down, or if. We shouldn't let *their* issues keep us from eating."

His heartless tone rankled Tom, but he managed to contain himself. "Are we ready, Barb? Do we need anything else from the kitchen?"

"No, this is it—let's start. They can eat later if they don't come down."

Barb took her place at the opposite end of the long table. She'd covered it with her favorite tablecloth and decorated it with a beautiful handmade centerpiece—inherited from her mother. The centerpiece was low and long and didn't get in the way of table conversation. Deep-green pine needles, three hurricane lamps, and red holly berries splashed a merry color against the lacy white cloth.

Tom thought it was overkill. He couldn't remember a less merry holiday season, save one.

They sat in uncomfortable silence for a few minutes, Tom not knowing whether to offer thanks for the food or a plea for help.

Barb met his gaze from the other end of the table. "Tom, why don't you go ahead and ask the blessing."

He nodded and they bowed their heads. "Dear Father—"

Tom heard the shutters rattle upstairs. "Mom, I don't want to!" was followed by the sound of something heavy hitting the floor.

He started to rise but stopped when he saw the warning in Barb's eye. He sat down again, biceps flexing. Then he heard a step on the stair and Susan's soft voice. He relaxed against the back of his chair. Maybe it'd be okay.

A few seconds later Susan and Joanie came down the stairs together. Susan sat down at Barb's end of the table, and Joanie took the middle seat next to Bill. She plunked down, sat back with her arms crossed in front of her, and pointed her scarlet face to the ceiling.

Bill leaned close to her. "Thank you, honey. I'm sure this isn't easy for you."

Susan shot him a hellfire missile glance, her fists knotted on either side of her plate.

Tom waited a few seconds, then cleared his throat. "Let's thank God for a good night and this good food, shall we?" As he bowed his head, he caught Joanie's scowl. He restrained himself with difficulty.

Tom prayed aloud, thanking the Lord for all the bounty and the company—and added a silent plea for peace at his table.

He looked up and met Barb's warm look of approval.

He smiled back and forked a bite of breakfast casserole. He knew it was his grandmother's special recipe. "Mmm . . . good casserole, Barb."

"Thank you."

Silence. The only conversation came from the ticktock of the clock in the corner.

Okay . . . now what?

Tom relaxed against the back of his chair.

"Hey, Bill—I noticed you have a marine corps hat. Didn't get a chance to ask you about it last night. Were you deployed?"

"Yeah. Iraq."

"Really?" Tom asked. "I was in 'Nam. Seems like a lifetime ago—most of the time, that is." He bit off his remark, seeing a wary expression on Barb's face—and its twin on Susan's.

Bill responded with a nod. "Yeah, I know what you mean. It's the same for me. Some things you can't let go of." He glanced at Susan.

"Maybe you and I can talk later—you know, compare stories," Tom suggested.

"Yeah. Guess so."

Tom noticed Joanie's bored expression. He expected her to make some smart remark, but she didn't open her mouth.

"Mommy, please?" Samantha begged. She and Sally had been whispering, foreheads together.

"Oh, I don't know." Sally pursed her lips. "Maybe now isn't the time, honey. We're eating and talking."

"But, Mommy, you promised I could practice my song—"

Joanie grunted. "Oh brother—"

Susan squelched it with a glare.

"Sure, kid—let's see what you've got," Joanie grumbled.

Tom chimed in, wanting to encourage the child. "We're done eating. It's okay, Sally."

"Would the rest of you mind? Sammie's practiced so hard these past few days. She wants to sing it for my mother," she said, frowning at Steve.

"Knock yourself out, little girl," from Bill.

Barb patted Sammie on the shoulder. "You can sing for us anytime, sweetheart."

Samantha stood up behind her chair and gave a flawless rendition of "Jesus Loves Me." It brought tears to Barb's eyes, and even Tom's eyes were moist. Everyone clapped for Samantha, and she gave a prim little bow, then sat down again by Sally, who gave her a tight hug.

"Very good, Sammie. I'm so proud of you."

Samantha's face glowed at the praise.

Tom remembered the day they'd taught the words to Katie, her babyish voice lisping each line after them. He caught Barb's expression of tenderness and pain in his direction and jerked his eyes away.

He looked back at her, but the moment was lost—she'd disappeared into the kitchen with an armload of dishes. He stood and grabbed some plates, almost colliding with Barb when she came back through the door.

"Susan, would you like to see those quilts we talked about?" Barb asked as he reentered the dining room a few minutes later.

"You're going to look at quilts? Now?" Tom said. At Barb's expression, he put up his hands in surrender. "Okay. Just asking. What's everyone else doing?"

"Joanie stomped up the stairs a minute ago—she's made door slamming an art form." Bill shook his head. "That kid . . . I don't know what we're going to do—"

"I'd love to see the quilts," Susan interrupted, pushing past Bill. She stopped and put her hand on his arm. "She'll be fine. At least she came down to the table. Let's give her some space."

Bill glanced at Tom and threw up his hands in surrender. "Women—"

"Hey, I'm in favor of giving her space. You won't get an argument from me. As long as the space is upstairs away from—"

"Tom!" Barb looked daggers at him. "Be nice—"

Bill put up a hand. "Hey, don't worry. I get that." The two men gave each other an air high-five.

"We promised the kids a game of Pictionary after breakfast," Sally said. "We noticed you had one. Is it all right if—"

"Of course. That's what it's there for. You can use the card table—it's folded up in the closet," Barb said. "I'll show you. Come on, Susan. I'll get them settled at their game first."

Tom glanced at Bill and decided to bite the bullet. "Hey, how about a cup of coffee out on the back porch. We could have that talk—"

Tom caught Bill's wary expression.

"I cranked up the heat earlier."

"Okay, yeah, I guess."

This is going to be fun . . .

 # Chapter 23

Tom and Bill drifted out to the enclosed back porch. It was Tom's favorite thinking place, with its tall windows giving a view of the creek and the woods beyond. If he couldn't be out enjoying nature firsthand, at least he could invite the beauty of it into this room. His favorite spot was near those windows, where Barb had placed their two chairs side by side with a table between them and stools for their feet. They faced the floor-to-ceiling windows with an unhindered view of the soaring mountains and majestic pines to the north of the inn.

These chairs were special to Tom. They had belonged to his grandparents, and Barb surprised him one birthday by having them reupholstered.

Whenever he sat in his chair, he could almost feel Grandpa's knees under him and his arms around him, wrapped in the roughness of his long-sleeved red-plaid work shirt. On some days, Tom could even see the thin curl of smoke from Grandpa's favorite brand of pipe tobacco, and smell the rich spiciness of it.

Sometimes they'd just sit and talk. Grandpa was a wealth of storytelling—everything from the Great War to his latest conquest on his fishing boat. Even after so many years and so much creek water under the bridge, Tom still half expected Grandpa to stomp up the back steps to take him hunting or fishing or out to build a snow fort.

He carried two steaming cups of coffee and set them down on the side table. Then he stepped to the far window and pulled aside all the draperies. He gestured to Bill to take a seat.

Bill leaned over and picked up his cup, took a sip, and sank down into the chair. "You've got a great setup here. I wouldn't mind retiring to a place like this—after I make my first million, of course," he said with a laugh. "What do you do for fun, anyway?"

Tom joined in his laughter. "The million I could handle. But this isn't exactly retirement. There's a lot of work to maintaining and running this place. Sometimes it's hard, but it's what we always dreamed of doing, and now we're doing it. And as far as fun, there's a place out near Little Diamond Lake where I throw my line in and catch our dinner. It doesn't get much better than that."

"I'm getting pretty close to making that first million," Bill boasted. "My bank account's pretty healthy right now, and I intend to keep it that way. That is, if Susan doesn't spend it all. Now she's talking about setting up an account for Joanie's college tuition. She's only fourteen—and I'm not even sure she's college material. That's women, though—all they think about is spending your hard-earned money."

"You never know about kids. Maybe she'll surprise you."

Bill shrugged and didn't answer.

"So, Iraq. How many tours?"

"Two."

"Whereabouts? What was your duty?"

"It was Iraq, Tom. I'm sure you read all about it in the papers. Not much of a story." Bill rubbed his hands together. "How much is your overhead here? Must not be much with you and Barb running it and no employees. And a serious tax shelter."

Tom was on to Bill's blatant change of subject. He decided not to be a quitter.

"That's all true, but let's talk about you. Two tours, you said. How many months?"

"Okay. If you must know—about twenty months. I was injured by an IED and mustered out. Worst year of my life. But I got over it, like everyone else does. There. That's it. Now you know the whole story. How long were you in 'Nam?"

"I did three tours. Saw lots of action. Glad when my tours were over," Tom said. "And I *never* got over it."

Bill didn't answer, but Tom noted his tightened jaw. Holding his coffee cup in his right hand, Bill swirled his left index finger around and around the rim intently, as if it was his primary mission.

Tom watched, hesitated before speaking. "And I suspect you never got over it either."

"What do you know about me, Tom? Nothing. Yet here you are making judgments. Leave it alone."

"I don't intend to pry or preach, I promise. But I'm hoping we can talk as brother marines and try to help each other. I lost buddies over there, and I bet you did too. Sometimes it feels good to talk to someone who knows."

Bill inhaled sharply, like a boxer who'd been sucker punched. Tom knew he'd hit a sore spot. He hoped he hadn't punched too hard. He remembered the first time a counselor had tried to talk to him.

"Aren't those the memories that bind us together, make us brothers? It doesn't matter whether the battles were in the jungle or on the sand, does it?"

Without warning, Bill slammed his coffee cup down on the table, sloshing it over the sides. It ran across the small table and dripped to the floor.

"That's enough, Tom. Just because we were soldiers in another life doesn't make us brothers, and it doesn't mean you know anything about me."

He stood, then leaned down, one finger extended in Tom's face. "Hear me. I appreciate everything you and Barb are doing for us right now, but we'll be on our way before long. We'll probably never see each other again, so let's not get too deep here."

Not waiting for an answer, Bill stalked to the door, his footsteps echoing through the kitchen and up the stairs.

Tom swiveled and watched him go. That went well. He wondered what else he could screw up.

He rose and stood in front of the window, hands on his hips, eyes focused on the gathering clouds over the peaks of the farthest mountains.

He remembered the time his assigned counselor cut a little too close to the quick, right after he'd finished his last deployment. Tom had punched him in the face and drawn his personal weapon from his ankle holster. He didn't go so far as to point it at the skinny guy who'd never seen more action than a forced march during boot camp, but Tom's butt was fried just the same. He was led away in handcuffs and locked in an interrogation room on the base until the base shrinks determined he was no threat. He was lucky they didn't press charges against him.

Tom had a hunch that Bill was close to a breaking point, although he'd been home for a long while. Some things just don't go away . . . they hid in the darkest corners of the mind, waiting for an opportunity. Bill's current family dysfunction fed into it.

Tom wondered. What would be the key to unlock Bill's emotions? How could Tom help him realize that he was in a dangerous frame of mind, that he would take his family down with him?

Tom knew. He'd been there.

And he wondered something else.

Had Bill brought a weapon with him?

 # Chapter 24

Tom wandered out to the kitchen. Barb was on her knees in front of the freezer, surrounded by frozen chickens, roasts, ribs, and two massive turkeys.

"Lose something?" he said right behind her, laughing when she jumped. "Or taking inventory?"

"Tom! You scared me to death. You could at least clear your throat or something."

"And spoil the fun?"

He didn't notice the wet washcloth in her hand until it caught him right under his chin. He backed away, hands up in surrender. "Okay, okay, I promise never to do that again."

"Right. Just like the last time you promised." Barb handed him a package of stew meat. "What's everyone doing?" she asked. "I showed Susan the quilts. She liked them—said they reminded her of her mom and grandma. I guess they used to do quite a bit of quilting together." Barb sighed. "It's a lost art." She rose to her feet and put the stew meat in the microwave to thaw it out.

"You mean like shucking corn and snapping peas on the front

porch? We could revive those lost arts instead of going to the grocery store if you want."

"Now don't make fun of me. We've become so . . . I don't know . . . impersonal these days. You know what I mean. I saw you and Bill talking out on the back porch a few minutes ago. Remember porches? It was the place for families and neighbors to talk face to face. Nowadays, we text people who are sitting right across the room. We've lost something."

"Are you talking about 'people,' or us?"

"Both, I guess," she admitted. "We're raising a generation who can't look each other in the eye. And . . . *we* seem to have lost that somewhere along the way too."

Tom stared at his wife. She was right, as usual. He didn't deserve her after . . . He thrust that thought back down in the foxhole where it belonged.

"You're right." Tom put an arm around her. "I'm sorry I teased you."

"I was serious." She took the thawed meat out and put it into her Crock-Pot. She added a vegetable medley, potatoes, water, and seasoning, put the lid on, and turned it on.

She turned, hands on her hips. "And mind you don't lift that lid, mister—"

Tom contrived a wide-eyed innocence. "Of course not."

"Uh-huh, like you always don't." She glanced out the window, her tone serious again. "I know it sounds archaic, but I want to get back to front porches."

"You sound a bit nostalgic."

"Don't you? Miss front porches, I mean?"

"Yeah, you're right, I guess. Grandpa and I spent a lot of time on his front porch—taught me how to tie flies—right out there." He jerked his thumb over his shoulder. "Wouldn't trade it for any-thing."

They stood together for a moment, looking out the kitchen

window. The snow drifted down again, adding another layer of white purity to the landscape.

Tom's thoughts swung back around. The drifting snow was pretty. But the dead stuff was still under it, and come spring all that muck would be back. Like life, he guessed—couldn't hide stuff under a pretty facade . . .

"What were you and Bill talking about? It seemed serious—then Bill stomped through the kitchen and went upstairs. He looked angry." She pulled her favorite cookbook out of a cupboard and laid it on the counter. It was old, one her mother had used, the familiar red checkerboard cover now faded.

Tom shook his head, hand in his pocket, jingling his keys. "What's for dinner?"

"Stew, biscuits, and salad. Stop changing the subject."

She flipped through the cookbook, stopping on a well-worn page splattered from decades of use by her mother and grand-mother. "Did you say something to make him mad?"

Tom exhaled. "Yeah. I guess I pushed him too hard. We were talking about 'Nam and Iraq, nothing too deep. But then he gave me what I thought was an opening to go a little deeper. He said, 'I got over it, like everyone else.'"

Barb raised an eyebrow. "I see. And you told him no one gets over it. You haven't. And neither have I."

Tom started to say something, but hesitated. The moment fled and was lost . . . *again.*

Barb ran her finger down the biscuit page, then closed the cookbook. "Susan told me how hard it was when her mother died. One moment she was there, and the next moment it was like she walked out of the room, turned a corner, and was gone."

"What's that got to do with Bill? Surely you're not comparing war with losing a mother. They're worlds apart. Not to say it wasn't hard, but losing parents is a part of life, right?

"Like losing a child?"

The sting of her words hurt like the slap so long ago. "Katie has nothing to do with this."

"She has everything to do with this."

She strode to the sink, picked up the cup fragment from the sill, and held it out between them, nestled in her palm.

"As I listened to Susan's grief, I remembered . . . I remembered losing Katie. I still remember every detail of that day. She was only two—" Her voice broke.

Tom reached out and drew her into his arms, instantly transported back to the darkest days of their married life.

"I don't know why God took her from us," Barb said, voice muffled in Tom's shirt, "but listening to Susan, I felt what Susan was feeling in that moment. That devastating sense of loss—a hole in the soul—one that will never be filled. The feeling that life will never be right again, that God isn't here with us—maybe never was—but somewhere *up there*. That he snatched her like some . . . some kidnapper, then walked away and left us with her toys and tiny clothes . . . and her empty crib."

Tom tightened his arms around his wife, sad that he was unable to feel as a mother felt when a child died. He remembered his helplessness to protect his baby daughter. The panic, the nausea in his gut, the paralyzing fear that he'd never left the jungle. That right around the corner, the enemy waited to spray his family's blood over the jungle floor.

He stiffened, certain he saw movement off to the left in his peripheral vision.

Barb moved away from him. "Tom, what are you thinking? I'm sorry I brought Katie up, but—"

The black-clad enemy faded into nothingness, and Tom refocused with difficulty. "No . . . no, it's okay. It was hard for both of us, in different ways. We couldn't stop what was happening to her. We couldn't stop what was happening to us. And . . . and it seems odd to me that so much time has passed, yet here we are, going over the same ground like it was yesterday. I still hear Mack's screams, and you . . . you still hold Katie in your lap, listening to her struggle to breathe, feeling for her chest to rise again. And then it doesn't."

Barb's jaw clenched. "It *was* yesterday—for me."

Tom took her hand and opened her palm. Katie's plump cheek and one eye gleamed at him. He closed Barb's fingers over it and brought her hand to his lips, kissing her knuckles.

"I know." He breathed hard. "Barb, you've given me an idea—about Bill."

"Oh? What?"

"I want to think about it first. I have an idea we're not that different."

Her forehead crinkled.

"He reminds me of someone I used to know."

"Oh?"

"Me."

Chapter 25

"What are we supposed to do now? Sit around and twiddle our thumbs or what?" Joanie's whiny voice grated on Tom's nerves.

Everyone except Joanie had helped clear the table after lunch. She scowled and picked at the last of her food—tuna salad sandwiches and chips. With effort, he ignored her as he went back and forth between the dining room and kitchen.

Tom thought for the hundredth time since yesterday what he'd do if she were his daughter. Then he watched Bill ease over and pick up her plate and silverware and carry them through to the kitchen. He shook his head and stepped over to the window to check the weather.

Joanie pushed harder. "Isn't anyone going to answer, or what? I asked—"

Susan bristled. "Joanie, stop it. I'm sure that—"

"Hey," Tom broke in over the brewing argument. "I was thinking about getting the sleds out of the shed and taking the kids up the hill. Doesn't look too bad out there right now, and it might be the only chance we have to get out and play. There's a great sledding place a mile or so away. How about it, Bill? Steve?"

Stevie gave a shout of glee. "Can we, Daddy? Can we?"

Steve put a finger to his lips. "Let the grown-ups discuss. You're eagerness is noted."

Stevie scratched his head. "Huh?"

"So you don't think the roads will open today?" Sally asked.

"Don't think so. It's still snowing, but not very hard. It might take the county another day to get all the way out here."

Bill cleared his throat. "I . . . I don't know . . ." He stopped and threw up his hands. "Oh, okay. How about it, Joanie? You up for some sledding? I dare you to say no."

"Oh brother," she began with a frown. "Can I stay in my room? I'm not going out there in *that*, with *those*." She pointed at Samantha and Stevie.

"Come on," Bill cajoled. "You can show us how it's done. Remember the trip to Canada last year? You were awesome on skis."

"Yeah, but this is sledding, not the Olympics. I don't feel like going." She looked at her mother. "I promise not to get in the way, so you *girls* can gossip all you want."

Bill walked over and whispered in her ear. Joanie frowned, then threw up her hands.

"Oh, all right. I guess so, if you put it like that. It's better than sitting around here."

"Okay then, it's settled," Tom said. "I'll go get the sleds out right now. Guys, you want to help me? They're packed in the shed up on a shelf hanging from the ceiling—kinda hard to get to. Kids, you'd best hang back until we get them all cleaned up and organized. And dress warm. It's pretty cold out there."

In spite of agreeing to go, Joanie kept up a steady stream of loud complaints as she stomped up the stairs, followed by Sally and Susan.

Susan tapped her daughter on the shoulder. "Would you please knock it off? You might have some fun, you know—"

Joanie answered full voiced. "Right, Mom. I see you're not going. Put your money where your mouth is for a change."

This was going to be a jolly time of it. Tom had never met such a bad-tempered kid. Maybe a little snow rub would take the edge off her.

Tom plotted his revenge as he led the men out to the back porch.

Chapter 26

Barb followed the men into the kitchen to put some snacks together for the hikers. She heard stomping and giggling upstairs.

She paused in her work and went to the kitchen door to listen to the cacophony of noise overhead. Sadness crept over her once again. Sadness that she and Tom had never had another child. She'd have liked to go sledding with a large family—she'd wanted at least four when they first got married—but more children never came. At the time, with Tom's problems, it was probably best.

She stepped back to the kitchen window and caught sight of Tom standing by the shed, gesturing to Bill and Steve, pointing up the hill through the trees. His coat swung open, and she was glad to see his .44 tight against his right hip. She didn't worry as much knowing he was armed.

As she watched Tom banter with the other two men, she knew he could have been a great father. In the two years they'd had Katie, he'd proven that. Tears filled Barb's eyes. Then she shook herself, squared her shoulders, and reminded herself that God had Katie in the palm of his hand—she shouldn't feel sorry for herself. Soldier on.

Barb had learned from her soldier father to take what life gave. She'd never wasted too much time on *what ifs* and *whys*—that was, until Katie. Her carefully groomed stoicism had crumbled the day she'd looked into her dead baby's face. Life lessons she'd learned at her father's knee hadn't prepared her for that. Barb closed her eyes and rubbed her finger lightly over her own cheek. Not soft like Katie's, the day she was born—and the day she left.

Ah, Katie, what I'd give to touch your cheek just one more time . . .

Tom's loud laughter outside brought her back to the present as the three children whirled into the kitchen. Susan and Sally rushed in behind them, scurrying and flapping their hands like cricket herders.

Stevie hopped around, not watching where he was going, and managed to knock over the full garbage can at the end of the counter. The lid shot off, and two days of trash fanned out on the floor.

Barb grabbed the broom and scooped it back into the can.

"Sorry," Sally said, then jerked her arm out, managing to catch Samantha before she walked into the mess. With a "Stevie, will you please be more careful," she guided the two through to the sitting room and out the back door.

Barb trailed her, carrying the snacks and water in two backpacks.

"Now, you two be careful out there," Sally said, tying Stevie's hood again. "And do what you're told. I don't want any broken bones." She released them with a kiss on the tip of each nose.

As Sally stepped back and stood on the steps shivering in the cold, Joanie pushed by and almost knocked her off the porch. Sally grabbed at the railing to keep from tumbling into the snow.

"Joanie, watch where you're going," Susan said from behind.

"Sorry—umm, what's your name again?" Joanie mumbled.

Susan shook her head, exasperation filling her voice. "What's wrong with you? We've been here a day and a half, and you can't remember her name?"

Sally held up a hand. "It's okay. Joanie, my name is—"

"Sally. Oh yeah—forgot," Joanie said. "Now can I get out of here and get this *fun* over with?"

Susan reached around Sally and grasped Joanie's shoulder. "You call that an apology—"

Barb handed the two backpacks to Joanie. "Would you mind taking these snacks over to Tom? He'll distribute them."

"Yeah, whatever."

Barb handed them to her, then stepped back to stand next to Sally in the doorway.

After dumping the bag at Tom's feet, Joanie trudged over and stood next to her dad, hands shoved in her pockets, familiar disgruntled scowl stamped on her face.

Susan closed the door and stood for a moment, head bowed, forehead against the door. Then she pivoted. A small smile crept over her face. She sagged back against the closed door and erupted in unrestrained laughter.

Barb grabbed at Sally's shoulder, and they collapsed together on the sofa, laughing until the tears came.

"Oh, my—that felt good, didn't it?" Barb exclaimed, gasping for air. "My house hasn't seen so much drama for years and years. I truly feel for both of you." She wiped the tears out of her eyes.

Sally grinned at Susan. "At least now I've got a better idea of what I'm in for when Samantha turns thirteen."

Susan shook her head. "They aren't all like Joanie. I know I wasn't." She wrapped her arms around herself, a faraway look in her eyes, the corners of her mouth downturned.

"It's no excuse for bad behavior, I know, but she's had a lot to overcome."

Sally leaned over and grasped her hand. "So have you, I think."

A moment ticked by. Barb felt a soft ribbon flow into the

room, swirling around them, binding their souls together in the commonness of womanhood.

She clapped her hands with a cheerful smile. "Come, my friends. We mustn't waste this time. The drama team will return much too soon for the second act of *Murder at the Master's Inn.*"

Barb held the door open, and they trooped back into the kitchen.

"Let's get this mess squared away, then I'll make some tea. Susan," Barb said, "maybe you could help me load the dishwasher. Sally, would you get a clean kitchen towel out of that drawer over there? If you wouldn't mind, you could help by drying those dishes in the drainer. If you'd set them on the counter, I'll put them away later."

Twenty minutes later, Barb said, "Okay, let's go relax in the living room while we wait for the kettle to boil." She followed the other two women out, leaving the door open.

Susan stood at the tall windows overlooking the road and fields beyond, her arms wrapped around herself.

"Sometimes it seems winter will never be over," Susan said, voice flat and devoid of emotion.

Barb patted her back, guessing she meant more than just the weather. "Especially here. I know what you mean. Coldness seems to settle into every floorboard and cupboard and wall. Spring and summer are welcome sights for me, but they don't last long enough."

Sally wandered about the room, examining knickknacks and pictures. She paused before the heavy buffet—the kind with a hutch sitting on top—and zeroed in on a collection of small ceramic figurines arranged on the wide bottom shelf behind glass doors. Each figurine, no more than three inches high, depicted a miniature of a young girl costumed in colorful eighteenth-century dress, complete with lace, frills, and bonnets. One sat on a stool reading a book, the child's tiny finger poised in the act of turning the page. Another flew a gaily hued kite suspended over her head by a string clutched in her palm, her rapturous face upturned. Yet another led a white curly-haired dog on a leash. There were fifteen in all, each uniquely posed. Sally opened the glass doors for a better view. Her eyes widened.

"These are exquisite, Barb. Such elaborate dresses. Tiny, but so detailed. This one—you can see the words—she's reading Shakespeare. Where on earth did you get them?"

"Those have been handed down in my family for several generations. My grandmother gave them to my mother, and my mother left them to me. I believe, though, they go back much further than that."

"Who will get them next?" she asked, closing and latching the glass doors.

The innocent question sucked the air out of Barb's chest. "Oh, maybe a niece, or . . ."

Barb noted their curious expressions. She gulped and headed for the kitchen. "I hear the kettle. I'll be back in a jiff."

Chapter 27

Tom dragged two vintage Yankee Clipper sleds, four saucer sleds, and two inner tubes out of the shed. After strapping a tube and a saucer to each big sled, then handing a rope to Bill, he led them across the footbridge and up the hill behind the inn. The path was narrow and slippery, pine trees hugging each side.

Steve kept a firm grip on Stevie's collar. Samantha was in front of him. She walked with her arms wrapped around herself, clutching the sides of her heavy coat. Bill and Joanie trudged behind Steve, Bill dragging a big sled and Joanie carrying the other two saucer sleds.

They crested the hill and paused at the breathtaking view spread out before them.

Joanie stepped forward, clearly enthralled. "Wow! Dad, this is great, isn't it?"

Bill's expression registered surprise at her enthusiasm. "Yeah. I haven't seen so much forest real estate in a long time. Beautiful."

"Why don't we take trips like this more often, Dad? You know, fam time, not to impress your clients. Even that ski trip to Canada was business—you spent more time schmoozing those bigwigs from Atlanta than you did with us. In fact, I don't think you had dinner once with Mom and me."

"Somebody in the 'fam' has to work, you know. Can't get around it. Not if you want to continue living the way you're used to—"

"That's so lame," Joanie accused. "You find time to golf with your friends and go to casinos." Her gaze roamed over the vista below. "This is way better."

Bill shoved his hands into his pockets, his face pointed at his feet.

Tom thought for the umpteenth time that Bill was just marking time being a dad. He wished he could shake him, wake him up, make him see the time he could never reclaim. Wasted time was something he was familiar with—and it was easy to spot in someone else.

"Okay, pay attention." Tom pointed to his left. "The path going that way leads back down the hill and comes out about a mile and a half west of the inn. We're going this way." He gestured to the right. "There's a great sledding hill about two hundred yards through those trees."

"Is the hill safe enough for Stevie and Samantha?" Steve asked.

"Yes indeed," Tom replied. "There are two starting points and two tracks. The speedsters can ride the right side, which starts clear at the top and is much steeper. The younger ones can use the left side, which starts about halfway down and is a much gentler slope. You'll see—there won't be a problem. We often take our winter folks up here, and no one's been hurt yet. Okay, troops, let's go."

As they started out, Samantha ducked around a big tree out of sight.

"Samantha," Steve called to her, "what are you doing? You're going to be left behind."

She bounded from behind the tree, laughing. "I wasn't doing anything. Just looking around."

Steve gestured to the rest of the group headed down the path. "Point yourself that way."

He caught Tom grinning at them from up ahead, and grinned back. "We're coming."

Samantha ran over and took her dad's hand as they started off through the trees.

After walking another fifteen minutes, they broke through a stand of trees fifty yards from the bottom of the hill. Bill clapped Tom on the shoulder.

"Hey, this is great. You weren't kidding."

"Daddy, I'm going." Stevie tried to grab a saucer sled from Joanie.

Steve nabbed his collar and jerked him to a standstill, then knelt in front of him.

"Now hold on, little guy. I'm going to walk up the hill and check things out. You wait here."

"Yeah," Tom said. "You kids just hang out right here so we can make sure there's no rocks or limbs where you'll be sliding. Bill, why don't you corral the kids while Steve and I scope it out?"

After a few minutes of careful examination, Tom and Steve pronounced the hill safe, and the party started.

After making a couple of runs at breakneck speed, Tom stood at the bottom and watched as Joanie and Bill careened down the hill, serried together on one sled, going faster and faster until they reached the bottom of the hill and hit a small bump.

The sled flipped and dumped them off together. A snowball fight ensued, ending with Joanie sitting astride Bill's chest, shoving snow in his face. He gasped for air, digging snow out of his mouth, then turned the tables on her.

He grabbed her under the armpits and lifted her over his head as easily as if she were a doll, then rolled over. Joanie was now the one on her back having snow shoved in *her* face. At last Bill rolled onto his back, and they lay side by side laughing hysterically.

Now that's *what I'm talkin' about*, Tom thought. *Nothing like kids, sleds, and a snowy hill. Maybe there's hope for 'em yet.*

# Chapter 28

Barb brought the teapot, sugar and cream, and three cups and saucers into the dining room. Sally and Susan sat in the living room. They rose to move to the table.

"Stay right where you are, ladies. I'll bring this over there to the coffee table—much more comfortable," she said. "Would you please move all those magazines aside?" She set the tray on the coffee table.

"Tom subscribes to so many bed and breakfast magazines, and would you believe he reads all of them? I use them for decorating ideas, but I think he reads every word."

Sally made a wide gesture. "They've sure paid off, because your place is stunning. Steve and I were talking last night about maybe coming back here with the kids next summer for some fishing and hiking. We're sure the kids would love it."

"Oh, that would be wonderful. We love repeat guests. But you'd better book soon because we're filled up for the summer months by the end of February. I'll give you contact information before you leave. And you too, Susan, if you're interested."

"I'm not sure if Bill . . . I guess it'll be up to him," she said. "And Joanie—"

Barb noticed her discomfort and picked up the basket of tea-bags. "Now, you ladies pick your poison here."

"This is nice," Susan said a few minutes later. "I needed this—it isn't often that I get time for myself. My friends back home are as busy with their families as we are. This is a gift, even if an unplanned one."

Sally dipped her teabag. "I agree. Folks are too busy these days. I belong to a mother's group at our church. We get together twice a month. Child care is provided, and all the moms sit and gab for a couple of hours. It has saved my sanity more than once." She hesitated, then asked with an impish grin, "Do you have anything like that in your church, Susan? A 'mothers of all-knowing teenaged girls' or something?"

"Bill and I don't attend church. We used to, but we've gotten out of the habit. Anyway, I don't think Joanie would go with us unless we hog-tied her and threw her into the car. Bill's never been much into it either, so we stay home on Sundays."

"There was a time right after Tom came home from his last tour when he refused to go to church. He'd been through a lot over there, and with one thing and another, he didn't want to go. He had the idea that church is for sissies. I stopped asking him."

"So you know what I mean, then," Susan said. "Sometimes it's easier to go with the flow, not make waves."

Barb sipped her tea, choosing her words. "I do agree with that. But there was a point when I had to go to church by myself. Tom didn't want to go. He was wallowing in memories of the war, losing himself trying to make sense of what happened over there, and I couldn't help him. And I couldn't help myself either, after we lost . . . anyway, so I decided I needed to do something different, something for me."

Susan averted her eyes from the other two women. She fixed

her gaze on the frigid landscape out the window, face taut, lips pressed in a thin line. Her hands gripped her cup, knuckles white.

Then she faced Barb. "Maybe you're right. But you're married to a different man. I'm not sure Bill would stand for . . ." She rubbed her forehead. "But I do wish I could find my way again. Sometimes I think Joanie's paying the price for our rebellion," she finished, tears glistening in her eyes.

Barb leaned over and patted her hand.

"The first step in a new direction is always the hardest. I know. But you need to take that first step. But maybe think about this too. Joanie's rebellion is hers—she's old enough to take that first step for herself. You can't beat yourself up, blame yourself because of how she behaves. God will work on her—let him do it."

Sally cleared her throat. "I've been there too. Steve and I went through a very rough five years right after we were married, but we didn't 'drift' away from God—we put on our running shoes and didn't look back for a long time."

Barb was glad she didn't have to do all the talking. "Running shoes? Do tell."

Susan nodded in agreement. "I'm hooked. Let's hear it."

"We wanted children so badly, lots of them, but I couldn't conceive. We went to doctor after doctor and tried everything, but nothing worked. I kept after Steve to keep trying, to keep spending thousands we didn't have. It wasn't Steve's problem. It was mine, and I blamed myself for disappointing him. Sometimes I'd catch him watching me with a look in his eye—I knew he hated me. Finally, after . . . after . . . he packed up and moved out. I was actually glad. Without him there, I didn't need to think about my failure."

"After? After what?" Susan asked.

Barb gulped hard, desperately trying not to interrupt Sally's flow of words, but she thought she'd scream if this story ended where she thought it would.

"I . . . I was finally pregnant, and we were so happy. But she . . .

she . . . was stillborn. I lost it completely then. I . . . I told Steve it was his fault. He'd given up because of the expense, and he'd been nagging and harassing me to just stop trying. The tension was so unbearable that I blamed him for the stillbirth. I told him I wasn't going to stay married to a murderer. So you see, we're not so different," she added. "Under the skin, we're all flawed in some way."

"Okay, I get it." Susan massaged her temples. "But I don't see what—"

Barb's hand shook, the teacup rattling against the plate. She leaned over and set it down before she dropped it, tea dribbling over the sides and pooling in the saucer.

Sally and Susan watched as she wiped it up with her napkin.

Barb leaned back again. She slowed her breathing and tried to control the bile rising into her throat.

"Are you okay, Barb?" Susan asked. "You're sweating. Can I get you anything?"

"I'm fine. Please, Sally, I'm sorry I interrupted you." She attempted a smile. "I'd like to hear what happened next."

Anything to move on past this.

"Okay. Steve couldn't live with my depression and blame anymore. While we lived apart, I came to my senses and consented to see a counselor with him. Looking back, it seems so stupid that I acted that way. I almost lost everything. And even now, with my mother's illness, I blame him. As if he planned the storm or something. I . . . I just want to see her one more—" Sally covered her face with her hands.

"And here Bill and I thought you both were so together, the perfect parents," Susan said.

Sally lifted her head out of her hands, her shocked eyes swimming in obvious pain.

"Sorry, but that's how you came across to us. Even your names all start with the same letter—I mean, really? Who does that anymore?"

"But we didn't—"

Barb, surprised at Susan's tone in the face of Sally's obvious grief, leaned over and patted Sally's hand.

"Sorry—go on. I interrupted you," Susan said, clearly trying to dial it down.

Barb leaned back and picked up her cup. "Yes, what happened then? How did you put yourselves back together?" She hoped Sally could ignore Susan's criticism.

"That's about all there is. Steve moved back in—he'd been gone about six months. We found a church we liked, and slowly healed over time. And then"—a huge grin split her face—"God answered our prayers and along came Samantha and Stevie."

"Oh . . . how long after you reconciled did you get pregnant?" Barb asked.

"That's a whole different chapter in our lives. Let me tell you—" She looked at Susan.

Susan picked at a thread on her sweater. "Oh, don't mind me. Let's hear it."

Barb wondered if Susan knew how much her sour expression resembled Joanie's.

Sally sat back and crossed her legs. "It happened like this . . ."

 Chapter 29

Tom called a halt and gathered the group at the bottom of the hill where there were some stumps and logs to sit on. After an hour and a half of sledding, Tom was exhausted. Many trips up and down the hill, carrying sleds, helping the two younger children, and keeping order when they argued over who got to ride the big inner tube next or whose sled went the farthest took its toll on him. Bill and Steve looked as tired as he felt.

Tom unzipped the backpacks. "Before I get the snacks out, I'm going to tell you they're all the same, so there's no need to argue, okay?"

The children rewarded him with blank stares.

He sighed. "This is the audience-participation part—you know, where you all nod your heads and say, 'Yes, sir.'"

Samantha and Stevie complied, but Joanie turned her back on him and found a log to sit on.

He ignored her and doled out the snacks and water.

"This is great," Steve said. "Sally and I discussed bringing the kids back here this summer for some hiking and fishing."

"Hey, that would be great," Tom exclaimed. "There are so many great trails not too far away, and places to fish. And I've fished them all—"

"Yay!" Stevie yelled. "How long before we come back, huh?"

"Let's let the snow melt, okay? So we can *find* the fish?" Steve chucked him on the shoulder. "Here, buddy, better put your hood back up. If you get sick, Mom'll have my hide." He secured the hood, retying it under Stevie's chin.

Joanie, now sitting next to Bill, leaned over and bumped his shoulder playfully. "Hey, Dad, could we? Come back, I mean?"

He was slow to answer, frowning and rubbing the back of his head. "Well—"

She broke in with a scowl. "Oh yeah—you're too busy working, golfing, whatever. No time for vacations. It doesn't matter." She turned away, crossing her arms and staring into the trees. "We'd bore you to death anyway, since you can't impress Mom and me anymore."

Staring at the back of Joanie's head, Bill answered. "I guess we'll have to see—"

"Yeah, I know what that means. Dad, you're so predictable—"

"Hey, kids, want to go exploring?" Steve broke in.

Samantha and Stevie jumped up.

Joanie didn't react, throwing a peek at Bill, who sat apart and stared at his feet.

Tom didn't miss Joanie's quick scan of her dad, so he raised an eyebrow at Steve and cocked his head in her direction.

"Hey, Joanie, want to come?" Steve asked. "I could use some adult help with these two ankle biters."

With an eye roll at Bill, Joanie rose. "Oh, yes please. I'd *love* to go exploring with you. Come on, Stevie. Hold my hand. I'll keep you safe." She took his small hand in hers.

Tom breathed a sigh of relief. At least she'd be out of his hair. "Bill and I'll stay here and spruce this place up before we hike back. Steve, if you head right through those trees ahead over there," Tom said, pointing, "there's a path—do you see how the trees on either side mark it? Stay between the trees, and you'll come to an old unused cabin hidden down in a hollow with a solid rock wall behind it. The path makes a bend in front of the cabin, then meanders back this way. Stay on the path, between the trees, and you'll be safe. It'll bring you right back here. Should take you about an hour or so, longer if you let Stevie do any 'exploring.'"

"Sounds good. Kids, get water and a power bar in case we get lost."

Tom saw Joanie's eyes widen. "No, he's kidding—you won't get lost."

She shrugged. "I wasn't worried."

But her knotted fists and tense expression said it all.

Right. Not so brave after all, are ya?

Chapter 30

After they disappeared through the trees, Tom picked up the trash left on the ground and stuffed it in his backpack. Bill helped, and soon they had the area squared away and pristine again.

The desire for Bill to open up to him weighed on Tom. He cast about in his mind, wishing Bill would give him an opening. It came sooner than he expected.

"How do you and Steve do it?" Bill challenged, back turned and posture rigid.

"Do what?"

Bill stared in the direction Steve and the children had gone.

"You both have such great marriages, and Steve's kids are so . . . so . . . oh, I don't know. Well-adjusted, I guess, is what I'm trying to say. By comparison, Susan and I are almost strangers, and Joanie's, well . . . what can I say?"

Tom laughed. "A teenager?"

"Yeah, I guess." Bill scuffed at the icy rocks under his feet.

Then he pivoted on his heel, facing Tom again, fists balled up at his sides. "How do you do it?"

"It wasn't always this way," Tom said. "We've had our difficulties, like any married couple. There's still times when Barb could cheerfully strangle me and throw me down the hill. And she'd be justified, too."

Bill's expression hardened. "Nothing's been right with me and Susan for years." He flexed his fingers as if trying to grasp at some unseen object. "All she does is spend my hard-earned money and bug me about spoiling Joanie. And I'm left wondering if this is all there is."

Tom noted Bill's tight jaw muscles and recognized it for it was—unrestrained, unmitigated anger and misplaced blame. He also noted something else. That key he'd been wishing for last night, the one that would unlock Bill's emotions, had just fallen out of his pocket.

"She expects me to forget what happened in Iraq, pretend what happened didn't, to suck it up and move on, be a normal husband and father, even though . . . even though . . ." Bill swung around again, facing the wilderness.

Tom knew Bill wanted in the worst way to tell him what happened but was afraid it would make him look weak. He knew because he'd been there.

"Even though what? Tell me what happened."

The result was like the lid blowing off a pressure cooker.

Bill backed up and whirled around, face grim but determined. "My best friend since grade school died in my arms over there," he yelled to the sky, both fists raised as if warding off a blow from an unseen celestial enemy. His face suffused into blotchy purple, neck veins bulging.

Tom braced himself.

"I tried to stop him from dying. All I could do was hold him. Watch the light go out. Michael and I did *everything* together, all through school—and he's gone, just like that, blown to bits."

As Bill spilled his agony, Tom relived in quick patches the days and nights in the muddy, bug-infested jungle, away from Barb—those years he tried to squeeze away somewhere in his brain but would always live on in his memory. A smell, a sound, a voice triggered those memories once in a while even now, although the harshness of them had lessened.

As his mind traveled back, Tom recalled the worst incident. Barb was young, naive, and hadn't understood how close he'd been that day to drawing his sidearm on her.

A hawk screamed in the distance.

The sound brought him back. He shook his head and stepped closer to Bill. The two men stood five paces apart, one in the white hot sand, the other in the murky green jungle.

Tom ran a shaky hand over his forehead and looked at the ground for a moment.

"I'm so sorry," he began without looking up. "Buddy, I know exactly how you feel."

He heard a moan and looked up. Like hearing the ominous click under his boot, Tom knew he was in trouble.

Bill's face crumpled, rage hurtling out of his mouth like a runaway freight train. He thrust a shaky index finger in Tom's face.

"No. You don't get to do that. You don't know. And I'm not your buddy—we don't know each other—"

Tom blanched. "I—"

"And I don't care if you did three tours in 'Nam. You weren't where I was. Iraq was a hot, dirty hellhole with sand everywhere—in your boots, in your pack, in your coffee—and it wasn't your war. We didn't know who the enemy was. It could be the man walking down the road with a cart full of melons, or a faceless woman holding a baby—"

"I do know—"

"Aww, just shut up!" Bill threw up his hands and shouted to the trees. "I get so tired of the brothers who say they know. You can't know unless you were wearing my boots, man, unless it was you holding Michael's messed-up body, watching his blood drain away into the sand."

Bill whirled back around, raising his fist. "So shut up. Unless you can tell me you wore your best friend's blood and guts on your face, had to tell his wife that it was your fault he—"

Tom recalled saying the same words to someone who'd never stepped off a transport plane in Vietnam yet was trying to tell him to buck up and get busy living again. He rushed to cover his mistake.

"You're right . . . you're right. Iraq wasn't my war," Tom said. "I'm sorry I said such a trite, meaningless thing."

Bill threw up his hands and backed a few feet away, a disgusted look on his face as he raked Tom up and down with red-rimmed eyes. "You know nothing—"

Tom thrust his chin out and raised his own fist. "But I lost men over there." He took a step forward. "So knock it off, Bill—I do know about that. You can't take that away from me. 'Nam was a hot, dirty hellhole with soggy muck everywhere. And we didn't know who the enemy was either—it could be an old farmer or a teenage boy—"

Bill's shoulders stiffened, and with a warrior's guttural cry, he charged. Head down like a bull, both fists raised, he covered the ground between them like a lightning bolt jumping from tree to tree.

# Chapter 31

T om sidestepped, letting Bill beat the empty air. But his recovery was quick, as Tom had anticipated.

Bill spun back around and shoved Tom's chest with both hands, sticking a boot out behind him at the same time.

Tom knew he was going down hard. Hanging on to Bill's forearms, he brought the other man with him, who landed on top and knocked the air out of Tom's lungs. For a split second they lay there, trying to breathe. Then Tom grabbed Bill by the shoulders, raised both of them up with a mighty effort, and butted his head up under Bill's chin, hard enough to throw the other man backward and get him off balance.

As Tom's head connected with Bill's chin, Bill grabbed the front of Tom's coat. Bill was thrown backward, but Tom was lifted off the ground in the process. Then as Bill fell back, he dropped Tom, his head hitting the ground again.

"Ahh—" Tom didn't move for a moment.

Then Bill fell on him again, screaming unintelligible words.

Tom rolled first one way, then the other, avoiding Bill's punches. Most of them landed on Tom's well-padded coat.

Geez, this guy won't give up. Tom didn't know how much longer he could hold out.

"Why'd ya have to do it? He was my friend, and he never even hurt a fly—" Bill's scream of fury soared to the mountains and returned in a muted echo.

Tom knew he was not the enemy Bill battled so furiously. That enemy was still in the desert. Or, more likely, in the heavens.

Finally, Tom was able to roll away, where he lay gasping for air. He rose to his feet and took off his coat, raking the snow out of the hood. The churned-up ground at his feet reminded him of the death battle he'd witnessed between two bull elk.

He watched Bill warily—splayed out facedown on the ground, back heaving with each breath. Tom stepped around him and put his coat back on and zipped it up.

"Come on, Bill. This is crazy. What're we doing here? Get up." He stepped closer and nudged Bill with his boot. "Get up. That's an order."

Bill rolled over and stood with effort. His back to Tom, he brushed snow out of his hair and off his jacket, stamping his feet to shake it out of his boots. "Hope I didn't hurt you," he mumbled, glancing back at him.

Tom pushed his coat aside, revealing the .44 on his hip. "Right. Like I'd let you."

"Maybe you shoulda used it."

Without warning, Bill collapsed to his knees, leaned over, and beat the frozen ground with his fists. "It should've been me . . . it should've been me—"

Tom sank to his knees beside him. "What do you mean?"

"We traded places in the truck that day. If we hadn't, Michael would be alive and I'd be dead, and Joanie wouldn't—" Bill sagged against Tom, sobbing, sucking in great draughts of air.

Tom tried to work out in his mind what Joanie had to do with it. "Bill, I'm so sorry." The weight of guilt on Bill's shoulders wouldn't be taken away by anything Tom could do or say.

Bill dropped back to his seat on the snow.

Tom followed suit, oblivious to the cold seeping through his jeans. He braved a glance at Bill's face, and seeing nothing but sadness there, he laid his hand on Bill's shoulder.

Bill wiped his face with his gloved hand.

"I remember it like it was yesterday. One minute we were in the truck, laughing at some joke Michael told. Always telling corny jokes, always makin' the guys laugh. I punched him on the arm, then he . . . he wasn't there. I don't remember getting out of the truck, but I must've. Couldn't hear a thing. The boys all piling out of their rigs, yelling and running over to us, and I couldn't hear 'em. Dust everywhere. About five yards away from me, I see this leg leaning on a rock. I checked mine—yep, still had both of 'em. I checked Michael—his right leg wasn't there. What was Michael's leg doing clear over there? It still had his boot on it, for crying out loud."

Tom tried to find words, any words, but couldn't. Bill's torment washed over him, flooding him like the rivers of the Mekong Delta, where Tom had almost drowned during a storm while on a combined security operation with a Navy SEAL team. He could still taste the brown brackish water.

"His leg was blown off, his head bashed in. There was blood everywhere, his flesh sticking to my helmet, my jacket. I crawled through the dirt and picked up . . . the leg . . . and like an idiot, tried to put it back on him. Stupid, huh?"

"You were in shock—" Tom couldn't manage any other words, lost in the putrid jungle, holding Mack in his arms.

"Michael was on the ground right next to me, and I hadn't even seen him at first. All I could focus on was his leg on that stupid rock. Then he must have felt me trying to shove his leg back on, and he grabbed me. A medic came over and took one look at him and shook his head. Michael had a hole in his gut you could drive a tank through and—"

"I *am* sorry for your loss. I've been there, believe me—"

Bill's vacant stare drifted over Tom's shoulder and scanned the mountains behind him.

"—and the last thing Michael said to me was to take care of . . . take care . . . and—" Bill broke off. Then, "And I haven't done a good job of either."

Take care of who? Done a good job of either? The look on Bill's face didn't invite questions.

"So don't tell me you understand, Tom. Nobody does."

"I lost my buddy Mack in the jungle—the best friend I ever had. You think I never have nightmares about that?"

Bill stood and stared down at Tom, then put out a hand and helped him up.

"And I know about guilt too, how destructive it is." Tom hesitated, then plowed ahead. "I'd like to give you some encouragement, if you'd allow me to." Tom waited for Bill's response, which came as a quick nod.

"Barb and I almost threw in the towel a long time ago, when I first came back from 'Nam. I'm sure I don't have to tell you what we went through, attempting to put our life back together after being apart for so long, and me relearning how to behave like a normal human being in civilized society. It was the hardest work we ever had to do. It nearly killed us."

Tom waited for some sign of agreement from Bill, but it never came.

Bill stood stiffly, hands on hips, forehead pointed at his boots.

"Anyway, we got pregnant after about a year and a half—a beautiful baby girl we named Katie."

Bill jerked his head up. "But . . . we thought—"

"We had her for two years . . . Then God took her." Tom gagged on his words.

Chapter 32

"**T**om—"

"Barb was devastated. Mothers shouldn't lose their children. But I . . . I wasn't so much . . . devastated, I mean. You see, when Barb told me she was pregnant, I wasn't that thrilled. I wasn't ready for that. I thought it was too soon, and I let Barb know it. As you can imagine, Barb was hurt. I even tried to get her to have an abortion. And now . . . geez . . . I can't believe I did that to her. Kill our own child—who does that?" Tom said miserably. "She kicked me out for a while. I thought we were over."

An owl hooted somewhere high overhead. Bill turned his face away, then swung his head back around to face Tom. His expression flattened, voice a monotone.

"What did you do?"

"After she let me come back, I took care of her—you know, did my duty. But we'd lost our connection to each other. That cursed jungle was always between us." He stopped, his eyes misted over, his next words stuck in the dry briar patch of his throat.

"I don't know whether I felt worse about Mack dying or his killer dying, but it sure killed things between me and Barb. I couldn't let go of it. My entire existence danced on the point of a pin called Vietnam, over six thousand miles from home. Only three years out of my life, and it changed everything for me. Nothing here made sense because nothing over there had made sense. You get that, don't you? Wasn't it the same for you?"

Bill swallowed hard and wrapped his arms around his chest, then gave a quick nod.

Finally. A connection.

Tom drew his next breath from the abyss of his soul. "And then Katie was born. She changed everything for me. She was the most beautiful thing I'd ever seen. The war ended for me that day—the jungle was gone from my head. She was so tiny and pure and soft—a miniature version of Barb. I fell in love with her instantly. I pretty much made a fool of myself over her, especially when we had guests or took her anywhere. It was like Barb and I had fallen in love again—"

"And then . . ." Bill prompted.

"And then God took her—an acute form of leukemia. He let us have her for two years, and then he took her back. Her last three months were spent in a hospital bed, pumped full of drugs—her beautiful hair gone and the light in her eyes fading, one day at a time. By the last day, she was almost a skeleton. It darned near destroyed us all over again. I even moved out for a short time."

Tom looked away and mumbled, "I couldn't stand seeing Katie's eyes on Barb's face."

Bill bit his thumbnail. "You must have been suicidal."

Tom scrubbed his face with both hands, as if trying to scrape the memory away.

"Yeah. Alcohol, Russian roulette, all of it. I didn't see the point of living a day longer."

Bill growled through clenched teeth. "Been there. Still there."

"I moved into an apartment. Barb and I still saw each other occasionally, still tried to work through the grief, but we weren't on the same page—not in the same book. Heck, not even in the same library. We even saw a divorce attorney, but never followed through. I was so far gone, I didn't even want to make the effort to do that. But God had a big idea about that."

"God?"

"Yeah, God. Barb started going to church, and pretty soon I saw the difference in her—"

"Hey, no preaching. I'm done with all that."

"Just hear me out, okay?"

Bill shook his head. "Fine, proceed. But don't expect me to follow you on this."

"I wanted what she had. The only way I can describe it is peace in her soul. So I started going with her. And slowly, over time, the healing started. We're not there yet—won't be until this old earth's gone—but it's not the monster it used to be."

Bill stared at him, then lifted an eyebrow. "And you're not mad at . . . at God?"

"Are you kidding? I'm a marine—and no one, not even God himself, messes with my men or my family. Of course I was mad at God. Who wouldn't be? After thirty-six months of 'Nam—watching my boys die, their families ignored by our own government—then riding in the saddle of survivor's guilt all the way home?" He paused to get a grip on his emotions.

"Of course I blamed God for that. And for Katie—when I wasn't blaming myself. I blamed the very one I didn't believe in. Crazy, huh? I still get mad at him. And it shows—ask Barb."

Tom lifted his face to the darkening sky. "There were times I literally beat my fists on the walls, pretending it was God's face. It was like a gnat beating an elephant. I don't do that anymore, but I've sure got a list of questions I'm gonna ask him when I see him."

"Guess I'll be standing in that line right behind you."

Tom took his hands out of his pockets and made a sweeping gesture, taking in the entire landscape and sky.

"You'll find God has infinite patience, with an infinite supply of love and mercy, if you'll take him at his word."

Bill's brow furrowed, hands limp at his sides. "I don't even believe God exists."

"Yet here you are, talking about him."

"Huh, never thought about it that way." Bill shoved his hands into his pockets and grimaced. "I don't know. I've never been one to buy into too-good-to-be-true, pie-in-the-sky promises. I'm a salesman. I know all the tricks—and I use 'em. I know you mean well, but I'm a born cynic."

"Noticed."

Tom decided to switch gears and give Bill some breathing room. "Tell you what. Let's get a fire going while we talk. Steve and the kids should be back soon."

"Is that an order, Lieutenant?"

"It's whatever you want, Soldier."

Tom had brought some small kindling in his pack, and they managed to find some pinecones and pitchy branches. Soon the fire burned hot. They stood nearby, hands extended to the warmth.

"I thought Barb was the most beautiful girl I'd ever laid eyes on," Tom mused, leaning over to stir up the kindling again. "We went to different high schools, but they were small schools, so they combined for big dances. I'd seen her around at games and stuff. You could have knocked me over with a feather when she said she'd dance with me. That was it for me. There's never been another woman I ever wanted to be with." He stopped, envisioning the younger version of Barb in her pink dance dress.

"How about you? How did you and Susan meet?"

"I . . . I . . ." Bill stopped, then started again, his voice cracking. "Tom, what should I do? My family's a mess, and I don't know how to fix it. There—how do you like that for honesty? I don't know what to do."

Tom shrugged. "Yeah—I died on that hill a long time ago." He chose his next words carefully, not wanting to come off preachy again.

"The best thing I can tell you is to talk to—"

Bill's anger erupted again.

"No. I've had it with counselors. They sit behind their fancy desks with their fancy words and their fancy drugs, all the time saying how they understand. It's a lie, Tom, and there's not a word they can say or a drug they can shove down my throat that's gonna do any good. I'm through with that. If that makes me a loser, then so be it. I'm a loser." Bill walked a few paces away.

Tom stumped after him and planted himself two feet from Bill, hands loose.

He kept his tone even. "You're no loser, Bill. I was going to say, talk to God—you know, the guy you don't believe exists—about Michael. And about Susan and Joanie." He paused. "And let him talk to you. See what happens. What've ya got to lose, Marine?"

Bill's shoulders relaxed, chagrin written all over his face.

Tom stuck his hand out.

Bill hesitated, then grasped it in a firm handshake.

"All right, Tom, I'll give it a try," he said in a husky voice.

Tom nodded and grabbed Bill in a stiff, manly bear hug, careful not to let it last too long.

Stepping back, he cocked an ear north. "They're back," he said, hearing "Frosty the Snowman" floating through the pines. "We should pack up and skedaddle back to the inn as soon as they warm up by the fire." He glanced up at the sky. "I figure we have about an hour and a half of daylight left."

Bill's head jerked around. He grabbed Tom's arm. "Hey, what's up with that? Tom, look out—"

Chapter 33

"Adopted on the same day—that's a beautiful story, Sally. Blessed twice over." Barb sneaked a peek at Susan, who hadn't reacted.

"Susan?" Barb prodded. "Earth to Susan . . . isn't that a great story?"

"Oh, sorry. I was wondering . . ." Her voice broke, eyes filling.

"Wondering?"

"When he'll get around to answering my prayers."

Barb pursed her lips. "In his time frame, not yours, I suspect."

Sally added, "That's what I had to learn, too—"

Susan jerked her head around. "I'm not you. It's not the same."

Cupping the warmth of the teacup in her hands, Barb sensed Susan slipping away. She couldn't break Susan's confidences from the previous evening. She pushed her long hair from her forehead, feeling the moisture there. She glanced again at Susan, a self-contained island in the midst of a storm. Barb knew what she had to do, but the thought of going there brought bile to her throat.

She gripped the sofa arm. "I know firsthand about grief, loss, and waiting for things to be right again. As I've tried to tell you,

Tom and I have been through some things, and I'm not proud of who we were back then. You told me you and Bill made some colossal mistakes. We did too, and some days we still reel over them, still suffer from them. You and Bill don't have a corner on that market."

She stopped then and waited to make sure Susan was tracking.

Susan's eyes narrowed to slits, her face impassive. "Go on. I'm listening."

"I told you that when Tom came back, he was a mess. But there's something else." Barb paused. "May I go on?"

"I told you—I'm listening. Say what you need to say."

Barb took a sip of tea and cleared her throat. "Tom came back from his third tour in 1974, and after a few months he seemed to come back from the darkness a bit. He saw a counselor for a time. He had PTSD, and I couldn't deal with that. He still has mild flashbacks sometimes. Once when the furnace came on, it made a clicking sound, and that's all it took. To him, it sounded like the click of a booby trap under his boot. And there were other things—the sound of a plane landing, the sound and smell of rain, fireworks." She picked at the fabric of the sofa arm. "It was hard for a long, long time. He . . . he lost his best friend, Mack, over there. We weren't the same people we were before he shipped out. Him more than me."

Susan stiffened. "You're not telling me anything new, you know."

"I know that. Anyway, about a year after he came home, we started to talk about having a family. He seemed a bit reluctant, but at least he was talking about it. And when I told Tom I was pregnant, I thought he'd be happy."

"He wasn't?" Barb heard the compassion in Sally's voice.

"Not so much. He . . . he wanted me to have an abortion. Can you imagine? I was so angry, I kicked him out. I couldn't stand to even look at him. It seemed like his answer for everything back then was to kill—"

"That was Bill too. And now he's all salesman. He thinks the answer to everything is the latest gadget and a fat bank account."

"With Tom, everything that happened to us always boomeranged back to 'Nam."

"Steve's answer for everything when we were separated was to get me 'out' more, as if by going out somewhere, I'd forget I couldn't get pregnant. Men—they're fixers, aren't they?—except for when they can't."

Barb nodded at Sally's comment. "I think they come by it naturally. But they don't understand that some things can't be fixed by a human hand. Time doesn't heal all wounds, but it does put some distance between us and the hurt. That's something, I guess."

Barb roused herself and looked at the clock in the corner of the room. "Ladies, I still have to make a salad for dinner. And there's biscuits to make. The stew's been simmering all day, so nothing to do there. Care to help? We can talk in the kitchen."

They gathered up their cups and the teapot and headed into the kitchen.

Barb set the cookbook out again and showed Susan which biscuit recipe to use. While Susan mixed the dough, Sally and Barb cut vegetables for the salad. When she judged the time was right, Barb took up her story again.

"I kept Tom away for several weeks," she continued, dicing carrots. "Then, I don't know, I guess I needed him—didn't want to be a single parent or something—so I let him come back home. For a while, on the surface, things were sort of normal. We didn't argue much, but that was because we didn't talk much. But there was no more talk of abortion."

"Arguing is all Bill and I do. It wasn't always that way . . . before—" Susan bit her words off and cut out another biscuit, grinding the cutter through the rolled-out dough and into the floured board.

"Anyway, it wasn't long before we had our beautiful little Katie."

"Oh—and where does she live? Does she have a family?" Susan asked.

Barb's dicing took on a frenzied sound, the knife slamming into the cutting board, carrot pieces flying.

"Had. We *had* a child."

# Chapter 34

Barb laid the knife down and took a ragged breath, relaxing her shoulders. She carefully scooped carrots into the salad bowl, some slipping through her fingers to the floor.

"Here, Barb, I'll get those—you go on and finish your story." Sally moved around the island and knelt at her feet.

Barb leaned against the counter, watching her.

"Anyway, I was so thrilled, and finally so was Tom. The moment he saw her, it was like my Tom had come home from the war." Her voice gurgled and broke. "And then . . . when she was two, they told us she had leukemia."

Susan dropped her spoon with a clatter and grabbed at her throat. Biscuit dough shot all over her shirt. She picked it off and wiped the counter, not looking at Barb.

"Did she—" Sally leaned forward, gripping the counter.

"She was gone in a few months. They stopped her chemo. There was nothing more they could do."

Susan glanced around the room. "But . . . Barb, there aren't any pictures of her. We assumed you and Tom never—"

"We couldn't bear it. Would you be able to? They're stored away in boxes, along with her other things, some here and some . . . in another place." She rubbed her temples. "And the longer we didn't open the boxes, the easier it was to leave them be. Maybe that's wrong, but that's how it is."

Choosing a tomato, Barb laid it on her cutting board. "Sally, would you mind getting the serrated knife out of that drawer over there?"

As Sally handed it to her, their fingers brushed. "I'm so sorry," Sally whispered, then resumed breaking lettuce into small chunks.

"Anyway," Barb continued, "it was a long time before Tom and I could even relate to each other. Our life together was sliced and diced into pieces. I couldn't deal with his anger. And he couldn't deal with . . . me. Can you understand how I felt?" She stabbed another tomato. "He wasn't angry at the doctors or even me—he was angry at himself for not protecting her. Like Mack, his buddy who died in his arms."

Susan put a floured hand to her mouth, the other fist knotted on the counter.

"We were both grieving in our own way. But I thought he mourned more for Mack than Katie. I was so . . . angry. He was so broken." Barb paused, gazing out the window, allowing the silence and the gently falling snow to soothe her.

She brought her thoughts back. Susan had filled the baking dish with small, round biscuits. "Looks like those biscuits are ready. There's some cellophane wrap in the third drawer down to the left of the sink. Let's cover them and stick them in the refrigerator until it's time put them in the oven. Then you can get some broccoli out and wash it. We'll add it to the salad."

Susan did as she was told and started cutting broccoli. "What happened then? I mean—"

"There came a day when I knew I couldn't continue the way I was. It was on the day we would have celebrated Katie's third birthday. While Tom was out that day, I'd decorated the entire house for a huge party—"

Susan stopped mid-cut, her hand frozen in place, gaze like twin full moons on her face. "What were you—"

"Balloons, streamers, posters, the whole works. When Tom came home, he took one look and walked out the front door and didn't come back for two days. I had—still have—no idea where he went. I sat in the living room alone, surrounded by pink balloons and party favors. I couldn't even go to bed that night. I lay down where I was on the sofa and cried myself to sleep."

"Oh, you poor thing." Sally reached for her hand.

Barb let her squeeze her fingers, but withdrew quickly. Now that she'd started on this road, she wanted to be done with it, without breaking down completely.

She picked up a stalk of celery, examined it, then whacked off the end. "That night I knew. I had to decide—to get well or get worse. I remember opening the closet where Tom kept his guns. I even took his short-barreled shotgun down and held it. Tom had taught me to use it early in our marriage."

Barb looked up at an audible gasp from Susan. She'd clapped a hand over her mouth, small green fragments of broccoli clinging to it.

Sally groaned and leaned over on the counter, head in her hands.

"I'm sorry," Barb whispered. "I don't mean to frighten or upset you."

Susan heaved a shuddering sigh. "It's . . . it's . . . this is so familiar. I can't tell you how many times . . . well, there were times. I'll leave it at that. If I hadn't had Joanie . . ." She looked away, clearly unable to continue.

Sally nodded her agreement. "There were times when I thought if I couldn't have a child, what was the use of living?"

Barb continued. "I held that shotgun for . . . for an hour, it seems like. I still remember the coldness of it, the smell of the gun oil, how the metal shone in the moonlight coming through the window. I stroked it—it was like hard silk. I put my thumb on the trigger, pointed it at my face, and looked down the barrel. It was like looking into heaven . . . or hell. I don't know which."

"You wanted to be with Katie," Susan whispered.

Barb stared at Susan. "Yes." She picked up the celery ends and ground them up in the disposal. She paused at the sink, her back to them, eyes locked on Katie's.

"I couldn't do it though. And I never did that again. It scared me."

"What happened? Was it a counselor or something?" Sally prodded.

"No." She returned to the counter and threw the celery chunks into the salad bowl. "I think this salad's big enough to feed the whole county, ladies."

Barb noticed Susan's tense face, waiting for her to answer Sally's question. "Believe it or not, it was one sentence spoken by a vet that Tom knew at the time. He said, 'After seeing what happened in 'Nam, especially to children, I had to give God my shovel and give him permission to dig up the bones one by one. Only he knows where they're buried.'"

Sally let out a breath. "And did you? Give him the shovel?"

Barb's gaze strayed to the window again. "Well, yes, but I started with a spade. Had to work up to a shovel. It took a long time."

Susan flinched. "So everything's perfect now for you and Tom? All kittens and roses?"

"Yeah, right." Her voice held a twinge of sadness. "No, things aren't perfect for me and Tom. Of course not. In fact, we spent most of yesterday, before you arrived, arguing and sniping at each other—because losing a child can never be healed in this life. Perfect? Hardly."

Susan stared at the mound of chopped broccoli in front of her.

Barb gentled her voice. "We're a work in progress, but we're learning to depend on each other." She drew back and watched Susan's face, chiseled in stone, but saw a tear slip out the corner of her right eye. In the background, the clock chimed the hour, and the Crock-Pot's hiss filled the kitchen with the fragrance of beef stew.

Susan broke the silence, her voice gruff with emotion. "Kind of like this salad. It took all of us to make it happen." She added the broccoli to it, mixing it in.

Barb nodded and covered the salad. After placing it in the refrigerator, she turned around with the milk carton in her hand. "Hey, girls, how about some milk and cookies? Like when we were little, right? And maybe we can talk about something else for a while—something less traumatic, like a world war."

Their beaming faces were like the sudden appearance of the sun from behind a dark cloud.

She shooed them into the living room. "You go on and get comfortable. I'll be your hostess again instead of making you work."

After the door swung shut behind them, Barb stepped to the windowsill and stroked Katie's cheek. Her eyes misted over, thinking again that her beloved little Katie was just around the unseen corner, waiting for her to arrive. The deep yearning in her soul longed to gather Katie's baby softness into her arms and protect her as she couldn't before. If she listened hard, she could just make out her giggle . . . the day she'd discovered ladybugs.

Barb drew a ragged breath. If only it wouldn't take so long to get there . . .

 # Chapter 35

At Bill's yell, Tom whipped around to see Steve and the kids burst through the trees, running pell-mell in their direction, yelling like wild banshees. They fanned out, surrounding the two men.

"Bill! Quick, we need to arm ourselves—"

"Got it," Bill yelled back.

Digging deep into the snow, they formed their weapons. Soon, the air was filled with snowballs flying in both directions, the kids darting forward and sideways under Steve's barked commands. When the kids ran out of the white ammo, Steve opened his bag and the four of them rearmed themselves.

Tom and Bill retreated out of range, breathing hard and brushing snow off their coats.

Tom eyed the advancing enemy. "Okay, here's what we'll do. We'll flank 'em. You see how they're bunched up now? Big mistake. If they don't spread out again, this'll be a piece of cake."

"Great idea, Lieutenant. Where do you want me?"

"You go left. I'll go right. Make snowballs on the way, and stuff your pockets. When I give the signal, move in, and we'll take 'em in the middle."

"What signal?"

He thought for a second. "I'll point and yell, 'Bear!' That'll distract them long enough. Go, go, go!"

As the enemy advanced to within firing distance, Tom and Bill ran in opposite directions. The enemy gave chase, and at the right time, Tom enacted his diversionary tactic.

He pointed dramatically at the trees to the north. "Hey, watch out! A bear!"

It worked. Steve and the kids pulled up short and rotated as one in the direction he pointed, their backs to Tom and Bill.

They moved in for the kill, pummeling the enemy with snowballs until Steve finally raised his hands and yelled, "We give up. You win!"

In a last effort, though, Stevie disobeyed orders, ran forward, and launched a snowball smack into Tom's face, then giggled through a victory dance until he slipped and fell down.

The game devolved into laughter, snow flung into faces and Stevie trying to tackle his dad. Steve picked him up with one hand and dropped him in a snowbank, the small boy coming up laughing and spitting snow. Exhausted, they plopped down where they were to catch their breath.

Tom stood, brushing snow off his coat and hood. "Did you find the cabin I told you about?"

"Yeah, we did. It's a little worse for wear after we used it for target practice."

Tom frowned. "Target practice?"

"You know, target practice. You know what that is, right? Weren't you a marine?"

"I didn't hear any shooting. Explain."

"We had to get ready for the war."

Stevie piped up, his expression stern. "Yeah, Mr. Masters. We practiced with our snow bullets."

"Oh, of course," Tom said with a straight face. "And I'd say all that practice paid off. I know you hit me at least half a dozen times, little guy."

Steve cuffed his small son on the shoulder. "Next time we'll work on battle strategy more instead of marksmanship, okay?"

Stevie nodded vigorously. "Yeah, Daddy, but what's that mean?"

"It means we'll practice tricking them, like they did us—"

"Ohhh . . . okay. Tomorrow?"

"We'll see."

Joanie extended her hands to the flames. "Mr. Masters, this fire is nice. Can we stay for a while?"

"Only for a few minutes. It'll be dark soon, and it's time to head back before your moms call out the rescue dogs. So let's have a quick snack and get going."

They dived into their packs and gulped their power bars and water.

Steve helped his kids bundle back up, then pronounced them ready to go. They looked like miniature sausages in their bulky zippered coats, hats, and gloves. After checking the ground for trash and loading up the sleds again, they formed a line and started back.

The snowflakes pelted them again, and Tom, wanting to get back to the inn as soon as possible, set a brisk pace. If they hurried, they'd make it in plenty of time before sunset.

As they walked, he enjoyed hearing the banter between Steve and his kids, who were bringing up the rear.

Tom also heard Bill and Joanie trudging along right behind him, talking quietly together. He had hopes that his connection with Bill this afternoon would bear fruit, that eventually Bill and Susan could begin the healing process. He knew the road for them would be hard—he'd walked his a long time. But all in all, Tom thought it'd been an encouraging afternoon.

He began a Christmas jingle in his deep baritone voice, the others joining in one by one.

# Chapter 36

"What's that?" Barb asked, carrying the milk and cookies on a tray. She set them down on the table and stepped to the big window overlooking the front veranda, listening first one way, then the other.

Sally stopped flipping through the magazine she'd picked up. "What?"

"I heard something. Don't you hear it?"

Susan and Sally joined Barb at the window, but the sound was gone. And then in the hush, a large section of snow slid off the metal roof, landing right in front of them with a *whoosh!* Startled, they jumped back from the window as one. The tension broke like a burst water balloon as they laughed at each other.

"I guess I was hearing the snow slide. But I was sure I heard singing coming from somewhere . . ."

Sally winked at Susan. "Someone on the roof—singing? Santa Claus?"

Barb's face held a look of mock severity. "Funny. I hope it wasn't in my head."

She glanced at the clock. "I wonder when they'll be back. It's three thirty already. It'll be dark soon."

Sally touched Barb's arm, her brows pushed together in an anxious furrow. "You think they're all right, don't you? Sam's not much good in—"

"Now, don't you worry. Tom knows these hills like the back of his hand. He'll keep everyone safe." She patted Sally on the shoulder.

"Come on, worrywart. I'm not going to eat these cookies by myself. I'm sure they'll be storming the gates soon enough, and then there'll be no peace . . . again."

"You're right," Sally said. "It'd be a shame if these cookies molded on the plate."

"No chance of that, I think." Barb passed the plate, and each grabbed a tall glass of ice cold milk.

Settling down against the back of her chair, Barb glanced out the window again. The gloom deepened, and she heard again the odd sound carried on the wind.

Then she turned her attention to her guests, who pored over one of Tom's magazines, their heads together, exclaiming over the beauty of a stone fireplace.

She hoped, for their sakes, that God would bring their families home safe and sound.

# Chapter 37

As "Jingle Bells" wafted over the treetops and faded, Tom glanced back at Bill and Joanie, walking right behind him. They walked hand in hand, laughing together.

Mission accomplished. Tom's soul high-fived and did a back flip.

The inn was over the next hill. They walked in silence now, no longer able to sing and walk uphill at the same time. Tom was glad they'd made it before dark with no mishaps.

He cocked his ear, listening to the quiet conversation opening up behind him.

Bill's voice held uncustomary gentleness. "This was fun, wasn't it?"

Tom didn't want them to know he was listening, so he kept his face forward.

"Yeah. I guess I'm glad we came. But don't think I'm glad I'm not at Ginny's." Joanie paused. "But it's sure way better than being at Mrs. Brewster's."

"On that we agree, sweetie."

Bill seemed to hesitate. When he continued, Tom had to listen hard to catch his words.

"You know, honey, I'm sorry the weekend didn't go as planned for us. But this hasn't been so bad. I know *I've* had some fun. And I think your mom really likes Barb and Sally. She's enjoying herself, except for *our*—yours and mine—shenanigans." Then, pointedly, "Your mom needs friends, Joanie."

Tom didn't hear Joanie's reply, but he was gratified at Bill's effort to connect with her.

"I've made a decision." Bill's voice held a note of finality.

"You're always making decisions. In fact, don't you make all of them?"

"Now don't start on me, young lady—"

"It's true, Dad. Mom bows to anything you want—"

"Would you hear me out for once?"

Tom couldn't see her face, but he guessed the scowl was there.

"I'm going to stop working so much and spend more time with you and your mom. I haven't been there for you, and I want to change that. I can work more from home than I have been—after all, I *am* the top salesman at the company. That should be worth something."

"Oh, great. So you're gonna lurk around the house, spy on me, and make me behave?"

"Yep, that's my new business plan. Any objections? No—don't answer that."

Tom couldn't resist a quick glance back at them. They'd stopped walking. Bill leaned over and kissed her on the cheek. She closed her eyes, a look of sweet contentment on her face.

Then she brought a snowball out of her pocket with lightning speed, smashing it down on Bill's head.

Backing away, she shrieked with glee as Bill scooped snow out of his jacket hood and wiped his face.

"You sure you want to spend all that time with me, Dad? Are you really sure?" she teased.

Bill moved without warning and grabbed her around the waist, picking her up like she was a toddler. He dropped her in a snow bank with a soft thud, then turned and gave Tom and Steve a thumb's-up. "Yep, I'm sure."

Stevie jumped on Joanie as she was getting up, almost managing it—then she was pinned back down as Samantha jumped on Stevie.

Bill glanced at Tom and nodded. Tom reached out and squeezed his shoulder.

It's a good day.

Together they helped the kids up, brushing snow off their coats and faces.

"Hey, let's get going, okay? We've got lots of snowbanks back at the inn, and I don't fancy being buried out here when that storm comes whippin' back on us."

They started up the hill again, the trail leading through deep-green pines frosted with snow, branches bent to the ground. As they reached the top of the incline and rounded the last corner on the path, they paused, and Samantha once again darted behind the same massive tree as she had on the way out, hidden for a few moments.

Tom saw her reach up.

Then she hopped out and took her place beside Steve.

"What were you doing, honey?"

"Nuthin'."

"Somethin'," he retorted, trying to grab her hood. She skipped away from him.

They arrived at the crest of the hill and started down the final leg to the bridge. Tom heard the rush of ice-covered water as it spilled around boulders and brush. The path here was treacherous, with small stones embedded in the ice. He stepped aside and let the others go ahead of him.

Steve took Samantha's elbow to steady her. She clutched her

bulging coat around her middle in an odd way. He tried to pry her elbow away from her side to get a purchase on her, but she resisted, her face strained with the effort.

"Samantha, what are you hiding there?"

The others turned.

Samantha shook her head, not answering. She glanced up, face scarlet, and stepped back from Steve, gaze darting like a caged animal looking for a way out.

"Daddy, that hurts," she whined as Steve leaned over and pried her arms away.

"What is it?" He pulled harder on her elbow.

Something slipped from under her coat, revealing a silver edge. She clutched it tighter, backing away from him. She shot a nervous glance at Joanie, eyes pinched against the sunlight low over the hills.

"Samantha, what do you have there? Give it to me." Steve held his hand out.

"Yeah, twerp, what is that?" Joanie shoved Stevie aside and took a menacing step toward Samantha.

Tom stepped in front of her, blocking her way.

Joanie tried to push him aside, but she might as well have tried to uproot one of the nearby western white pines, some standing over a hundred feet high. He put her in front of him and grasped her shoulders firmly, pinning her there as they watched the drama between Steve and Samantha.

Bill stepped up beside Joanie, putting a calming hand on her arm.

Samantha stood miserably, face reddened in shame and frustration. Steve waited for her to hand over whatever it was.

Stevie broke away and ran over to his sister, trying to reach under her coat. "Come on, Sammie. Let me see it—"

Joanie's iPad tumbled to the snow.

Tom had grabbed at Stevie as he darted past and lost his grip on Joanie.

She charged at Samantha with an angry shout. "Give it to me, you little brat—"

Samantha sidestepped and snatched the tablet from the ground. She clutched it to her chest and ran down the path toward the inn, fifty yards away. Hotly pursued by Joanie, she reached the footbridge.

Joanie caught up with her and tried to grab her arm, sending Samantha to her knees on the bridge.

The iPad flew out of her hands, fell to the creek, hit a rock, and bounced off. Then it slid downstream on the ice a few feet. Spinning around, it fetched up against a downed limb and was held there, undulating slowly with the movement of the water under the ice.

Joanie bellowed in anger and flew by Samantha, who was now sobbing, flat on her belly on the bridge. Joanie ran off the end of the bridge and down to the bank. She found a spot where she could get right down to the water, just opposite the iPad. Joanie went to her knees on the slippery bank, stretched her arm out, and reached for it, her body wobbling.

"Joanie, get away. You'll fall in!" Bill ran down and across the bridge past Samantha, who'd stood to watch Joanie. In his haste, he pushed by her, knocking her against the bridge railing.

She lost her footing, fell to her seat, and promptly wailed again.

Bill ran off the bridge, stumbling over rocks, and slid down the bank. He yanked Joanie backward by her hood and hauled her away from the water. They watched helplessly as her tablet broke away and slid to the left, away from the bank. Then it slipped into a hole and floated out of sight.

Joanie glared at Samantha, standing next to Steve on the bridge. "You're going to pay for this—and I'm not talking about money."

Steve slipped an arm around Samantha, drew her in, then directed a tight-lipped stare at Joanie. "Stop with the threats. It's gone. We'll buy you another one—"

"Don't you tell me what to do."

Bill had his arm around Joanie. He tightened it and leaned over, whispering in her ear.

She jerked away from him and pointed at Samantha. "Yeah, sure, Dad. Buy me another one, but what about her? Who's gonna punish her? Her parents? What a joke—"

Tom stepped forward, one hand extended, palm out. "Okay, that's enough—"

Samantha's yell cut him off. "Joanie, I didn't mean to drop it. You made me—"

"Shut up. You stole it!"

Tom dropped his arm in disgust. *So much for peace and camaraderie. It was good while it lasted.*

Chapter 38

"Ah, this hits the spot, doesn't it—" Barb jerked herself forward in her chair. "What in heaven's name is that racket?"

A cacophony of angry voices rushed at them from the direction of the back porch. Barb stood and put her milk down with a clatter. The melee sounded now in the kitchen—stomping, a door slamming, and then the sound of something crashing to the floor.

Joanie's voice bellowed. "Get your hands off me, Dad."

"Joanie, stop it." Bill sounded weary and frustrated.

Susan put her hand to her forehead and closed her eyes.

"Joanie, stop pinching me!" Samantha yelled. "I'm sorry I—"

Steve yelled next. "Let go of her."

Sally started forward, but Barb held her back with a calming hand on her arm.

"Wait. The men are out there. Let them handle it for now."

Sally shook her hand off and sat down on the arm of the sofa, face working. "Barb—"

Barb shook her head. "Just wait." This was like listening to a radio program—*Father Knows Best* meets *The Shining* . . .

And then Steve's voice again. "Stevie, here, get out of the way. You're going to get run over. Tom, can you grab him, please? Kids, stop fighting."

Joanie lost it. "Shut up, twerp! I told you I'd hurt you, and I meant it!"

Sally jumped up and started for the kitchen again but was stopped in her tracks as the door flew open and crashed against the wall. Tom and Stevie fell into the room, tripping over each other. Stevie ran for Sally, who knelt in front of him.

Before the door swung shut again, Barb caught a brief glance of Bill, flanked by Joanie and Samantha. He was keeping them apart with a grip on each of them. Steve stood behind him trying to haul Samantha away from the fray by the back of her coat.

"Tom, what—"

Barb fell silent when he held up his index finger and shook his head.

The door burst open again. Joanie charged through first, held back by Bill's grip on her hood from behind, trying to yank her back, almost choking her.

Steve and Samantha stumbled in behind them. Samantha made a beeline for her mother, sobbing hysterically.

Bill pulled out a chair at the table and gestured to Joanie. "Now, sit down, young lady." He wrenched her hood again while gripping her arm and shoved her toward the chair.

Joanie flung herself down, shaking the table and upsetting a heavy silver candlestick. It fell over with a crash. She jerked out of Bill's grasp, scowled at him, then turned a malevolent eye on Samantha—still sobbing in Sally's arms.

Tom plopped down in his recliner.

By the tight-lipped anger on his face and red-tinged eyes, Barb knew he was probably wishing himself somewhere else—anywhere but here. She'd seen that expression before and usually made herself scarce. No chance of that today though.

Sally drew Stevie and Samantha to the sofa, an arm around each. Steve stood behind them, hands on hips, clearly daring anyone to come near his family.

Susan and Bill sat down at the table, one on either side of Joanie. Susan tried to put her arm around her daughter, but Joanie stiff-armed her.

"Don't even, Mother—"

Barb righted the candle, then took a seat near Tom in the living room. "Is someone going to please explain what happened out there?" she said, breaking the glacial silence that had wrapped itself around the room.

Joanie pointed at Samantha, her finger extended like it was a weapon. "She—"

"Mommy, Samantha threw Joanie's toy in the creek," Stevie squealed, thrusting out his chest with obvious self-importance.

"It's not a toy, you dumb kid. It's a tablet—"

Bill took her arm and pinched her to silence.

Sally gasped and looked down at her daughter. "You didn't, Sammie."

"No, I didn't." She flung an arm in Joanie's direction. "It's all her fault."

"You little liar!" Joanie bellowed again, rising from her chair. "You threw it. And what were you doing with it anyway? You're such an idiot. Who takes a tablet sledding? And you never even asked me—you stole it out of my suitcase, you little thief."

"No I didn't. It was on the bed where you left it—"

"Yeah, *my* bed. *My* tablet. That makes you a thief—"

Steve leaned forward, hands gripping the back of the sofa. "Now see here—" He put his hands over his small son's ears. "Will everyone be civil, please? This is ridiculous—"

Bill stood and shoved Joanie back down in her chair.

"Joanie, I've had enough out of you. Now be quiet."

Sally's stern voice broke in. "Would you take Stevie upstairs?

He doesn't need to hear this."

Steve stepped around the sofa and knelt down in front of Stevie. "Hey, buddy, let's go upstairs and get into some dry clothes."

"Aww, Dad, I wanna stay and watch. Sammie told me that Mr. Brown isn't even—"

"No, Stevie, it wasn't a suggestion." He grasped the small boy's collar. "We're going upstairs now."

He lifted an eyebrow at Sally, gestured toward Samantha, and pointed upstairs.

Sally leaned forward and kissed Stevie. "No, I think Samantha needs to stay down here."

He bent and whispered in Samantha's ear.

She puckered her lips and gripped his hand. "Okay, Daddy. I promise."

He patted her head and guided Stevie toward the stairs, hand still gripping his collar.

"Aww, Dad, geez . . ." His dejected voice trailed away as he trudged up the stairs in front of his father, grumbling all the way.

Tom stood in front of his recliner and looked at his guests.

"Okay, can we start again—"

Barb stood and waved a hand in his face, hands on her hips. "Now, what in tarnation happened out there?"

# Chapter 39

Joanie stabbed her finger in Samantha's direction. "She—"

Tom gritted his teeth. He knew this wasn't over, and he was dangerously close to the limit of his tolerance.

Waving Joanie to silence, Bill ran his fingers through his hair. "Here it is in a nutshell," he said with practiced smoothness. "It seems little Samantha here took Joanie's iPad outside under her coat. She left it in the crook of a tree while we went on to the sledding hill, then on the way back, she got it again and put it back under her coat. Now, she's young and all, but surely you and Steve have taught your children not to steal—"

"St . . . steal?" Samantha's voice ended on a squeak.

"Oh, you *do* know what it means. At least that's a start."

Sally jerked around and faced him. "Steal? That's harsh. Of course we've taught them not to steal." Clearing her throat, she added, "And have you taught your daughter not to bully little girls?"

Joanie snorted. "Whatever. I didn't bully her. I gave her what she deserved." She looked daggers at Samantha, jabbing her finger at her. "And I'm not done with you. You better not close your eyes tonight—"

"Joanie!" Susan whirled around and yelled at the same time Bill swatted the teenager on the shoulder.

"What? She did deserve it. Dad," she wheedled, "I know you paid a lot of money for it. Aren't you the least bit upset?"

"Of course I am, baby. Those aren't cheap. But we'll buy you another one, right, Susan?"

"I thought you told me you won it in some sales contest—"

"Thanks a lot. Do you have to spill everything?"

"Geez, you guys, do you have to fight about everything? This is about *my* iPad, not *your* issues."

Bingo. She's no dummy.

"It doesn't matter about the iPad, sweetheart. We'll buy you a replacement. We'll get the latest and greatest, okay?"

Susan, red faced, threw up her hands in obvious resignation.

Tom looked at the floor and shook his head.

Bill noticed and raised his voice again. "What, Tom? This isn't your business."

"It may not be my business, but it's my house," Tom challenged. "And frankly, I'm a bit weary of these constant theatrics."

"Tom!" Barb exclaimed. "These are our guests—"

"Oh Lord—" Sally cut in, grasping Samantha's chin. "Sammie, look at me. Did you really throw the iPad in the creek? If you did, your Dad and I will have to replace it, and it will come out of your allowance for a long time to come."

"No," Samantha said, desperation in her voice. "I didn't throw it, Mommy. I promise."

"What happened then?"

Samantha buried her face in her mother's waist and sobbed, unable to answer.

"Okay, Sally, it was this way," Bill said. "As I said before, Samantha stole . . . umm . . . *borrowed* the tablet—without permission—and took it with her. Joanie was upset. Can you blame her? Samantha wouldn't even hand it to Steve when he asked for it, for crying out loud. She hightailed it down to the creek and tossed it over the railing. Joanie tried to get it, but it sank before she could. She almost fell in the creek trying to grab it, by the way, which might not have ended so well for her. I had to run down and pull her back before she slipped. So you see, Joanie's justified in being angry. It was a stupid kid's prank that went wrong, and now *someone* will have to pay for it."

Sally looked down at Samantha. "Honey, you must tell Mommy the truth."

"Mommy—" Samantha buried her face again. "I didn't do it."

"Oh brother, kid. Come clean, why don't you?" Joanie groaned. "Geez—"

Barb frowned in Tom's direction. He knew what she wanted.

He gulped a breath. "Uh, I don't mean to argue, but—"

"But what?" Bill jerked around to face Tom, head thrust forward.

"I think you left out some key details," Tom started mildly. "You forgot the part about Joanie *chasing* Samantha down toward the creek, trying to grab her from behind, causing Samantha to fall, and *then* the iPad flying out of her hands. Samantha didn't throw it into the creek on purpose," he declared. "Joanie grabbing at her arm caused her to drop it."

"You don't have a clue—"

"I agree," Tom interrupted, "that she definitely shouldn't have had it out there to begin with. Samantha is partly responsible, no doubt in my mind. But, the whole thing could have been avoided, don't you think, if Joanie hadn't flown off the handle?"

"Tom, just back off. I'll handle my own family." Bill raised his hands, fists clenched.

Tom read the signs and watched him warily, his biceps tightening. Out of his side vision, he saw Barb carefully replace her coffee cup on the side table.

"Tom—"

He waved her to silence. "I got this."

Bill paced around the table, past Susan, and stood in front of Tom.

Susan reached for his arm. "Bill—"

"Stay out of this, Susan."

Tom waited, watching Bill's face. He looked like a bull moose ready to charge at the least provocation.

"Tom, I'll try to be civil here. Don't make it hard for me. I think my daughter has a right to be angry. Just because the little twerp . . . uh, girl, is young doesn't mean she has to be protected and coddled. She should have to face the music. She should be punished—severely."

Sally drew Samantha closer to her, stroking her hair.

"See? Coddled—"

"Now see here," Sally said. "You have no right to—"

Tom took a step closer to Bill and took care to lower his voice. "You forget. I was there. I saw everything. Your version is your version. It seems Joanie's not the only one who has trouble with the truth." He leaned toward Bill and poked a finger at his chest. "Didn't the Marine Corps teach you anything about honesty, Soldier?"

"Stay the hell out of this. It doesn't concern you. And I'm not your soldier—"

"You tell 'em, Dad," Joanie said with a sneer. "Make 'em pay."

Susan shushed her with a firm hand on Joanie's arm. "Who pays is not your concern. Let the adults handle this." Turning to Sally, she said, "I'm so sorry about this. I'm sure she didn't intend to destroy the tablet, and I know we can come to some agreement over the matter."

"Oh sure, Mom. Take her side. Sometimes I wonder if you're even my mother, the way you blame me for everything."

Susan gasped, her hand to her chest. "Joanie, how can you be so hurtful?"

"You make it easy for me."

Susan appealed to Bill with a glance, but he ignored her and stepped back to stand on Joanie's other side, putting his arm around her shoulders.

Susan slumped down in a chair, head bowed.

Come on, Bill—what is it with you? Tom wanted to shake him.

Sally looked down at her daughter, cupping her chin and tipping her face up.

"Samantha, honey, have you apologized to Joanie?"

Samantha nodded, curls bouncing. "She wouldn't listen to me. She pinched me, and it hurt—a lot." She pointed to her upper arm.

Sally frowned at several small bruises forming. "Oh, honey—"

"She deserved it," Joanie growled. "And I'll do it again."

"Joanie, stop this!" Bill tightened his grip on her shoulders.

Samantha shrank back against Sally, trying to hide her face.

"Never mind that for now, honey," Sally said. "We'll put some ice on your arm in a minute. Right now, you owe Joanie and her parents a big apology for taking her tablet without permission. How would you feel if she'd taken something of yours, like your doll that you brought with you?"

"Yeah, like I would—" Joanie interjected.

Sally cut her off with a palm thrust in her direction. She knelt in front of her daughter.

"Do you understand? Daddy and I have told you we should always admit our mistakes and say sorry, remember?"

Joanie huffed. "Oh brother. What is it with you people? Just smack her—"

Bill tightened his grip on her shoulders again. "Joanie—"

Sally placed her hands on Samantha's shoulders, turned her around, and gave her a gentle push in Joanie's direction.

Samantha took a timid step toward Joanie.

"You come any closer to me, twerp, and you *will* be sorry."

Bill let go of her and slammed his palm down on the table.

"Joanie, it wouldn't hurt you to listen for once. Hear her out, for crying out loud."

Tom moved closer to the table. He wanted to defuse the situation but was unsure how. This wasn't a squad of soldiers he could knock around if need be. He glanced right and saw Steve standing on the bottom stair. He wondered how long he'd had been listening.

Tom leaned down to whisper in Barb's ear. "Honey, maybe you could—"

A moment later, his idea fled, as every eye in the room stared in shock at Samantha.

Red faced, she stamped her foot. "You're so mean—all of you. Anyway, *he's*"—she stabbed her finger in Bill's direction—"*he's* not even your real father. Your real father's dead. So there."

# Chapter 40

Tom felt as if the air in the room had been sucked out in the wake of Samantha's outburst. He watched helplessly as the drama reached its climax.

Samantha burst into tears again and ran back to the shelter of her mother's arms.

Steve charged down the last step and over to Sally's side, drawing her and Samantha across the room, away from the erupting chaos.

Barb moaned into her hands. "Oh no . . ."

Tom scratched his head in confusion. "What?"

Barb grasped his arm. "Tom, maybe we should—"

Joanie jumped up, knocking her chair against the wall behind her. A large picture crashed to the floor, splintering glass in several directions. Eyes wide, she stared at Bill and Susan, mouth open but no sound coming out.

Susan cowered, head buried in her arms.

Bill unloaded on her. "You and your big mouth. You can't keep anything to yourself, can you. You're pathetic."

Joanie's voice broke. "Mom? What's going on—"

"Honey . . . I . . . I'm so sorry—" Susan began.

Joanie raised a fist at her, cutting her off.

She stepped toward Bill, glass crunching under her feet. "Dad?"

Bill lowered his eyes to the floor, hands limp at his sides.

The miserable silence stretched, backed only by the loud tick of the grandfather clock and Samantha's soft whimpers.

Joanie's face flattened, her voice deepening in fury as she flayed her mother. "You're nothing but a pathetic liar. I hate you."

"Joanie . . . I . . . I . . ." Susan's hands fluttered at her sides like the wings of a dying butterfly.

Joanie squared her shoulders and spoke in a chilling, emotionless voice.

"I hate all of you." Her rage-filled glare raked the room. She paused on Samantha, who cowered behind Steve. Her voice rose with each enunciated word. "You come near me again, brat, and I *will* make you sorry."

Then she turned her full wrath on Bill, eyes like flaming charcoal, grilling him.

"And you." She hammered each word. "I don't know who you are or what you've done, but you can stop pretending to be my dad."

Bill said nothing—didn't even look at her.

Tom thought he looked smaller, frail, like his heart and soul had leaked away through the floorboards.

Joanie spat her next words. "Yeah, I thought so. You two have no excuses, no explanations. Everything's all about you. As usual."

She pushed her chair out of the way and stumbled to the foot of the stairs, kicking shards of glass from the broken picture out of her way. At the last moment, before escaping up the stairs, she swiveled toward Bill one more time, red-rimmed eyes boring into his.

"You're nothing but a hypocrite, *Bill*. You're nothing to me. I'll never call you dad again."

Joanie whirled and left the room. She stamped up the stairs, each footfall punctuating her fury.

Bill groaned and dropped into a chair at the table, head down.

Susan tried to take his hand, but he jerked it away and turned his chair away from her. She hesitated, then rose and trudged up the stairs, stiff backed. A knock, and a muffled voice shouting "Go away!" wound its way down the stairs. Then Susan's voice. "Joanie, let me in. Please, let me explain, honey." The click of a doorknob and the soft closing of the door.

Muted voices through the upstairs floorboards, then a door opening.

"Get out!"

Door slamming. "Joanie, please. Don't do this—"

Tom peeked at Barb's strained face for a split second. He knew where her mind was—in a dim hospital room, keeping vigil over another death.

After a few moments, Susan returned and sat down. She stared in silence at the back of Bill's head.

Steve gathered Sally and Samantha and retreated up the stairs.

Bill scraped his chair backward, stood, and slammed through the kitchen door. It creaked on its hinges, swinging back and forth in his wake. Then the sitting room door opened and banged shut, rattling the walls.

After a few minutes, Susan rose. Her hands traveled nervously over the table, straightening placemats that didn't need straightening.

Barb approached her and stilled Susan's hand with her own. "Susan, I'm so sorry—"

Susan shook her head and fled upstairs. Another door slammed.

Left alone in their frigid dining room, Tom leaned close to Barb. "Did you know about this?"

Her face flamed. "Yes."

"Great."

"But—"

"Shh . . . later. I think we'd better let everyone calm down."

She backed away and fled to the kitchen. Tom turned to the window and stared into the gathering gloom as the darkened skies threatened a fresh unleashing of snow.

His thoughts were circular, like buzzards over a dead carcass. He tried to snare one idea to put all of this right, to bring even a fragile peace back into his home, but he simply did not know what to do about this family who'd become . . . unfamily.

His take-charge, leave-no-stone-unturned mentality that had served him in the jungle had failed again in the real world. He leaned forward and pressed his forehead into the icy cold of the window.

He didn't think he'd ever heard so many slamming doors in his home, cutting everyone off from each other.

Tom groaned in his soul. He felt his helplessness and remembered the gut-wrenching pain of it from another time. He knew Bill was on the edge, because Tom had once teetered there and looked over that same precipice. And he knew the lengths to which Bill might go to stop the pain.

Tom was determined to help Bill, but didn't have a clue where to start.

Chapter 41

Tom's hope that Barb's delicious stew and biscuits would make for a pleasant meal with their guests was soundly dashed.

Bill and Joanie didn't make an appearance at the dinner table. Tom and Barb ate in uncomfortable silence, while the Elliotts made small talk at the other end of the table.

Samantha's face was red from crying. Sally sat next to her, occasionally patting her back or smoothing her blond hair back from her face. Eventually she calmed down and took an interest in her food.

Stevie chattered away as usual, too young to comprehend the tight undercurrents swirling around the Master's Inn. Steve had to curb the chatter so his son would finish his meal.

Susan sat midtable between the Masters and the Elliotts, picking at her food, not making eye contact with any of them.

Not knowing what to say, Tom kept quiet and ate his dinner.

"I'll help you clean up," Tom said a little later. He'd been lost in his own thoughts while eating and hadn't noticed the table had emptied. Their guests had drifted away.

"Thank you. I guess Susan and Sally don't feel like helping, but that's okay. I hate to say it, but I've had my fill of everyone. What about you?" Barb started into the kitchen with a load.

"I think you know the answer to that one, don't you?"

Tom went out and came back with the last of the dishes. "I wiped the table down and put the centerpiece back. Is that it?"

"Yes. I'm done in here. Let's go relax in the living room."

Barb took one end of the sofa, and Tom sat at the other end, the distance between them filling him with unease. It wasn't only the people upstairs who had issues.

"Looks peaceful out there, doesn't it?" He loved the way the full moon—alternately framed, then hidden by building storm clouds—shone through the window and bathed them in light.

"It does. But it's freezing cold—like in here. Even though it's quiet upstairs, everything has fallen apart. And you . . . we . . . did nothing—"

She turned to him, an accusing look in her eyes. "What's the truth about what happened out there this afternoon, now that it's just us?"

"It happened like I said." He leaned forward in his chair. "Bill was lying through his teeth. I can't figure it out. Does he think I'm blind or something? And listen, there wasn't anything we *could* do, don't you see? And there still isn't. I wish the weather would clear so they would all leave and take their baggage with them."

"That's not very charitable of you," she said. "They're here, and probably for a while yet, so we should at least *try* to help them. Maybe it's why God brought them here. Isn't that what we decided?"

"I thought you wanted them gone."

"I do. And I don't."

Tom stared at his hands. He knew where he wanted to go, but he didn't know how to get there.

He swallowed hard and looked up. "Maybe you're right about trying to help, but we have enough problems of our own. I certainly don't have any answers for them. I . . . I don't even have answers for us." He saw her flinch, but he wouldn't take it back.

"Tom—"

He didn't care for the pain in her eyes again. The thought of that conversation, *again . . .*

"Never mind that now." Feeling cowardly, he switched gears. "How do you think Samantha found out about Joanie—I mean, that Bill's not her biological dad? It's obvious Joanie didn't know before they arrived. I can't figure it out."

Barb lowered her head. "I think I know. When everyone first arrived and there was that awful scene with Joanie and Bill ganging up on Susan—remember?"

"I remember I was thinking Bill acted more like a buddy to Joanie instead of a dad."

"Yeah. Susan poured her heart out to me right after that—you know, when we had tea together. She told me the whole story of Joanie's real father being killed in Iraq and then how she and Bill got together. Bill and Michael were best friends. It's sad—"

"Whoa there. You lost me. Did you say Joanie's real father was Bill's best friend, Michael? You're kidding, right?"

"No. Why would I kid? What do you know that I don't?"

"Something Bill and I talked about when we took the kids sledding. But . . . what does this have to do with Samantha?"

"It was while Susan and I were talking. I thought I heard a noise, and Susan did too. We both looked up. But there was no one there. I think Samantha must have eavesdropped from the stairs. That's the only thing I can think of. It was the only time Susan mentioned it. It had to have been then, don't you think?"

Tom considered her words. "You're probably right."

Barb leaned forward and put her head in her hands. "I'm so darned sorry it happened. We had no idea. And now Bill and Susan will have to deal with the fallout. I told Susan they shouldn't have kept it from Joanie, that she'd find out some day. I just didn't think someday would be here, with us."

Tom reached over and patted her knee. "There's nothing—"

Barb looked up. "She found out in the worst possible way—in front of all of us—and it might ruin their family. *Truth* is what people need to hear, and Joanie should have been told the truth a long time ago."

Truth. Yes. People needed to hear the truth . . . Barb needed to hear the truth. Maybe it was time. He'd put this off far too long.

Chapter 42

Tom moved to Barb's end of the sofa and sat close to her, folding her hand into his own.

"I agree, but Bill thinks it's none of our concern, and he's probably right." He cleared his throat and said, his voice gruff, "You know, I'm going to say something here. Maybe it's the wrong time and all, but here goes."

Barb tried to remove her hand, but Tom tightened his grip.

"Hear me out, okay?"

She stiffened and looked away.

He gently turned her face toward his. "Please look at me, honey."

She resisted at first but then gave up.

"Tell me. Do you think God is wringing his hands over the proverbial cat being let out of the bag tonight?"

She looked at him in confusion. "What do you mean?"

"I mean, do you believe God is in control? Of even this fiasco?"

"Of course I know God is in control. But . . ."

He pressed harder. "But what? Either he is or he isn't. There's no *but*, no in between. Either he's God with a capital G or he's not."

"This is a fine time to get all preachy with me. Where's this coming from?"

"I don't mean to preach. You asked where this is coming from. Bill and I had quite an . . . experience out there today. We were alone for a little bit while Steve took the kids hiking. It brought back some things. I'll tell you about it later. But watching him this afternoon and tonight, I realize that I'm . . ." He stopped and cleared his throat. ". . . him."

"What? Who? You mean Bill? You are not—"

He leaned toward her, clutching her hand harder. "Shh—"

Barb lowered her voice to a fierce whisper. "You're not a blow-hard like him. And you'd never have been that kind of father. I don't believe it."

"Hey, wait a minute. What I meant was, I'm him because of what I put *you* through. And I don't recall ever apologizing to you—a real apology—not one dragged out by a counselor. Yeah, we've talked over the years, and cried sometimes, but you're smart enough to know I was only going through the motions most of the time so you'd . . . you'd leave me alone."

Barb raised her head and allowed her eyes to slide over his.

"Do . . . d'ya think God was in the room that night when Katie . . . when she . . . she stopped breathing? If he's in control—" He choked out the words and could go no further.

Barb wrenched her hand out of his.

Oh no you don't, mister. You're not taking me there again.

"What does it matter now? And if he was . . . there in the room . . . then what kind of loving God is he? The kind that gives us the most precious thing in the world, then takes her away from us? Do you even remember how much she suffered? That's love? If it is, I don't want any part of it, thank you very much."

She turned a stiff back to him, arms crossed in front of her.

"Barb—"

"Look, I'm tired of trying to figure it all out. It happened. We need to move on."

"That's just it—we haven't. I don't think we can. And watching the Browns tonight, I know why."

"Oh really? Okay then. Let's hear your newfound wisdom."

He raised his voice a notch. "You're sure making this hard, aren't you?" He looked toward the ceiling at a sound, then leaned over, lowering his voice. "Give me a break here."

She looked at his face—anguish in every line and crease—the way it was the day Katie had died. But now it was more than four decades later, and she knew the truth. She'd done that to him. And that truth hurt.

"Fine. Proceed. I'm all ears."

Tom angled toward her and leaned forward, elbows planted on his knees, chin supported by his curled fists. His eyes narrowed as he stared her in the face.

She tried to look away but found she couldn't.

"Remember the night when Katie was about three months old and we knelt by her crib and gave her—lock, stock, and barrel—to God? Did we mean it? Or not."

Barb's retort stuck in her throat. She knew where he was going and couldn't bear to go there again, but she felt like a pinned bug in a display box. Knowing what came next, she shrank from it.

Tom hammered home his point. "I guess we didn't really, did we? I guess we didn't know what we were saying—that we gave God permission to do whatever he wanted. Even take her from us."

Barb felt her face dissolve. She leaned over, head in her hands. "I didn't mean *that*. I didn't give him leave to make her suffer like that, to take her." She looked up at him. "And what I remember is what you said the day she died, that I shouldn't have had her—that I should have 'done something about it before.' Weren't those your exact words?"

Tom's face drained of color.

"Tom, I—"

He looked ready to vomit, and she wished she could snatch her words back.

"We haven't moved on, have we, Barb? It's that day in 1976 every morning we wake up. Every day of our lives—from that one to this—is *that* day. And I think we won't . . . move on . . . until we acknowledge that—"

The sharp words shot out of her mouth. "Maybe we're not supposed to move on—"

"I'm sorry. I know I caused this—"

So now he thinks he can wipe it all away with another "sorry"?

"No need to be a martyr over it. And anyway, taking on all that guilt isn't good for either of us." She couldn't help her heartless tone. "It was God's decision to take her. And I guess he doesn't have to consult us."

"I've been ashamed for telling you to do . . . that . . . since the day I first said it, but I was too proud to own up to it. Barb, honey, I was afraid—afraid I'd ruin a child if I became a father then. That somehow the jungle, all that hatred and brutality, would become part of her DNA. And then to say that after she . . . she left—"

Barb squeezed her eyelids together. She heard the agony in his voice and felt the thaw begin—like early spring when tiny green shoots under the snow announced warmth and life was just around the corner.

He lowered his head over her hands, pressing his forehead to her fingers. "If I could go back and erase those words, I'd do it in a heartbeat." He stopped and cleared his throat. "Will you—can you—forgive me?"

Barb had never heard such brokenness in his voice. For the first time since he'd crushed her with those words, she believed him. She took his hand in hers and raised it to her lips and kissed his rough, calloused knuckles. She caressed them and tucked his hand under her arm.

He curled next to her, his head on her shoulder.

Looking out the window, she listened to his breathing and heard the soft pings of a video game drift down the stairs, chased by childish giggles.

Barb relaxed and closed her eyes again. Images slipped past her eyelids as she relived the wretched past in the space of a few moments.

The day she found Tom sitting on the porch, gripping his service weapon, a bottle of Jack Daniels by his side. The separations, the move from Boise, trying to stay married.

And then . . . sweet Katie was born. Tom hadn't had one flashback while Katie was alive, until she got sick. Her frail body fighting for life and breath the day she died. Tom yelling at the hospital staff to *do* something.

And then the flashbacks returned with a vengeance. For a year or more, he'd had several a week. She didn't know which was worse—Katie's death or what it'd done to him.

Now, something in her soul moved. It heaved deep inside her—something that had lain heavy and rotten in her gut for so long. She'd nursed it, cultivated it, suckled it—it'd kept her alive since the day Katie had died. She felt it wrench away and almost tried to snatch it back.

But as her fingertips brushed it, she let it go and watched it float away. The relief was rich and heady. Something else drifted in and took its place—something soothing, like the sound of the creek out back or a warm cup of spice tea on a wintry afternoon. It settled in like a cozy quilt—lavender, with bumblebees sprinkled on it—draping itself softly around her soul.

And Katie was there, her tiny hand covering the angel's head, her sweet smile and bright-blue eyes lighting the room.

Chapter 43

Tom shifted next to her, and the wretched past faded. She looked at him and remembered he'd asked her to forgive him and she hadn't answered him—maybe the reason for the dread on his face now. Compassion welled up in her, compassion for this broken soldier who was her husband.

"Yes, Tom. I forgive you. Thank you for saying what you did."

His gruff voice was clogged with four decades of pain. "Should've said it a long time ago." He sank into the sofa, head against the back, legs stretched in front of him. "What a colossal waste of time."

Moisture popped out on her forehead—she knew they weren't finished. "Can I be blunt with you?"

"Fire away," he said, voice raspy, lashes wet against his rough cheek.

Barb searched for words, not wanting to hurt him but knowing he needed to hear the truth and she needed to tell it.

She took his hand and leaned into him. "I hated you. You killed us with those words, as surely as if you stuck your bayonet into my womb. And it hurt for so long, here." Her voice cracked as she covered her belly with her palm.

The tears now spilled over and flowed down to Tom's chin.

She reached and wiped them away with her thumbs.

"It stopped hurting when she was born, but when she died . . . it all came back." She looked away from him. "I blamed *you* when she died, not the disease, not the doctors. You. As if you not wanting her was the reason she got sick. If I could take *that* back, I would."

Tom sat up and gathered her in his arms then and pressed his cheek against her hair.

"*I* blamed me. I did want her, but I was afraid. Afraid I couldn't protect her. Like I couldn't protect Mack and the boys who died over there. And then she got sick, and I found out what *helpless* is. Somehow it got all jumbled in my mind, and I couldn't fix any of it." He paused, then whispered so low she had to strain to hear his words. "I should've been able to fix it."

"We've torn our house down with our own hands and left it in ruins. There've been good times, sure, over the years, but they could've been better. Is that what you're trying to say?"

"Yes, that's it. But," he went on, "I think I have to—we have to—acknowledge the hardest thing of all—"

"That God was kneeling in the jungle with you next to Mack's body?"

Tom hardened against her, then relaxed.

"Yes, that, too. And he watched me empty my gun into Mack's killer—a teenager doing what he was trained to do. I think . . . I know . . . that God loved that young soldier the same as he loved Mack. And that maybe God watched that young boy drift off to somewhere he wasn't. And that's on me." Tom shook his head. "It changed me. I can't explain it. I'll never be able to."

She took his chin in her hands and turned his face to hers. "Remember? War always changes the warriors. That's what we wives learned when you boys came home. The ones who did come home."

She pulled away from him then and sat up straighter, her grip on his arm tightening. "And he *was* kneeling . . . next to . . . next to—" The sentence she'd tried to finish for decades lodged in her throat again, like an immoveable boulder.

"Katie. Is that what you were going to say?" Tom asked.

"Yes . . . next to Katie."

Now that she'd finally finished that sentence, the words tumbled out like a thundering avalanche.

"Next to me as I held her and watched her go. He heard the machines stop beeping, the nurse say how sorry she was. He watched us weep. He saw me lift her eyelids and look for the light that used to be there. He saw you take her from me, lay her in your lap, and try to shake her awake, heard you yelling at the doctor when he rushed in. God watched all of that and did nothing."

Why didn't you stop it? Why? You gave us the most precious thing. You saw how much we loved her, and you took her anyway.

"Why didn't he stop it? Why? He saw how much we loved her and he took her anyway," Tom said, his eyes great pools of misery.

With those words—Tom saying out loud what she couldn't— Barb felt a seed drop into her soul and a hand tenderly planting it, replacing the rotting mess that had been there before.

She realized now that Tom had always understood . . . and he'd loved both mother and child with a warrior's fierce devotion.

And she knew they would heal, they'd go on, and the seed would someday bloom if they diligently cultivated it. The peace that had drained away so long ago now seeped back into her being like water flowing into the dry places of her garden, soaking to the roots of thirsty plants. She drank deeply.

Her voice filled with childlike wonder. "He was there. He never left us."

Tom leaned over and kissed her forehead, stroking her hair. "And he's here now."

Barb didn't want the time to end. They sat like that for a long time, Tom's head on her shoulder. She watched the wild white landscape outside, glad the storm inside had quieted.

For the first time in forty-four years, she thought of Katie with joy, and smiled.

Chapter 44

"Oh, so sorry . . . I . . . I didn't mean to interrupt."

They twisted around to see Susan at the foot of the stairs, her hands clenched in front of her. Barb thought she looked ready to fly apart at the seams.

"No, no, it's okay." Tom rose to his feet. "We were just talking."

"Oh. I was going to the kitchen—you don't have to get up. I was going to get some of that tea Barb introduced me to." She looked from one to the other, backing toward the kitchen.

"Okay . . . say, do you know where Bill is? I thought I'd go, you know, talk to him for a few minutes," Tom said. "Is he upstairs?"

"No, I don't know where he is. Maybe he ran away—Lord knows he has a right to." Her voice dragged.

Barb caught his eye and cocked her head toward the kitchen. "I think he went out to the sitting room when we cleared the table. I'm sure he's still out there—he didn't have his coat."

Tom nodded and slipped into the kitchen.

Barb stepped to Susan's side and put an arm around her. "How about that cup of tea now?"

Susan pressed a hand to her forehead, rubbing between her eyes. "If we stay much longer, I guess you won't have any tea left in the house."

"You don't have to worry about that, my friend—I have a secret stash. Come on. Difficult conversations go better with sweet tea."

She led Susan to the kitchen, hoping the difficult conversation would bear fruit.

Tom strode through the kitchen, stopping to fill two coffee cups, then paused at the back door overlooking the sitting room. The window in the door gave him a clear view of Bill.

He stood across the room in front of the big windows, hands on his hips. Tom noticed a tremble in one hand. He watched as Bill leaned against the window, forehead on the glass. Even though Bill's back was to him, Tom sensed the weight of guilt on the younger man's shoulders.

Then Bill slapped the window hard enough to shake it, and spun to face him. Rage etched on Bill's face caused Tom to take a step back from the door. Bill's expression looked wild—unfocused and out of control—like a man intent on nothing but the kill. Tom had seen the same look in Vietnam on his own men and on the faces of the enemy. And in the mirror.

In that instant Tom knew Bill didn't suffer from guilt at all—he denied it. The fury in his eyes gave him away.

Bill twisted around again and sat, fists knotted on the chair arms.

Tom sucked a steadying breath and, carefully balancing the two cups in one hand, opened the door, shutting it as Barb and Susan entered the kitchen. He paused to pull the curtain across the windowed door for privacy, glimpsing the concern on Barb's face for a brief instant. Then he stepped down and treaded lightly across the room to the chair beside Bill's and sank down, settling Bill's coffee next to him.

Bill sat forward stiffly, elbows on his knees and chin in his hands. He stared, unmoving, at the frosty window glass, clearly trying to get a handle on himself.

Tom sipped his coffee, then relaxed and sat back in his chair, content to let the other man lead the conversation.

He heard Barb and Susan through the door, the rattle of dishes and the whistle of the kettle.

Bill turned his head slightly at the sounds, his face darkening.

And then silence drifted in again as the women retreated to the dining room.

Bill leaned into his chair and settled against the back, his knuckles stretched white against the chair arm. Some of the redness on his face had lightened, but his eyes were puffy and anger-glinted. He glanced at Tom, then away, the darkness outside reflected on his face. "Welcome to my world."

The sound of the creek rushing under its icy cap, usually soothing to Tom, now sounded discordant and angry, not unlike the man sitting next to him.

"Your world might be new to me, but I can guarantee you it's not new to God. He's been trying to get your attention for years, but you haven't been listening," Tom said, surprised at the challenging words that came out of his mouth. But he wouldn't take them back—he was relying on God to put words in his mouth that Bill needed to hear.

He expected an angry retort, but none came. He stared back with vacant eyes, focused on something only he could see. Tom had the curious sense of being just the audience to the wrestling match between this man and his creator.

"Tell me more about Michael. You said before that you were best friends all the way through school. What was he like?"

Bill's hard expression softened. He held his cup in both hands, staring into it, as if seeing images in the blackness.

"He was better than me. Even as kids, he always protected the underdog. He never put himself forward about anything. Always looked out for the other guy."

"He sounds like someone I would like to know, so help me

know him. Paint me a picture, Bill. Friends like that are hard to come by."

Bill's voice sounded far away as he called up memories. "Loyal to the bone, always had my back." He swallowed hard.

"One time in the ninth grade, we were in the local minimart, and I stole a candy bar. It was a stupid thing to do. I stuck it in my pocket, and Michael saw and tried to make me put it back. I laughed at him and told him not to be a geek. When we got up to the cash register, it dropped on the floor when I got some money out for something else I wanted to buy."

"But—"

"Yeah, I know what you're thinking. Why did I steal it if I had money in my pocket? I told you I was stupid."

"What happened then?"

"The cashier—a high school jock—was the local police chief's son."

Tom slapped a palm to his forehead. "What? Oh no—"

"Yeah, go ahead and say what a moron I was. You wouldn't be the only one. The clerk heard it fall out and hit the floor. He came around the counter and grabbed it before I could. He knew it was off their shelf because it had their store label on the wrapper. He grabbed me and threw me down on the floor like I was a murder suspect or something, yelling that he was going to call the police and his dad. He always was a jerk, full of himself."

His voice broke a little. "Then Michael . . . he said *he'd* stolen it, that it had fallen out of *his* pocket. That's the kind of guy he was. And I . . . I didn't say anything. I let him take the heat for it. That's the kind of guy I was—kinda like 'will the real jerk please stand up?'"

"Michael was a good friend—"

"The best. Michael took the blame, got in trouble at home, and had to do community service. He had to clean the back room of the minimart for a month and other odd jobs, whatever they could lay on him. And the police chief's son—Eddie, the cashier—treated him like dirt, bullying him, taunting him, making him clean the bathrooms two or three times a day. In all that time, Michael never once complained. And I, his best friend, said nothing. When I finally did try to apologize, tell him I'd come clean, he wouldn't let me. He said 'what's done is done, and the work isn't that bad anyway—and that's what friends do.' I've never forgotten that. And I never stole anything again either."

"He sounds like a great guy. I'd like to have known him."

"Yeah, well, he's dead now," Bill said, his face working. "And it's because he took the heat for me—again."

Tom thought back to the tender conversation he'd just had with Barb. "He's not the only one. Tell me, have you ever considered the heat Christ took for you?"

Bill didn't respond to that. He shrugged his shoulders and walked to the window.

Tom wondered if he'd gone too far. He forced himself to wait.

After several moments, Bill whirled around, taking his glasses off and wiping his face with his arm. "You sound like Michael."

The intensity of his words hit Tom like a burst of napalm.

"Michael? What do you mean?"

"I mean, that's what Michael always used to say to me. Don't you get it?"

"Michael . . . Michael was a believer? He followed Jesus?"

Bill nodded, stepped back to his chair, and plunked down, head in his hands.

Tom leaned back. It was unbelievable how God worked a puzzle. Every piece fell into place at just the right time.

"Wanna hear his last words? The last thing he said to me . . . was . . . 'Believe in Jesus, Bill. He's the only one you can trust.' And then he was gone." Bill pushed the words out, gagging on them, covering his mouth like he would vomit. "I held him, tried to stop him from leaving without me, but there was nothing I could . . . could do . . . nothing . . ."

Anger now spilled over again. "Where'd he go, Tom? He died without my permission. Trust God? How can I trust a God who kills my best friend and allows him to bleed out in my arms? And don't give me that 'he's a loving God' crap. I'm sick to death of it."

Bill set his coffee cup down with a heavy smack that sounded like a gunshot. His head dropped into his hands, clearly shutting down again.

Tom stiffened at the sound of the cup hitting the table. His vision narrowed and dimmed. The room disappeared, floated out the window. Then the window folded itself up and disappeared. He was surrounded by warm, moist green, buzzing with insects.

 Chapter 45

Which direction did it come from?

Lieutenant Masters heard the drip, drip, drip of the rain off the giant leaves of the forest that closed in around them. He looked down at his feet and watched the shiny green of a pit viper slither across his path, its tail disappearing into the dense foliage.

Then he heard the first rat-a-tat-tat of the M16s, and all hell broke loose. Tom dropped like a stone to the jungle floor. He saw his buddies' helmets bobbing between the leaves as they frantically positioned themselves to counterattack. He knew some were hit, heard their groans.

He looked left and saw Mack twenty yards in front of him. He'd stood for some reason, staring at his feet. Mack put a warning hand out in front of him and lowered the business end of his weapon. A smile crept over his face as he took a cautious step forward. He bent down and extended his arm, his weapon now in his nondominant left hand—useless to him.

Tom raised up and peered over the top of the wide leaves, trying to see what Mack was looking at. He saw a black-clad arm rise up out of the leaves, bloody hand extended. Mack reached for the hand. Then the barrel of an AK-47 poked up, pointed at Mack's chest.

"Mack—" Tom was cut off by the chilling sound of the AK's high-powered rounds smacking into flesh at close range.

Mack, driven backward, disappeared under the leaves.

Tom froze, then leaped up, rage driving the bullets from his M16 in short bursts. After spraying the jungle around him, he dropped again, breathing hard, listening for sounds of the advancing enemy over the groans of his wounded men. He knew Mack wasn't dead, because he'd seen his boots slipping away under the foliage.

The shooter was nowhere to be seen. Tom thought he'd gotten him.

Nothing else moved, so Tom started the slow crawl to Mack's side.

He called out as loudly as he dared. "Stay down, Mack. Stay still. I'm coming to you."

Before he'd gone even a quarter of the distance, a guttural cry sounded to his left. He popped up in time to see a black blur rush forward out of cover, then stop, scream, and raise his bayonet high, quickly plunging it downward three times.

Tom sprang up again and sprayed the soldier, killing him before he hit the ground, his torso falling over Mack. Tom no longer cared about stealth as he raced to Mack's side. Sliding to his knees and dropping his pack and weapon in one smooth move, he shoved the enemy soldier aside. As the body rolled off and turned over, Tom saw a boy—couldn't have been more than fifteen or so. He still gripped his bayonet, stained with Mack's blood and tissue. Tom stared, his mind in shut-down mode.

Then he forced his eyes away and took Mack in his arms, noting the grievous wounds to his shoulder, head, chest, and abdomen. Mack was still alive though, his large hands gripping Tom's jacket with unexpected strength.

"Mack, Mack, hang on, buddy. Hey, over here. I need the doc now!" Tom yelled, covered in Mack's blood as he gripped his friend's head against his chest.

He heard shouts in the distance but no more gunfire. With the tramping of feet, his men surrounded him.

The medic gently took Mack from Tom's arms. His hands shook as he took medical supplies out of his bag.

"Sir? Maybe you should go—"

"No. I'm not leaving him. Do what you need to do."

"Yes, sir." He loosened the clothing on Mack's upper torso and removed his helmet, now in three pieces, as one round had cracked it.

Tom cringed at the amount of blood. He looked up at his men. "Anyone dead?"

The nine men who stood in a tight circle around him were silent.

"Well? Give it to me," Tom growled.

"Gabe and Dan. They're over there in that filthy creek," Jimmy mumbled, pointing.

"Go get 'em," Tom ordered.

They turned as one and moved off.

Suddenly, Mack convulsed. His body arched and jerked under doc's hands, who tried to stem the bleeding from his gut and chest.

Tom shouted into Mack's face. "Mack, Mack, I'm here. It's Tom, buddy. Hang on. We've got to get you stabilized and out of here. Don't leave—"

Mack relaxed, eyelids closing.

Tom looked at the doc.

"No, he's still alive, but barely. I . . . I don't think there's anything I can do, sir. I'm sorry," he said, his hands still busy packing Mack's wounds.

"No. Save him, you hear me? You . . ." Tom commanded, shaking the medic's shoulder. "Save him—"

Tom felt his other hand gripped by a strength he didn't think was possible. Mack's mouth was open, blood bubbling over his lips as he tried to speak, choking on the foaming red fountain. Tom lowered his head to Mack's face. He gently wiped his buddy's mouth and nose.

He heard, as from a great distance, his men tramping back. He glanced at them briefly as they laid Gabe and Dan down in the mud a few feet away. He focused again on Mack.

"Tom . . . home . . . promise me you'll get home alive. Don't die in this godforsaken jungle. Promise me," Mack whispered through the gurgling red stream now gushing over his chin and down under his collar.

Tom put both hands on Mack's cheeks and nodded slowly, forehead to forehead, knowing he promised something he had no power to keep.

Mack's anxious face slackened. Then the corners of his mouth lifted in his characteristic crooked grin.

Tom's heart soared with hope.

Mack's eyes brightened, lit from some unseen source, as if he'd caught sight of a long-lost friend or the love of his life.

Then the light faded as the shine in his eyes dimmed and his glassy stare widened. He took a last shuddering breath, then lay still, his mouth open. His body sank into the jungle floor, his life draining into the thick, sticky mud.

Tom brushed his fingers over his friend's lashes and gently closed his mouth.

Doc stopped his frantic work and sat back on his heels. "I'm sorry, sir."

Tom lowered his head to Mack's chest. One sob escaped.

He laid his hand on doc's arm. "It's not your fault."

Chapter 46

"What?" Bill asked.

Tom's eyes snapped open. A stranger stared at him from the other chair. The jungle slid backward, like it was on a track, to the secret bunker in Tom's mind, disappearing as the warmth of his home and the rich smell of pine and good food brought him back.

"What do you mean?" Bill demanded. "Of course it's my fault. I told you before—I let him talk me into changing places with him that day. If I hadn't, Michael would be alive. Don't you get it? It's my fault he's dead and that I'm alive. It's my fault I'm married to a woman who still loves *him* and that *his* daughter hates me now."

Tom heard the words and the misery behind them, but couldn't focus.

Bill got in his face. "Hey, you okay?"

"Yeah, some memories I try to forget, that's all—"

"Oh, hey . . . I'm sorry. You want to talk about it?"

Tom sat up and reached for his coffee—it was cold. He set it back down again. He felt the moisture on his forehead and wiped it with a napkin.

Tom focused on Bill's last question. "Yeah, I do. If there's one thing I've learned since I came back from 'Nam, it's that the more times I talk about it, the less of a monster it is. Telling my story takes the teeth and claws from that monster." He paused to gather his thoughts and to let his words sink in. "Have you found that to be true?"

Bill fixed his eyes on his feet, fingers nervously picking at the arm of the chair.

Tom sat back in his chair. "The jungle's never far away, Bill. And I suspect you find yourself on the hot sand staring at Michael's body more times than you care to admit."

He sat up and looked straight at Bill. "I lost the best friend I'd ever had. Mack was his name. We'd grown up together. Played high school football together. Chased girls together. There was nothing we didn't know about each other. We lived in a small town where everyone knew everyone—a far cry from the jungles of 'Nam. I wasn't prepared. Nothing could have prepared a kid fresh out of childhood. Our parents were friends. We even went to the same church. I spent most of the time in church daydreaming about fishing and hunting. I never listened the way Mack did."

Tom paused, wondering if he should say what he wanted to.

"Mack and Michael sound very much alike. It's a very similar story to your own, just a different war."

"They're all the same war."

"Hmm—you have a point there. Anyway, that day, we were headed back to base camp when we were ambushed. Mack was shot. I tried to help—was crawling his way—when a boy jumped up and rushed him and bayoneted him over and over while I watched. I can still hear Mack's screams, can still see the boy's face. He was sobbing as he gutted my best friend."

Bill grimaced. "What did you do?"

"I shot him, of course. I gunned down a kid." Torment churned his soul. "And you know the worst part? Not Mack. I know where he is. He was a strong Christian, vocal about his faith even when we were kids. No, the worst part is wondering where that kid went. It's knowing that chances are, I sent a kid to hell. Try living with that."

The rush of the creek and the sound of the driving snow pelting the windows blanketed the room and softened the edges of Tom's guilt. For the thousandth time, he begged God to forgive him, for the hole inside him to close.

Bill broke the silence. "I'm sorry." He stumbled over his words. "I guess I get so . . . so wrapped up in myself that I forget other people have stories too."

Tom leaned his head back. "Quite a human failing. We forget how connected we are under the skin."

How could he keep Bill talking? How could he get him to open up more about his own failure with Susan and Joanie? "Did I hear you say that Susan and Michael were married?" He didn't want to add fuel to this smoldering fire by letting on that Susan had already told Barb. "And that Joanie is *Michael's* daughter?"

Bill squeezed his hands together in his lap. "I came home a few weeks after Michael died. I went to see Susan, and . . . and things happened. We were married a month later."

"A month—only a month?"

"Yeah. Susan was pregnant, and I felt obligated to help her after . . . after . . . anyway, we got married right before I went back to finish my tour."

"So . . . so—"

"Yeah, we never told Joanie. Stupid, huh?"

Unhurried, with the clear knowledge once again that he was not leading this conversation, Tom asked, "Would you like some more coffee?"

"Yeah, I wouldn't mind some more."

Tom took both cups into the kitchen and was glad to see the pot was still full. As he poured, he heard the soft voices of Barb and Susan in the dining room.

Still no sign of the Elliott family or Joanie, who presumably were hiding upstairs.

He took the cups back out to the sitting room and set them down. Seeing Bill out on the back porch, Tom grabbed his coat off the hook and stepped outside.

"It's peaceful here. I envy you and Barb." Bill chuckled. "As you've noticed, our lives are anything but peaceful. With my job—always having to be on the road—and Joanie's activities and . . . it sure keeps us running. I'd like to slow down a bit."

"Yes, it's peaceful. But our life wasn't always so. You'll get there."

"Yeah, I guess so."

"Let's go back inside before our coffee gets cold again, okay?"

The two men settled themselves back in their chairs and sipped the hot coffee. After a few moments, Tom picked up the thread of the conversation again.

"So tell me, Bill. Do you ever think about following Jesus, as Michael begged you to?"

Bill looked straight ahead, out the window at the building storm—mirrored on his face.

"How can I? He's the one who took Michael away from me, and from Susan and Joanie." His rock-hard face glowed red in the light from the windows.

Tom pressed on, sensing Bill was close to a breaking point. "God didn't kill Michael. The person who made and set that roadside bomb did."

"Yeah, that's what the VA counselor told me, that the one I should blame is the enemy. Not the government who sent us there, not God, not myself. Only the enemy."

"So you *did* see a counselor?"

"Sure I did. Susan made me. But those imbeciles have never seen combat. They blather on, wanting me to 'talk,' to 'share,' to 'work through it.' But none of it does any good—it's putting a dressing on a gunshot wound without digging out the round that's still in there."

"Hmm. Well said, and I agree. But here's the thing. The way to heal wounded warriors is to start from the inside out, and God's the only one who can do that. There's no doctor on this earth who can work *that* bullet out from the inside."

"He didn't have to kill Michael to tell me that."

"Did you ever listen to him before?" Tom challenged. Seeing Bill's face suffuse into anger, he added, "I'm not saying God allowed Michael to die to get your attention. God's plan for Michael is God's plan for *Michael*. But it got your attention, right?"

"Some plan, Tom. I won't follow a commanding officer who deliberately allows his squad to fall into enemy hands, to go into harm's way, to be blown to bits. What kind of leader is that? In my service, we'd call that officer a traitor."

"I get it. I wouldn't follow that guy either. But that's not who we're talking about, is it? No officer on this planet can see from the beginning to the end of a person's life and everything in between, or know what's going to happen on any particular day, tramping through a jungle or across a desert floor."

Tom gripped his cup. Bill would not want to hear his next words. "I think Michael got what he wanted."

Chapter 47

"Huh? What's that supposed to mean?" Bill sputtered, spraying coffee on his shirt. "He got blown to bits. You think that's what Michael *wanted*? What he wanted was to be with Susan. To have lots of kids. He told me that."

"Let me finish—"

"You're crazy. If ever anyone had something to live for, it was him, and he knew it. You've got rocks in your head, mister."

Tom leaned into his next words. "You're alive, Bill." He measured each whispered word. "You're alive, sitting here with me, talking this through. You still have a chance to make things right with God and with your family. *That's* what Michael wanted, right?"

Bill gaped at Tom, white-knuckling the chair arms again.

Tom couldn't tell if he was going to punch him or give in, but he finally sagged back into his chair, white faced, breathing ragged.

"Haven't you had enough of trying to go it alone? When I came home, then we lost Katie, we both tried that route. It doesn't work. It never works. What about it? Aren't you tired of trying to be the smart guy with all the answers? Trying to make Susan happy, Joanie happy, your boss happy, while you're drowning in bitterness over circumstances out of your control?"

Bill wiped his eyes with the backs of his hands.

"Say it with me. 'I didn't kill Michael. A bomb did.'"

Eyes locked on Tom's, Bill repeated the words soundlessly. Then he repeated them out loud. And again and again, leaning forward in his chair, then slipping to the floor, retching out his sorrow on his knees. As if he couldn't make himself low enough, he spread-eagled, belly down, pounding the floor with his fists—each blow hard enough to shake the walls. With each hammer of his fists, he groaned out the words.

Tom noted a flick of curtains in his peripheral vision. He looked and saw Barb's face.

She held his gaze for a fraction of a second, compassion and understanding mingled in her expression, then let the curtain drop.

The last blow landed. Bill dragged himself up and sat on the floor with his back against the chair.

Tom watched, remembering his own time—when he'd finally thrown in the towel. Bill was no different than he'd been, a boxer against the ropes, nowhere to go, pummeled by guilt.

"There's only one battle worth losing. We're old soldiers—we don't like to surrender. It's not in our makeup. Fighting until the last of our boys get home, until the last drop of spilled blood is avenged, that's what we're about. Am I right?"

Bill nodded.

"But there's *one* battle worth losing—the one you're fighting now. It's being waged over your head, between that wily serpent and the Christ who loves you and won't leave you on this battlefield in enemy hands. He's determined to bring you home, Bill. Don't fight *him*."

Tom sensed a clear shift in the room—almost a shimmering in the air—as years ago in the jungle, seeing the backward-moving enemy disappear stealthily through the wide green leaves. It was the moment he knew for certain the enemy had given up, the skirmish was won, and he and the boys could retreat to safety. He breathed a prayer.

Time to come home, Soldier.

Bill's eyes burned with intensity, his voice pleading. "I love my family. I don't want to lose them. But you're right—I can't do this alone. I know I can't. I used to be able to handle anything, but I can't handle this. I can't live with this guilt anymore. I know—have known all along—guilt made me marry Susan. And guilt kept me from adopting Joanie. How could I take Michael's daughter from him—I'd already taken his life. That's the way I saw it."

Tom grasped Bill's shoulder. "Let's stay focused on the real mission, Soldier. Is keeping your family what this is all about? Or is there a deeper agenda?"

Bill shook his head. "No, I guess that's not the whole thing. Michael told me over and over again that God loves me. And now . . . now . . . I know it's true. Why didn't I listen to him then? If I had—"

"No, don't go there, my friend. God's timing is God's timing. It has nothing to do with you—or me, for that matter."

"What do you mean?"

"I mean that I blamed myself for Katie's death. Stupid, huh? It was leukemia. I didn't cause that. But somehow I could live with it better if *I* took on that guilt—the guilt of not wanting her in the first place. And in the process I almost destroyed Barb."

"I guess we're not so different—"

"No, we're not. And something else. Soldiers or not, big, tough guys that we are, we're no match for God."

"I guess this weekend was no accident of the weather. He brought me here to talk to you, didn't he? Why would he love me so much?"

Tom threw back his head and laughed out loud. Then he noticed Bill's face.

"Sorry. Wasn't laughing at your question . . . just—"

"Just what? I really want to know."

"I was laughing because that's one question I can't answer. I ask myself every day why God would put on baby skin to come and rescue me. But it's true. That's what it's all about. He's the warrior's warrior."

Tom held Bill's gaze. "What about it, Bill? You want to shake hands with your true commander-in-chief?"

Bill didn't hesitate for an instant. He got up from the floor and took a deep breath.

"Yeah, let's do this."

Tom reached, and as they grasped and shook hands, he felt the sweet presence fill the room, hovering over the two of them as they knelt and Bill gave up the fight—the one that had started with a bomb blast in the desert on the other side of the world.

Tom recognized the surrender at once, for it had been the same for him. His fight had begun in a muddy, steamy jungle, clinging to a blood-soaked friend, and had continued at the grave of his sweet little Katie. His had ended this night, too, when he'd confessed his need and his guilt to Barb, at last able to leave his baby daughter, and Mack, in God's care.

Both men bowed their heads. Tom reached and gripped Bill's shoulder as he brought his new friend to the throne of grace. He listened as Bill, the warrior, sobbed aloud and laid down the weapons of his own self-sufficiency at the feet of the only one worthy of the honor.

As Barb finished praying with Susan, she looked up and saw Tom beckoning to her from the kitchen door. She hurried over to him, listened for a moment, then turned and motioned Susan over.

She approached timidly, with a wary look in her eye.

Tom laid a gentle hand on her shoulder. "Bill's waiting for you in the sitting room. He has some things he wants to say."

Barb noticed her anxious look. "It's okay," she whispered. "He needs you right now."

Susan swallowed hard and nodded, clearly nervous.

They followed her into the kitchen, and she stepped into the sitting room and closed the door behind her.

The curtain pulled across the window prevented Tom and Barb from seeing into the room or hearing what the two said to each other, but the brokenness in their voices came through loud and clear.

Tom pulled out two kitchen stools. "How'd it go with her?"

"She has a lot of hurdles to jump right now. She told me how Joanie's father died and all that happened after Bill came home." Barb's eyes welled up and spilled over. "It's such a mess . . . I don't see how they can come back from it, Tom. They—"

Tom put his finger over her lips and whispered. "Yes you do, honey. The same way we did."

He took her hand and tucked it into the crook of his arm as they bowed their heads.

Chapter 48

Joanie cracked open the bedroom door and peered out. The Elliotts sat at a small table playing a board game. Samantha leaned over and tickled Stevie, then was ambushed by Steve from behind, throwing her into a fit of giggles. Soon they were all tickling each other, shrieking with laughter, game forgotten.

Joanie pushed the door closed and leaned her forehead against it, teeth clamped so tight her jaw hurt. She hated all of them . . . hypocritical liars.

She turned her back against the door, gaze roaming over the cheerful room—Christmas knickknacks on the twin dressers, matching quilts covered in tiny snowmen on the beds, and two large guest baskets decorated with large red bows. Unwanted tears spilled over her cheeks. She brushed them away, rage building again.

False. This was a fairy-tale world—it had nothing to do with real life.

Reaching for a hand-held mirror on the dresser, she brought it to her face. An unfamiliar image stared back. Cheeks flaming, hair stringy and disheveled. A small sprig of pine needles still lodged over her ear. Bill had placed it there earlier when they'd hiked arm-in-arm back to the inn after sledding. Her focus zeroed in on that sprig. Joanie sucked air like she was dying, her chest heaving with effort. With a groan, she plucked out the branch and threw it across the room. The mirror went with it, crashing and splintering against the wall.

She jumped at the sudden rap on the door behind her.

"Everything all right in there?" Steve called.

"Yeah. Leave me alone."

"Are you sure you're—"

"Go away." She leaned her head back and closed her eyes.

Joanie heard Steve's retreating footsteps, then Sally's soft voice ask a question.

Who cares? Her thoughts shifted again to her parents. How could they do this to her? They're so stupid. *They're* not *my parents.*

She slipped down to her bottom, hunched against the door. A memory surfaced from a decade ago and played like a movie on the far wall, where she'd thrown the mirror.

The miniature pink bike with training wheels wobbled down the road, streamers fluttering from the handlebars in the fresh summer breeze, Joanie's unsteady legs pumping the pedals as Bill ran along behind with his hand on the back of the seat. And then the moment he let go of the bike and she sailed to the end of the block, never once stopping or falling. He raced up to her and scooped her four-year-old body up in a bear hug, congratulating her and promising to take her for ice cream to celebrate this rite of passage, her first taste of freedom.

He was a lying hypocrite, pretending to be her daddy that day. And Mom—standing on the porch with that silly grin on her face, watching him, letting him do it. She was worse. She was supposed to be her mother—she should have stopped him. She should have told her the truth about her real . . .

But she couldn't go there. This just proved to Joanie that she didn't need them—she didn't need anyone.

The movie fast-forwarded to a picture taken by her mother a year ago, Joanie and Bill on the night of her disastrous first middle school dance. She'd been wearing the prettiest dress she'd ever owned and a sparkling necklace presented to her by Bill that very evening, her hair piled on top of her head. She'd felt like a grown-up for the first time. As she descended the stairs, the admiration on Bill's face made her heart sing. Then he turned her around and put the necklace on her, his warm fingers tickling the back of her neck. He'd kissed her cheek, whispering she'd be the prettiest young lady at the dance.

Joanie's cheeks burned at the memory, because there was no dance for her that night. Her date was a popular older boy she didn't know well, who'd shocked her by asking her to go with him.

He'd stood her up. She waited over an hour, shifting nervously on the sofa, smoothing her dress and hair over and over, until she finally gave up and went upstairs and put her sweats and T-shirt back on. The pity on her parents' faces, watching the clock and trying to encourage her to be patient, now played on the screen of her mind. Her stomach churned.

When she'd gone to school on Monday, the boy wouldn't talk to her. One of the girls in the locker room that day after PE told her it was going around that he'd forgotten about the dance.

Forgot? How could he have forgotten? Like Bill "forgot" to tell her the truth. And Mom, she must've forgotten too—to tell her she was married before. Or maybe Joanie was the result of a one-night stand . . . nothing but an inconvenience.

Joanie's downward-spiraling thoughts threatened to drown her in a sea of unanswered questions.

She let him do this to me—play at being a father. He might as well have raped me . . . I have been raped. He stripped everything from me—and she let him do it.

Her agonized thoughts took a different turn, down an unknown, scary path she didn't want to tread but couldn't help herself.

Who was he? Did she look like him? Act like him? What was he . . .

Joanie couldn't finish the thought. She focused on two pictures in her mind. From earlier this evening, her mother and Bill glaring at each other, ignoring her pain. And next to that, the scene of the Elliott family just outside her door, laughing and playing together. Her own so-called parents hadn't even so much as glanced at *her*, the one they'd raped with their lies. They'd focused on themselves, as usual.

They hadn't noticed her until she'd forced them to. Maybe they didn't need to notice her anymore. Maybe she should disappear. Then they wouldn't have to be bothered with her—

Shaking herself angrily, Joanie jumped to her feet and jerked her coat out of the closet, knocking Samantha's coat to the floor. She stared at it, lying in a heap, then kicked it across the room.

She yanked the door open, letting it crash against the wall. The Elliotts stopped talking. Stiff backed, she walked past them, feeling their stares like needles in her back.

Sally's cheerful voice sounded forced and loud. "Umm . . . Joanie, do you want to play?"

Joanie didn't bother to answer or even turn around—she left the room and descended the stairs. Halfway down, Sally said something she couldn't hear, then Samantha's whiny response, loud and clear.

"Mommy, no, I can't."

Her high voice grated on Joanie. Reaching the bottom of the stairs, she whipped around toward the kitchen, intending to slip out the back door. But she heard Barb's voice through the swinging door, saying *her* name. She ground her teeth, rotated, and walked out the front door.

# Chapter 49

Joanie stood on the front veranda, feeling lost and wondering what to do next.

It was still early evening, thick clouds hiding the moon overhead and snow blowing sideways in the strengthening wind. The tops of the pine trees waved in the gale, giving a spooky feel—like watching a horror film and knowing bad things were hidden around the corner, ready to jump out at you. But it was too late for her—the bad things had already happened.

She was surprised it wasn't colder—she felt quite warm in her coat, mittens, and knitted cap, so she wandered over to the porch swing, brushed snow off the seat, and sat down. Leaning back against the cushion and closing her eyes, she punched rewind in her head.

Her parents—well, one was a parent—had been lying to her for her whole life. She couldn't grasp the enormity of it. She felt only hatred and loathing for them. She allowed it to fill her, resentment building like water behind a dam. The dam burst, and she felt it flow into the empty, lonely places. She let it come. She felt powerful with the filling. It was all she had left.

A tear slid down her cheek, then another. She put her hands to her face and sobbed, the sound muffled by her mittens. Every lie, every word spoken by Bill, every argument between them, every moment of companionship, every one of her fourteen years streamed from her eyes and soaked her gloves.

The answer popped into Joanie's mind like a magician waving his magic wand. She sat up and wiped her tears. She could run away, now, tonight. They probably wouldn't even miss her—that would be one problem solved for them. One inconvenience gone.

But then she realized she was in the middle of nowhere, with nowhere to go. She hammered her palm on the arm of the wicker swing.

Why couldn't they have told her? Cowards!

Joanie's thoughts dragged her around in circles again. She was sure of only one thing. There would never be anything they could say or do to justify their deceit. And she would never, ever forgive them—

"Joanie?"

Her eyes snapped open to see Samantha framed in the doorway, bundled up in her outdoor clothes.

Joanie groaned and slumped against the back of the rocker. "Go away—"

"Joanie, I . . . I'm sorry . . . about everything. I'm sorry I made everyone mad—"

Joanie stood and strode toward her, fist thrust in Samantha's face.

Samantha stepped backward, clearly frightened.

Joanie shoved her fist two inches from Samantha's nose. "I hate you, you little brat. Now get out."

She sat again on the swing, turning her face away. "Just go. I don't want to talk to you. Don't you get it? I don't want to talk to any of you." She waved Samantha back into the house.

Not hearing any movement, she looked up and saw Samantha rooted to the porch. "Fine. Have it your way. But don't expect me to say anything, ya hear?"

Samantha wandered to the porch railing, giving Joanie a wide berth.

Joanie watched her out of the corner of her eye—perfect blond curls peeping out from under her cap, her perfect little body, and her tiny feet shod in pink boots.

What would it be like to be her? Everything about her screamed contentment with life. The more Joanie dwelled on Samantha's perfections, the angrier she became.

Two perfect parents to give her anything she wanted. Even an annoying little brother wouldn't be so bad. Why couldn't Joanie have that? Why did she get stuck with a lying mother and a pretend father?

And . . . and my hair—it's ugly and never does what I want it to. And she's so tiny—why can't I be tiny like that?

"Why don't you go away and leave me alone? What do you want from me?"

"Why do you have to be so mean? Mommy says—"

"I don't care what 'Mommy' says."

"But—"

"Everything's perfect in your life, isn't it?"

"Mommy says God—"

Joanie boiled over. Heat surged up from her chest and she stood, towering over Samantha's small frame. She squeezed her fists at her sides, feeling her fingernails dig into her palms. The pain catapulted the words out of her mouth.

"God, God, God—I don't care about God and what he says, so shut up about it. I came out here to think, and I can't with you yammering on about God this and God that and your perfect parents and your stupid little brother, so go away and leave me alone."

Samantha backed away.

"I'm sick to death of all this God crap. Walk in my shoes for a little while, brat. Then you won't be so sure about—" A picture arose unbidden in Joanie's mind, from earlier in the evening, of Samantha sheltered in her mother's arms and Steve's hand resting on Stevie's shoulder. "—all these lovey-dovey, pie-in-the-sky lies about some God somewhere. There's a whole world out there you know nothing about because your parents—your *real* parents—protect you from every little hurt, anything that might upset you. Some of us don't have that. Instead they have . . . they have—"

"But, Joanie—"

"—fake parents. But you, you have two parents—not pretend parents—who cater to your every need."

"But, Joanie—"

"Your own parents. How would you feel if you found out your whole life was a lie . . . that the man you call *dad* wasn't really your dad? How would you feel if some brat, some stranger, knew more about your family than you did? And then told everyone?"

Samantha clenched her fists.

"Tell me how loved you'd feel if you woke up one day with no parents because they didn't care enough to tell you the truth about who you are."

"Me and Stevie, we're—"

"Yeah, you and Stevie—" Joanie said his name with a sneer. "You're so privileged. You live in a world I don't know, will never know. So go away with your perfect little family in your perfect little world and leave me alone. And take your perfect little God with you." Joanie dropped back down onto the porch swing, put her head back, and closed her eyes for a moment, then opened them.

"Are you still here? Don't you get it? Get out of here."

Samantha put one foot forward and jabbed a finger at Joanie. "You think you know everything, but you don't," she said. "Stevie and I are adopted, so there."

Joanie's head jerked up to look Samantha full in the face. "Adopted? But—"

"They aren't our real parents—"

"You're lying. Admit it."

"No I'm not. We were adopted when Stevie was a baby and I was three."

"Where's your real parents?"

"I don't know. Mommy says they couldn't take care of us, so they went away somewhere."

Samantha stared, wide and unblinking. Joanie knew she was telling the truth.

In that moment of unexpected connectedness, Joanie felt her anger take a turn. Samantha and her brother had been thrown away by people who should have loved them.

"So you think it's okay that they lied to me for fourteen and a half years? And *Bill* didn't even adopt me—he acquired me, like excess baggage when he married Mom."

"Parents shouldn't lie to their kids. But maybe they're sorry now—"

Joanie shifted her blank gaze to the wilderness beyond the inn. "Who cares if they are? And besides, being sorry now doesn't cut it. It doesn't make up for what they did. I'll never forgive them."

Samantha's whisper dropped into Joanie's lap without warning. "God forgives them."

Joanie bristled. "Don't you get all religious on me. It's too bad you got thrown away, but I don't want anything to do with your God. That hasn't changed. And, kid, you're making my face hurt with all this adoption talk. Go away before we get all sappy here."

"Does that mean you're not mad at me?"

"Geez . . ." Joanie slammed her body back against the cushion. "I guess so. If that makes you happy—and if it makes you leave me alone. But we're not friends or anything, ya hear?"

"Okay. But I have to go now."

"Haven't you been listening? Go already—"

Samantha hurried away, letting the door swing shut behind her.

Joanie stared at the closed door. She knew what Samantha was going to say when Joanie had cut her off—that God wants her to forgive her parents.

Forgive? Why?

As if that would make her life perfect or something. What a colossal mess they'd made. Bitterness played around the edges of her mind, thoughts of revenge, but what could she do? She felt imprisoned by the blackness of uncertainty, adrift without an anchor—the anchor that was supposed to tether her to someone, someone who would tell her who she was.

Forgiving them wouldn't change anything, wouldn't bring her real father back. All the stuff she'd been forced to learn at church was buried now, meaningless, under the garbage of the monstrous lie they'd been living.

Joanie's thoughts came full circle again. Samantha could believe what she wanted—it had nothing to do with what had been done to *her* by Mom and *Bill*. She covered her face with her soggy mittens.

The jagged cracks in her heart leaked out the plea before she could stop the words.

Dad, where are you? Why aren't you here instead of . . . instead of . . . him?

Her head jerked up.

She wasn't gonna sit here and cry like a baby.

An outburst of laughter coming from upstairs in the house fueled her next decision.

Joanie stood, jammed her hat back on, pulled her hood over that, and buttoned her coat up to her chin. After making sure her flashlight was in her pocket, she stomped down the front porch stairs as if trying to crush the lie with each punch of her boots. At the last moment before her feet touched the icy ground, she stiff-armed the decorative angel that capped the newel post. The angel broke off and dropped to the ground. She picked it up, flung it as far as she could, then trudged into the darkness.

# Chapter 50

Susan laid a hand on Bill's cheek. "Come on. We need to find Joanie and talk to her. Together."

He placed his hand over hers, caressing her fingers, then turned and stepped into the kitchen.

"Yeah, let's get this done. I can't imagine what she must be going through."

Susan, knowing Tom and Barb had come into the kitchen behind her, expected to see them. "Hmm, wonder where they went." She shrugged. "Oh well. Let's go."

Bill opened the door into the dining room and stood aside to let her through first. She started to ease past him, but he stopped her and took her hand.

"Let me do the talking at first, okay? I got us into this mess, and I want her to know that."

As they started toward the stairs, Samantha blew by them from the front door, pushing between them. She almost knocked Susan down in her haste.

"Hey! Watch out—"

"Oh, sorry, Mr. and Mrs. Brown." She ran up the stairs, leaving Bill and Susan staring after her.

"What was that about?" Bill took Susan's hand again, and they followed her up.

Susan peeked into the room Joanie and Samantha shared, then stepped out, shaking her head at Bill.

"Has anyone seen Joanie?" Bill asked.

Samantha peeked out from Sally's tight hug. "She was outside with me just now. We . . . we were talking."

Bill lifted an eyebrow. "You were talking? What about?"

Samantha looked at her father, who nodded his encouragement.

"I was saying sorry to her . . . you know, for what I did before. She wasn't very nice to me, but Mommy said I had to." Samantha shot a look at her mother. "So I did."

"Do you know where she is now?"

Samantha shrugged. "I guess still out on the big porch. She was on that swing with the flowery pillows."

"Come on, Sue. Let's go." He grabbed her hand, and they sped toward the stairs.

Susan reached the front door first and pulled it open. No one was there.

Bill came up behind her and grasped her sagging shoulders.

"Come on. Let's search the house. She's got to be here somewhere."

They hurried from room to room, then returned to the veranda.

Susan slumped against him. "Where in the world can she be? We've looked everywhere—" She couldn't keep the dread out of her voice.

"What's that?" Bill bounded down the stairs to the front walk.

"What?"

"This." He set the angel on top of the post. "It's been broken off—"

"Do you think Joanie did that? I don't remember it being broken before. She's out of control, Bill. What can we do?" She put her face in her hands. "Poor Joanie—we did this to her."

He put an arm around her and drew her close. "Yes, we did." He patted her back.

Susan refused to be consoled. "I can't stand the thought of her alone somewhere, trying to make sense of this. She's only fourteen. She can't possibly sort this out on her own."

"Try to stay calm, honey. Let's get our coats on and go out and find her. She's probably hiding somewhere, trying to make us worry. You know how she is. I'm sure she's fine." He stepped backward to the hall closet door and pulled out her winter coat. "And here's your boots."

She slipped into her boots and threw her coat around her shoulders. "Shouldn't we find Tom and Barb and tell them?"

"Not yet. I'd guess she's close by—maybe in that shed out back—and we can settle things with her without bothering anyone else. Don't you think that'd be best?"

He asked her opinion? Susan didn't know if she could get used to that.

"I guess you're right. No sense worrying everyone else yet."

They pulled on their gloves and went out into the night.

Tom and Barb came into the dining room from their private suite, where they'd retreated.

Barb stopped in her tracks. "What on earth is all that shouting?"

"I don't know, but I'm gonna find out. It sounds like it's coming from out back by the creek."

As they passed the staircase, they met Steve hurrying down the stairs, Sally and the kids bunched up right behind him.

Steve frowned and scratched the back of his head. "What's going on?"

"Don't know. Can't even tell where it's coming from."

"It's coming from out back by the bridge. I think it's Bill and Susan," Sally said.

"Bill and Susan?" Barb asked. "Why would they be out there yelling like that? Are they fighting again?" She threw a glance at Tom.

"They'd better not be—"

"Don't think so. They went out to the front porch to talk to Joanie. That's where Samantha said she was a little while ago." Steve's frown deepened. "I guess they didn't find her."

Tom sighed. "I'm going out there. Steve, would you come with me?"

They grabbed their coats and started out through the kitchen.

Barb plucked at Tom's sleeve. "I hope nothing's happened to Joanie."

"Nah—chances are, she's moping somewhere close by. We'll be right back."

# Chapter 51

Tom flipped the yard light on as they exited the back door. They saw Bill and Susan standing on the bridge, side by side, in the glow.

Through their cupped hands, the distraught parents yelled Joanie's name at the mountains to the north. The mountains responded with only the echo of wind rushing through snow-laden ravines.

Bill slewed around as Tom and Steve approached. "We can't find Joanie anywhere. Where in the world could she have gone?"

"Why in tarnation didn't you come and get us—"

Bill jerked his head toward the shed, padlock still in place. "We thought she'd be nearby, hiding—you know, to make us worry—and we didn't want to bother anyone."

"Okay, fine. Are you sure she's not in the house somewhere? Did you look everywhere?"

"Of course we looked everywhere."

"Okay—"

"She's not in her room, she's not out here, and Samantha told us they'd been talking out on the front porch. Her coat, gloves, and boots are missing. We looked inside everywhere we could, except in your room. Unless she's under a bed somewhere or in a closet we don't know about, she's not in the house. So we came outside. Where could she hide, other than the house and the shed?"

Susan tugged at his sleeve. "Honey, shouldn't we go in? I'm freezing—"

"We're not going in until we find her."

Tom knew better than to argue with him. He glanced at Steve. "Would you mind going back in to let Barb and Sally know what's going on out here? They're probably worried. And ask Barb to put on a fresh pot of coffee for us."

"On it." He bolted for the back door.

Tom stared at the ground, trying to see any impressions in the snow Joanie could have left, but he saw nothing. The snow pelted, becoming heavier by the second, so if she'd gone this way, her tracks would be covered. Glancing up at the dark sky, he knew they were in for it again.

Tom frowned. "Do you think she ran off? Would she do something so extreme?"

Bill ran a shaky hand through his hair. "If I had to guess—"

"We don't have to guess." Susan crumpled, sobbing into the front of his shirt. "She ran off because we've lied to her all her life. I guess we deserve it, don't you think? To lose her?"

Bill shook her by the shoulders. "Stop it, Susan. You mustn't think it, honey."

Tom stepped close to them. "Now hear me, you two. You've got to get hold of yourselves. This won't do you or her any good." His stern voice brooked no argument. "But Susan's right. No good us standing around out here without a plan. Let's get back inside."

They hurried to the back porch. Tom flipped the yard lights off again to conserve power.

Entering the dining room, he stopped. Turning, he put a finger to his lips. Crowding into the doorway as best they could, they heard the end of Sammie's prayer.

". . . and anyway, Jesus, please bring Joanie back to her mommy and daddy. Amen."

Tom tiptoed over to her and laid his big hand on her shoulder. "I don't think there's much of anything we can add," he said.

He stepped back and with a wave of his hand gathered the group around him.

"All right. It's going to be a long night, I suspect. Barb, did you start the coffee? I'm going to call some people and see what they suggest we do."

"Who? The police?" Bill asked.

"No, better than that. The local search and rescue group. My good friend Kenny will be all over this. I hope I can get through. If not, I'll fire up my shortwave radio." Tom looked at his watch. "It's ten thirty p.m. now. I'm guessing they won't advise starting a formal search now—they'll wait until first light."

"Why not the police?" Bill demanded. "And why wait until morning?" He threw a quick glance at Susan. "She's out there alone in the dark. We have to go now—"

Tom gentled his voice, resisting the urge to lecture. "The search and rescue group has deputies who work with them, and they know these mountains as well as I do. And as far as waiting until morning—here's the thing. It won't do any good to have a bunch of people stumbling around these mountains in the dark. I know it's hard for you to wait, but it's too risky. We might create more problems than one missing girl, and that wouldn't be of any help to her."

He saw Susan's stricken face and laid a hand on her arm. "Right now, we three guys will canvas along the road and across the creek a little farther, on the off chance we can find her. But you have to understand that we can't go off very far into this wilderness in the dark. If she's okay right now, wherever she is, chances are she'll be okay awhile longer."

His words had no effect on Susan. Her ghostlike face stretched tight around wide eyes glistening with tears. Tom threw a pointed glance at Barb.

She swallowed hard and nodded. "Susan, will you help me in the kitchen please? And Sally, I think it's time the littles were in bed, don't you?"

Sally took the hint and herded Stevie and Samantha upstairs, while Barb took Susan into the kitchen.

The three men followed them. Tom kept his shortwave on a specially constructed shelf above the refrigerator. While he tuned the radio, Barb doled out cups of coffee.

Tom got through to Kenny after three tries—no phone service yet. It was as Tom suspected—they'd convene at the inn at first light if the three of them couldn't find her tonight. Kenny promised to alert the rest of the team and to stay by his radio, should Tom call again.

They downed their coffee, then Tom led them to the living room and opened the closet door. Strapping on his sidearm and grabbing his Marlin, he gestured to the others.

They followed him to the front door and out to the porch.

As the screen door swung shut, Barb called from the kitchen doorway. "Be careful, guys—"

Tom nodded, switched the yard lights on again, and shut and locked the door.

"Good thing we refilled the generator. I'd hate to be out here in pitch blackness."

Bill eyed the Marlin. "Tell me the truth. Besides animals, what's out there? What might she . . . run into?"

"Hold that thought, okay? I want to check the perimeter for footprints. Why don't you two go that way and I'll go this way, and we'll meet in the back. Got your flashlights?"

Both men nodded and walked away, their flashlight beams bouncing in front of them.

Tom lit the ground, alert to any depression in the snow no matter how small. He looked up and saw nothing but driving whiteness in the yard light. They hadn't seen a snowfall like this in several years. He cursed the heavy downpour. Any possible footprints had most likely been obliterated.

He rounded the corner of the inn and met the other two men standing in the middle of the driveway. "Find anything?"

Steve gestured wide. "Nope. Not even bird tracks. Looks like we've gotten about eight to ten new inches since dinner. And it was so clear earlier. Didn't think we'd get much more."

"As you know, things can change without warning out here. And I think you're right—about ten inches on top of what we already had. We won't see any tracks."

Tom faced Bill, pushing his hood back from his forehead. "As to your question earlier, I won't lie. You remember what the terrain was like when we went sledding? The trees closer and closer together, the small streams, the drop-offs? It's ten times worse the farther up you go."

Bill took his hat off and ran his fingers through his hair. "We'd better keep that to ourselves, guys. I don't want Susan hearing that. She's in panic mode as it is."

Tom looked at the dark sky. "Joanie's pretty smart, right? She probably wouldn't go toward the mountains. Wouldn't she stick to the road, where it's easier walking?"

Bill shrugged. "I don't know. She's so upset right now, she's liable to do anything. I've never seen her like this. Sassy, rebellious, sarcastic, yes. But this . . . rage, no. And there's something else."

"What?"

"When we were on the porch just now, I saw the angel that sits on the newel post. It was broken and lying across the yard. Joanie must've done that. Sorry—"

"Don't stress. That can be fixed."

Tom swung around to face the end of the driveway and the road beyond. He'd been involved in a handful of mountain rescues in this area, and several had ended badly.

Not this time, he promised himself.

"I'd be willing to bet money she'd go down the road. Makes

sense—she'd know she couldn't survive very long up there. Maybe she thought she could hitch a ride somewhere. She'd be wrong though, since nothing's moving, but you never know how kids think—or don't think."

Tom could see his remarks did nothing to ease Bill's fear. Nor his own. In his mind's eye, he saw Joanie getting into a car with a stranger—and he was sure by their expressions that Bill and Steve imagined the same.

"Okay, let's not let our thoughts run rampant. As I said before, nothing's moving, so she's not likely to find a ride anyway."

Steve gripped Bill's shoulder and gave it a shake. "He's right. It doesn't do any good to borrow trouble. We need to stay focused. Okay?"

"Yeah, okay. You're right." Bill put his hat back on and buttoned his coat to his chin. Steve bent and tightened his boot laces.

Tom checked his sidearm and took the safety off, then slung his Marlin over his shoulder. "Let's go, guys."

They tramped down the driveway and out to the service road and the highway beyond.

They returned shortly after midnight, discouraged and empty handed.

Tom feared the worst—that even if Joanie had managed to find shelter, the blizzard-like conditions would make it impossible to find her, maybe for days.

How long would it take her to freeze out there? Mere hours. Or to be attacked by hungry wolves or a cougar? What if she fell into a canyon or the river? On unstable snow—she was a city kid and wouldn't stand a chance.

He kept these dismal thoughts to himself as he said good night to everyone. He knew he'd be awake a long time.

# Chapter 52

Tom barreled through the back door the next morning. "Looks like a war zone out there, and it's not even seven yet."

Barb filled disposable coffee cups and put them on a tray. She bent to pick it up, but Tom intercepted her.

"Here, honey, let me take that for you." He stepped to her side and reached for the tray.

She turned her back for a moment, shoulders shaking.

Tom put the tray back down and turned her to face him.

"I'm sure Joanie's fine." He knew it sounded weak. "According to Samantha, she was wearing a heavy coat, hat, gloves, and snow boots."

"But she went out there in the dark. She doesn't know the area. And you know as well as I do there are animals out there, icy trails, the river only a short way away . . . How are you ever going to find her . . ."

"Those fifteen or sixteen guys and gals out there know their stuff. If anyone can find her, they can. Now, listen to me. Bill, Steve, and I are going with them. I need to get out there and get some instructions. I'd like to think that you and Sally will stay with Susan, pray together, keep her company. She's going to need both of you. And you can help Sally keep the kids occupied. Okay?"

Barb was silent, tears flowing.

He put his hand under her chin and lifted her head. "Mrs. Masters, do you understand your orders?"

She wiped her eyes with her fists and managed a weak grin. "Yessir."

But her face grew serious again. "Please be careful." She grabbed his hand and pressed it to her cheek. "And bring her back."

"Yes, ma'am, we sure will." He picked up the tray of coffee and hurried out the back door.

Barb followed him as far as the outside porch. At least nine or ten four-wheel-drive vehicles were parked willy nilly between the back of the inn and the creek.

She tilted her head to the sky. The clouds were heavy with unshed snow—to add to the almost one and a half feet that had fallen overnight. The tramping of feet and the vehicles packed it down near the house, but beyond the bridge and creek, the snow measured a good two and a half feet up the tree trunks and bent the white-laden branches down until they were touching the surface.

Barb turned her attention back to the rescue teams forming. Samantha's and Stevie's shrieks of laughter as they weaved in and out among the searchers and chased each other with snowballs lent a bright contrast to the grim expressions on the faces of the adults.

Sally appeared at her elbow. "Uh-huh—I knew they'd be underfoot."

Barb moved aside so Sally could join her.

"Sammie, Stevie, come here please."

Steve looked up from the map spread out on the hood of one of the vehicles. He corralled the two children with some difficulty and walked them over to Sally.

"Hi, honey."

Stevie tugged on the bottom of his coat. "Daddy, I wanna go with you."

Samantha tugged on the other side. "If he gets to go, I get to go."

Steve knelt down in front of them. "No."

"But—"

Steve laid a finger over the boy's lips. "And that's final, young man. I expect you to stay with your mother and Sammie and behave yourself."

"Aww, Daddy, that's no fun—"

Steve squeezed his shoulder. "I need you to stay here and keep the girls safe. Okay?" He put his mouth to Stevie's ear in a stage whisper. "You'll have to be the man of the house while we're gone. Are you up for it?"

Stevie stood up straight and thrust out his chest. "Okay, Daddy, I will."

Samantha pushed Stevie aside. "I can help. I'm older."

"I'm counting on *both* of you to help and not be a problem. Now, get in the house and get your coats off. I'm sure there will be breakfast for you soon." He threw a questioning look at Barb.

"Umm . . . yes, I was going to make pancakes this morning, and I could sure use some help in the kitchen."

Samantha clapped her hands. "Pancakes? Yum—"

Stevie elbowed Samantha aside and crowded into the doorway behind Barb. "Can you make faces on them like Mommy does?"

Barb herded them through the sitting room. "We'll see about that. Go get your coats and boots off, then wash up so you can help. I'll be right back." She stepped back out onto the porch.

Sally looped her arm through Steve's and looked at Barb. "How are they?"

"They're okay . . . getting out of their coats. I told them to wash up before they help me with breakfast."

Steve spread his arms wide in a gesture of helplessness. "I don't know how much 'help' they'll be, but at least it'll keep 'em out of trouble for—"

Tom's voice interrupted him. "Steve, we're ready to go."

"Okay, be right there."

Tom looked up at the second-floor windows of the inn. "Where's Bill? He was right here a minute ago—"

Bill appeared and vaulted down the porch stairs, stuffing something into his zippered jacket pocket.

He hurried to Tom's side. "Sorry. Had to say goodbye to Susan."

Steve took Sally's hand. "This may take a while. Don't expect us back for lunch, and maybe not dinner either. You should see the terrain we have to cover. The map makes it seem positively treacherous—"

Sally's eyes widened, riddled with fear.

"But," Barb interjected, "Tom knows these mountains like the back of his hand. He grew up here, fishing and hunting with his dad and grandfather. And he's a soldier—he knows how to survive. And the others . . . the others have lived in this area for years and years. They know what they're doing." She gripped Sally's hand.

Sally let out a breath and searched Steve's face. "Be careful out there. And . . . and you know I'm worried about Mom. What if . . . and now we'll be delayed longer." Her grip tightened on his sleeve. "I'm so afraid . . . Please come back in one piece."

Steve leaned over and kissed her on the forehead. "I will. I promise. Maybe cell service is restored. You should try calling your mom's doctor. I gotta go now."

With a last pat on her cheek and an "I love you," he turned and strode toward Tom.

All three men waved as they picked up their survival packs and circled up with the searchers. Then they headed down the driveway to the road, while others fanned out in different directions. The two women watched until they were out of sight over the first small rise.

Sally's voice sounded like it came from far away. "Tom had his rifle over his shoulder."

Barb turned Sally to face her. "He never goes hiking without his rifle and his sidearm. It doesn't mean there'll be trouble—it's meant to avoid trouble." She patted Sally's shoulder. "Come on. Let's go in—I'm getting cold standing out here." Barb cast a look behind her at the sky above the ridge.

Sally's question held a tremor. "Are you worried?"

"A little," Barb admitted, shutting and locking the door behind her. "But not about Tom. I know he can take care of himself. But I confess I'm a little concerned about the weather. If it'd just let up for a bit . . ."

Sally nodded. "I'm praying in my heart right now, for Joanie and for the safety of everyone looking for her."

"So am I, my friend. Now, let's get busy on breakfast, shall we?" Barb went to the refrigerator and came back with eggs and milk. "Why don't you see if you can find Susan and ask her to help. We need to distract her—"

"Okay. I'll be right back."

Barb stood motionless for a moment, staring down at the eggs and milk, thinking of Joanie out there somewhere in the cold and the building storm.

She swiveled around and stared at Katie's blue eyes perched on the windowsill. Katie had gone away, and the only thing left of her that dark day was her tiny ivory body lying still in Barb's lap, the light gone from her eyes, fingers still clinging to her own. Barb gripped the counter edge behind her, swamped by despair. This must not happen again—she couldn't bear it to happen again. She loosened her grip on the counter and forced herself to relax, remembering who was out there with the searchers.

Eyes clamped shut, she heard tromping on the stairs.

Please don't let Joanie go. Please don't let this happen—that Susan should have to see her little girl like the last time I saw my Katie.

The rest of the prayer leaked out under her eyelids and she could go no further.

The door burst open, and Stevie's voice rang out. "Pancakes? Aren't they done yet?"

Samantha gave him a playful punch on the arm. "We have to make them, silly."

"Ow, Sammie!"

Under cover of their bantering, Sally leaned toward Barb. "I got through to Mom's doctor. The connection was bad, but he told me she's hanging on. In fact, he said her condition has improved somewhat. So that's one piece of good news. But right when I was saying goodbye, we were cut off. Guess we're back to no service. And Susan—"

Susan stood rigid beside the counter, hands to her face.

Barb hurried around the counter and gripped Susan's shoulders.

"Hey. Let's get some pancakes going—it'll keep us from worrying. What d'ya say?"

Susan took a deep breath and dropped her hands. "Okay, what do you want me to do?"

"Atta girl. Sally, you'll find an assortment of aprons in that drawer over there by the pantry, in case you want them for you or the kids."

She took her mother's apron off the hook, then reached for her grandmother's pancake bowl and the sack of flour she kept in the pantry. She glanced at Katie's plump cheek on the windowsill and heard the babyish voice sweetly singing the words to her favorite song.

Jesus loves me, this I know.

Barb thought of the long day of waiting ahead and forced the weariness and fear back into a corner of her heart. She mustn't let it show.

Chapter 53

T wo hours later, Tom called a halt. He'd directed them along the forest service road for about four miles, which ran parallel to the highway. He'd thought Joanie would want to stay off the main road—that was, if hitchhiking wasn't her goal.

They stood now at a fork in the service road—they could either follow it farther in the same direction, or up the mountain, where it snaked out of sight behind the trees. Voices drifted from the surrounding hills as the search teams, shouting Joanie's name, scoured the area.

After digging into their packs, they stood in a tight circle to keep warm while gulping water and energy bars.

Tom surveyed his team and noted their fatigue. He'd allowed Bill to take the lead, and he'd kept up a relentless pace, pushing them to move too fast for the conditions. It didn't help that the clouds now unleashed their burden of snow again—a soft beginning—but he knew it would get worse.

"Bill, I'll take lead now. I think we should slow our pace a bit. It won't do Joanie any good if we push ourselves so hard that we have to quit too soon." Tom glanced at Steve, who nodded his agreement.

Bill didn't answer. He put a shaking hand to his face, wiping moisture out of his eyes.

Tom grasped the other man's shoulder. "Bill? What do you say?"

Bill shook him off. "Yeah, I know." He rubbed a nervous tick on his cheek. "But we can't give up. We can't. I promised Susan I'd bring her back, and I mean to—no matter what. D'ya hear? I'm not breaking another promise to her."

Tom, concerned at the frenzied tone in Bill's voice, made an effort to soften his own. "We won't give up. If it's the last thing we do on this earth, we're going to find Joanie. I promise you that."

Tom watched the other man's face go from firm commitment to indecision to fear all in a blink as he stared at the unforgiving mountains in the distance.

Bill turned his back on them and walked a few feet away, his shoulders hunched against the cold wind blowing out of the northeast. He stood for a few minutes, his weary gaze roaming over the savage landscape, fists clenched at his sides.

Tom knew what was playing out in his head. There wasn't much distance in a soldier's mind between a buddy blown to pieces in the desert and a daughter splayed out, broken and frozen at the bottom of a ravine. He walked over and laid a heavy hand on Bill's shoulder.

"Hey, Soldier," he commanded. "Look at me."

Bill's unfocused eyes met Tom's.

"Joanie isn't Michael. You're here in Washington state, not in the desert, and we're going to find her. You must believe that. We won't leave her out here under any circumstances." Tom grasped Bill's shoulder tighter. "Think with us."

He motioned Steve to come over. "Think. Where would Joanie go? Is it even possible she's not out here? Maybe she went down the highway?"

Bill's face sagged. "I don't think so. Didn't that deputy say they'd been over the highway in both directions and found nothing? No footprints, no nothing. So she had to have come out here, right? But there's no shelter out here . . . except trees, that is."

Tom nodded. "They're still patrolling the roads in both directions. And another team took this service road in the other direction from the inn. So I think our best bet is out here. I have the walkie-talkie—they would've called if she'd been found."

Bill's eyes started to fill again. "She's everything to Susan. Everything. I don't know what I'll do if we find her too late . . ." He trailed off. "I took Michael from her—"

"That's not going to happen. We'll find her. You must get a grip on yourself—for Joanie's sake, and Susan's."

Tom noted the snow had thickened. They couldn't stand here and do nothing much longer. "What we have to do is think like Joanie."

Bill lifted an eyebrow. "I never thought I'd have to try that. Think like a fourteen-year-old girl?" Bill wagged his head and almost smiled. "Impossible."

"Yeah, scary, huh? But what I meant was, if you were Joanie, where would you go?"

Bill shook his head. "I don't know. I'd have thought—"

Steve waved a hand at them. "Hey, guys—"

Bill and Tom stopped talking and looked at him.

Steve hesitated, then continued. "I think I might have an idea. Maybe . . . but . . ." He stopped, staring up at the mountain where the service road disappeared through the trees.

"What?" Tom asked.

"That old hunter's cabin. Where I took the kids hiking. Joanie thought it was pretty cool, even mentioned how peaceful it would be to live there. She looked in the windows, walked around, seemed quite taken with it. Oh, and she said, 'This would be a perfect place to hide.' Or something like that."

Tom followed his gaze. "That's a long way for her to walk at night and in the snow. At least four miles from the back of the inn, and over rough terrain. I sure hope she didn't go that way. It seems to me she'd stay on the road because it's easier walking."

Tom's gaze pierced Bill's. "What do you think? You know her better than we do."

Bill rubbed his chin. "She's stubborn enough—that's a fact. I think we should at least check it out. Can you use the walkie-talkie and ask if anyone else has?"

Tom pushed his hood back and ran a shaky hand over the short gray stubble on his head.

"Tom, did you hear me?" Bill demanded.

Tom swung back around, his face grim.

Fear laced Bill's voice. "What is it? What's out there? Don't hide anything."

"I won't. I promise. Steve, did you notice the marker for an old well to the east of the cabin, about twenty yards away? It's a metal pole, about eight feet tall, with an orange flag on top of it. The wooden well cover is rotting away. If anyone didn't see it and stepped on it, it'd collapse for sure. I stuck the pole into the wood. Did you notice it still standing?"

"Yeah, I did notice it. I had to stop Stevie from trying to jump up and grab the flag."

"Good. If the pole was still standing, that means the lid was still intact, at least then."

Bill cleared his throat. "How deep is that well?"

"Not sure, but deep enough to break both legs in a fall—maybe twenty-five to thirty feet. There's no water in it—just some rocky shale at the bottom that would cut you up pretty bad."

Bill's face blanched as white as the landscape. "We have to go there. Now."

Tom took the walkie-talkie out of his coat pocket. After a short conversation, it was clear no one had searched that far behind the inn yet. Tom told the deputy on the other end they'd head that way now.

"About half the searchers have gathered back at the inn for some hot coffee," the voice said. "We'll be going out one more time, but we might have to call this off until tomorrow morning. The weather's closing in—"

"Yeah, okay," Tom cut in, walking a few steps away. He didn't want Bill to hear the deputy's words. "It'll take us a couple of hours, I think, if we push it, to get to that cabin. I know a shortcut from where we are, along the service road. You know where I'm talking about, right?"

"Yeah. You sure about that? It's a treacherous hike, even without a storm."

He heard the other two men approaching him from behind and lowered his voice.

"I'm sure. Steve thinks there's a good chance she went that way. No time to explain now. We'll check in with you again when we get there."

"Be careful. You need to get there before dark. You can't go over that ridge with no daylight, you know?"

"Point taken." Tom signed off and put the walkie-talkie back in his pocket and settled his hat lower on his head.

"Guys," he said, his gaze lifted to the wall of snow-laden clouds shrouding the mountains, "we have to move fast if we're going to do this. The shortcut I mentioned starts from this service road, then veers off from it. The path will bring us up over the ridge on the far side of that cabin, from the opposite direction of how you and the kids got to it before. It's shorter but riskier."

Steve exhaled slowly. "I'm not much of a mountain man, but I'm game. You know these mountains best."

Tom forced a tight grin. "Stay behind me and keep up. I don't need to rescue one of you in addition to Joanie."

Bill picked up his pack and tightened it around his shoulders and waist. "Are you sure about this?" He looked up into the gloom, deep lines etched around his eyes. "Can you find your way before it gets dark? In this?" His sweeping gesture took in the entire wild landscape around them.

"Since I was twelve, my friend."

He stepped off the service road, tightening the strap on the Marlin.

"Form up. Let's go."

# Chapter 54

Barb and Susan stood close together on the back porch in the waning light of the late-afternoon sun. The wind had calmed somewhat, but Barb guessed that wouldn't last long. Sally and the children banged around in the kitchen, cleaning up after a late lunch they'd served the search team.

They watched as the teams threw gear into pickups, loaded dogs into kennels, and rolled up their maps. The county sheriff strolled to the porch, hat in hand, his glance landing everywhere except on Susan's face.

"Ma'am, we're not giving up. But it's too late to continue, and we've been out there the better part of the day. I'm sending them home to rest. We'll be back at first light."

"Thank you, Herb," Barb said. "We appreciate everyone who's helping. Are there any of your people still out there?"

"Nope, everyone's accounted for—except your men. I heard from Tom right before we headed back here. They're going over the hill that drops down behind that old hunter's shed. They think there's a chance she might be holed up there. I don't know," he added in a voice that did not inspire confidence. "It seems like a long shot, but Tom knows what he's doing."

Barb threw an arm around Susan's stiff shoulders. She frowned and pressed her lips together, then gave Herb a slight jerk of her head toward Susan.

He met Susan's eyes. That his cheerfulness was forced was painfully obvious. "Now, don't you worry, ma'am. As I said, Tom knows his business, knows how to survive. If she's in that cabin, he'll bring her home, mark my words." He turned to go.

Susan found her voice. "Thank you, sir. I'm . . . I'm . . . praying you're right. I don't know what I'd do . . . if . . . if . . ." Susan couldn't finish her thought, hanging her head in despair.

The sheriff fingered his hat with jerky movements, then shoved it on his head. "Yes, ma'am."

Barb put her arm around Susan and hugged her tightly. "Susan, bear up. You must bear up. We can't see Joanie right now, but God has her in his sights, you can be sure of that. And as much as you love her, he loves her so much more."

She nodded at the sheriff over Susan's shoulder. Touching his hat and dipping his head, he backed down the path, turned, and trudged to his truck, obvious weariness in every step.

Barb drew Susan back into the sitting room and sat her down in Tom's chair. After lighting the wood in the old pot-bellied stove, she stepped back over to Susan and crouched at her feet, stroking her arm.

Susan's vacant stare fixed on the wild landscape out the window. Barb followed her gaze and noted the change from only five minutes ago. The wind had kicked up again. Barb felt a pang of alarm in her chest.

She recalled the time many years ago when Tom had first taken her to that hunter's cabin. They'd hiked over the back side, but it'd been early summer and the weather had been glorious that day— flowers and mountain shrubs in bloom, eagles calling high above them. There was no footpath, only animal tracks. They climbed over fallen limbs, boulders, and waded through a small creek to get there.

She'd asked him at the time why he took her that way instead of walking the path from behind the inn. He'd replied, "I want you to see where I used to spend time when I was young. My grandfather always told me I should have more than one way of getting where I need to be. So I went to the cabin one day, then climbed out this way, the way we're going. It's harder, but a shorter distance. Grandpa said that's how life is sometimes—the best path is often the hardest."

Susan leaned over in her chair and hugged Barb's neck, weeping softly.

"Susan," Barb said. "Tom's smart. I trust him with my life, and you can trust him with Joanie's."

She heard the door from the kitchen open. Sally tiptoed into the sitting room.

"Thank you for cleaning up after everyone. Where are the children?" Barb asked.

"They're upstairs reading their storybooks. They'll be fine for a few minutes on their own."

Sally took Barb's chair, then leaned over and enclosed Susan's hand in her own. "While we were cleaning the kitchen, the three of us prayed for Joanie and the men. Samantha, especially, prayed hard for Joanie." She hesitated. "I believe God will honor our prayers and will help them find her. If there's one thing I've learned from my own stupid mistakes, it's that he's always faithful."

"But when it's your own child, it's so hard. I should be out there looking for her, not sitting in here blubbering."

"Yes, I know. We think our children are our own, and then something like this happens and we realize they aren't—they belong to God. And isn't that best for them?" Sally asked.

"Best for them? What's best is that she's here with her mother.

And anyway, what does that mean? He *took* your child . . . and Barb's."

Sally let go of Susan's hands and hunched forward, obviously unable to answer.

Susan stared at the back of Sally's head, then unleashed. "Why? Why does God do this to us right when Bill and I . . . Bill was on his knees to me last night—on his knees. He was so broken. I've never seen him like that." She stood and walked to the window.

"He confessed the guilt he still feels over Michael's death." Her voice rose. "Do you even understand how hard that was for him? Do you? And for me to hear it? Michael was everything to me—"

She pivoted to face them. "How could God be so cruel as to bring us back to him, then take Joanie from us?"

Barb sat back on her heels. "Maybe this isn't about you and Bill."

"What on earth is that supposed to mean? It *is* happening to us—"

"Maybe it's about Joanie. Did you think of that angle? So many times we think only of how something affects us, and we think God is doing something for or against us. But maybe this is about Joanie."

Susan frowned. "You don't understand."

"I think I do."

"Right when Bill and I reconcile, when everything looks so . . . I don't know . . . hopeful, why would God allow this to happen to us? And we did this . . . Bill and I . . . *we* did this to her."

Barb's next words came hard, like shrieking nails pulled out of old boards. "I always have to remind myself that Katie is safe with him. But when she was so sick—going through chemo, with tubes sticking out of her, and we knew there was no hope—we struggled too. We can't give up our babies. We're not wired that way. It's like you tear your heart out of your chest, hold it in your hands, and watch it slow down to the last beat. And then . . . nothing."

Susan put an unsteady hand to her mouth. "Yes. That's it. And I can't do it." She leaned over and gagged. "I can't tell God he can have her. I can't—" Tears spilled out, sliding down her cheeks and splashing on her hands, now gripped by the other two women.

Barb was drawn back in time . . . she and Tom pleading for Katie to breathe just one more time. And further back, to her own mother on her knees next to her older sister Maggie's bed, begging God for her life. Maggie died a short time after that prayer. Barb had lost a sister, but her mother had lost a child, and the family had never been quite the same again.

Barb tipped Susan's head up and pressed their foreheads together.

"Ah, honey, you don't have to tell him *that*—he already knows you can't let go. He knows firsthand. Tell him you can't give her up, that you can't live without her. And keep telling him. Don't give up."

With Barb's words, Susan let go and allowed the violent tide of emotion to surge through like water over a breached dam. She sat back and raised her arms, yelling her anguish at the ceiling.

Barb felt the sweet presence of God move in and fill the room as they clung to each other and prayed. She didn't know how this day would end, but she knew God was already there.

# Chapter 55

T om slowed the grueling pace he'd set, then stopped, taking his compass out of his pocket to study it again. They were an hour into the hike, now at the base of the hill they had to get over. He looked at his watch—almost three o'clock.

He adjusted their course a bit, then surveyed Bill and Steve. Bill was strong and focused, but Steve, wheezing and dragging his feet, looked like he was wiped.

Tom clapped Steve on the shoulder. "You gonna make it? You look a bit overwhelmed, buddy."

"I'll be okay." He stopped for a coughing fit. "I know we can't stop."

"We can stop for ten minutes, no longer," Tom instructed. "Sit down on that rock over there and get an energy bar and some water out of your pack. Bill, you help him."

Tom scanned the darkening sky. His men would be fine after a short rest and some food and water, but he wanted to check out the conditions up ahead without them.

If they were caught up there on unstable snow, as green as they were, he might not be able to bring them out. Then what about Joanie?

He scrutinized the ridge ahead. It snaked away from them, winding all the way up and connecting to a higher ridge, ending at the top of the highest mountain in these parts. They'd need to stay on the downhill side of this smaller ridge—on this side—until they were right above the cabin, then start down. The hill smoothed out to a short climb down of about fifty yards, then a drop of about six feet to the right of the cabin.

He unslung his Marlin and handed it to Bill. "Hang on to this for me until I get back."

"Where're you going?"

"I won't be long."

A nervous tic jumped in Bill's cheek. "Sir, we need to know where you're going in case you don't come back." He locked eyes with Tom, clearly unwilling to let him off the hook.

"Okay. You're right. I'm going on ahead for a short way—I want to check that there aren't any rockslides or unstable snow we'll have to negotiate. I'll follow above the draw over there." He pointed. "You stay here and rest until I get back. Under no circumstances are you to follow me. If I'm not back in twenty minutes, head back the way we came, down to the highway, and get yourselves back to the inn. Understand?"

He waited until they nodded their agreement, then took off at a fast clip.

As promised, Tom hiked back through the trees nineteen and a half minutes later, breathing hard as he dropped his pack and grabbed his water bottle.

Bill looked at his watch. "Right on time, not a minute past. How is it?"

"Okay, for the most part. But there's a rough patch about half a mile up. Loose rocks under the snow, a couple of downed trees. We'll have to be careful. But the good thing is, the snow seems fairly stable, although there's a lot of it—at least four feet or more

282

in some spots. But if we take it steady, I think we'll be okay." He glanced at Steve. "You good to go?"

He stood and hefted his pack to his shoulders. "Lead the way."

Tom took his rifle back and checked the chamber out of habit. "Okay, let's roll. Daylight's on the way out, and we need to move fast. I want to get over the top before the light fades."

He'd decided on the way back not to mention the cat tracks he'd seen—a big one, if he was any judge. No sense adding another layer of worry.

Tom halted their climb after thirty minutes. "See the ridge ahead? That's where we're going. Another hundred yards and we'll be right above the cabin. We should be able to see it from there. Then we can start down. It won't be easy, but if we're careful, we'll make it. That place I warned you about is right up ahead of us."

"How long will it take once we start on the downside to the cabin?" Bill asked between gulps of water.

"Not more than a half hour, I'd think."

Bill looked surprised. "That long? I thought you said the cabin's right at the base of the mountain."

"Here's the thing. Going down *seems* like it'd be easier, but in this stuff you have a whole new set of problems," Tom replied. "Like if you fall going downhill, there's no stopping you. If you fall going uphill, you might bang your face or something, but you have a lot more control over how you fall. But either way, caution is the order of the day. The light's going fast. I think we'd better have our flashlights at the ready. I give it about a quarter of an hour or so, then we'll need 'em."

Tom slowed the pace, but the need to get to shelter while they still had daylight thrummed in the forefront of his mind.

They traversed the unstable area without mishap. As they came to the ridge overlooking the cabin, the sun sank below the ridge behind them, shrouding the landscape in shadows.

Tom could barely see the outline of the cabin behind the trees at the bottom.

"Come on, guys. This way." He picked his way between two large rocks poised on the edge of the hill. "See there? You can see the roofline of the cabin."

Bill peered ahead. "That's still a ways off. And this is pretty steep."

Tom nodded. "What did I tell you? But we saved about ninety minutes by coming this way." He put himself in front. "Be careful now. Stay together. We're close—almost there."

They started down, sometimes sliding, but grabbing at branches to keep themselves upright.

"You weren't kidding—there's no path," Steve said. "And it seems like we're going to end up way to the right of the cabin. You sure this is right?"

"I already told you—since I was in grade school. And we *want* to veer to the right of the cabin. There's a sheer twenty-foot wall of rock directly behind the cabin, with a drop ending on a bed of shale." He added with a wry smirk, "It'd be quicker to go straight down, but I don't recommend it."

"Okay then," Steve said. "To the right we go."

They scrambled down another fifty yards, using their flashlights in the gloom.

"Okay, guys, we're almost there. But we're not out of the woods yet. Sorry about the pun."

His voice broke off as Bill let out a yell and fell hard, right foot twisted under him. Before Tom could reach him, Bill careened down the hill, hands grasping at small tree trunks and branches on the way.

Tom stumbled behind him, trying to grab him from behind, but couldn't get close enough.

He heard Steve let out a yell behind him, then call, "I'm okay. Go after Bill."

After rolling downward fifty feet, Bill slammed head first into a boulder, rolled over on his face, and lay still.

"Bill, are you all right?" Tom knelt by Bill's head.

 # Chapter 56

Bill's eyes were closed, but his groans signaled he was conscious.

Tom shook him by the arm. "Bill?"

His eyes fluttered open.

He had a bleeding gash on his forehead where it had kissed the boulder, but Tom couldn't see any other injuries. He rummaged in his pack and came up with some gauze squares, quickly pressing one into the wound. He took Bill's hand and pressed it over the gauze.

"Keep pressure on this."

Steve arrived in a stumbling heap, losing his balance and banging into Bill.

Bill shifted and let out a yell. "My ankle—"

Steve sat up. "Oh, man, I'm sorry. I couldn't help it—"

Tom leaned over Bill. "Which one?"

"My right."

Tom gave his ankle a cursory glance. "Can you stand on it?"

"Yeah, yeah, I can stand."

He lumbered to his feet with Tom and Steve's help but then collapsed into them again, holding up his right foot.

"It's . . . it's worse than I thought. I can't do it."

They lowered Bill to a sitting position on the rock.

Steve searched in his backpack for a paper towel. He wiped the sweat off Bill's forehead, then handed him a water bottle.

Tom rolled Bill's pant leg up to his knee and unlaced his boot.

Bill grimaced as Tom touched his swelling ankle.

He gave it a close inspection, gently probing and manipulating while Bill winced and kept a grip on Tom's shoulder.

"Is it broken?"

"Don't think so. Bad sprain maybe. But you won't be walking on it, that's for sure."

Steve peered over Tom's shoulder. "Should we put some snow on it?"

"Good idea. Grab some."

After packing as much snow into the boot as he could, Tom laced it back up as tightly as he dared to help control the pain and swelling.

Bill's anger spilled over. "Ah, this is perfect. Now what do we do?"

"First thing is to calm down," Tom admonished. "Take it one step at a time."

Bill shifted his weight and nodded. "And that'd be about all I can manage right now."

"The bottom of the hill is only twenty feet away. Once we're there, the cabin is only thirty yards to the left. Let's go. I'll leave you guys there and come back for the packs. Then we can figure out the next step."

Tom showed Steve how to hoist Bill up and drape his arm over his shoulder. Tom did the same on the other side. They set off, ranged sideways down the slope—Tom on the downhill side—stepping cautiously over rocky areas. When they reached the bottom, they stopped to rest, settling Bill on the ground.

Tom set off to retrieve their packs, returning in short order.

Steve pointed to the six-foot drop to level ground. "How are we going to get down there?"

"Piece of cake." Tom chucked the packs down to the ground, then dropped himself over the edge and motioned for Steve to jump down.

"Okay, Bill, scoot over here where we can reach you, and we'll bring you down nice 'n easy like," Tom directed.

Bill slid down and let his legs dangle over the short precipice. The other two men lifted him down, easing him to a sitting position.

Steve took his own pack and Bill's, putting one on his back and looping the other strap over his shoulder.

"Okay, let's go," Tom said. "And none too soon. I hope there's still firewood inside that cabin, and some blankets."

"And Joanie," Bill said, reaching up to adjust the fresh gauze on his forehead.

"Did you change that gauze?" Tom asked, his voice sharp.

"Yeah, Steve did while you went after the packs. Why?"

"What did you do with the used one?"

"I don't know. Threw it on the ground, I guess."

Tom threw a questioning look at Steve, who nodded.

Bill repeated his question. "Why? What's wrong?"

Tom looked back up the slope, eyes narrowed. He glanced at the cabin, then at Bill. "Never mind. I'm not going back up there to get it. Let's get inside."

They hoisted Bill up again and carried him between them to the rickety porch steps.

Steve glanced to his right. "The flag's still on that old well. I guess that's something, huh?"

Tom didn't answer, his gaze pointed down at the boards under his feet.

"What?" Steve asked.

Tom waved a finger, indicating the floor of the porch where they stood.

Steve looked and saw wide scrape marks. Looking behind them, he thought he saw similar marks in the snow just off the edge of the porch.

"Tom, what—"

"Shh—"

Bill lurched forward and beat his fist on the door. "Joanie, are you in there?"

Tom cocked an ear toward the cabin. He heard nothing.

Bill's fear-filled eyes met his own.

# Chapter 57

J ust as Tom raised his fist to pound the door again, running steps sounded inside, followed by a thud and a loud grunt. The door flew open with a jerk, banging against the cabin wall.

Joanie stood before them, face pinched with cold, wrapped in a tattered green army blanket that billowed clouds of dust when she moved. Behind her lay a homemade side table—constructed of ancient planks and two-by-fours—on its side, one board hanging off at a crazy angle. She bent over and rubbed her shin, then stood up, eyes wide and shiny with tears.

"You came back . . . you came for me," she said, voice cracking. "I didn't mean to stay so long, but I was afraid to try to get back on my own. I heard a scratching sound outside right after I got here. I thought it was an animal, and I was afraid it was still out there—"

Tom held up his hand to stem the tsunami of words. "Joanie, can you move out of the doorway, please? We've got to get Bill inside."

They had to turn sideways to manipulate him through the door. More dust wafted into the air as they settled him in a cushioned chair by the fireplace.

Joanie slammed the door and turned around. "What's going on? Are you hurt or something?"

Bill coughed and rubbed his eyes. "I took a little fall. I'll be okay. Tom says it's not broken, just a bad sprain."

"But your head—it's nasty."

"No, it's okay. A scratch. It bled a lot, but it stopped—"

"But how did it happen? Were you guys fighting or something?"

"Joanie, can you help me for a minute?" Tom broke in. "I'm hoping there's still firewood inside that little closet over there. Would you bring me some, and some kindling? We need to get this place warm. And, Steve, please go out and get some more snow. We'll pack it on his ankle again once I get his boot unlaced."

After Joanie brought the kindling, Tom lit the fire, then knelt in front of Bill. He loosened the laces again and packed snow inside the boot, then retied the laces and wrapped it in a blanket.

Joanie watched. "Aren't you going to take it off?"

"No. It'd hurt like the dickens, and the boot helps keep the snow in and the swelling down."

"But in my—"

"Joanie, would you grab a few more blankets, please? We need to get him warm."

She brought an armload. Tom took two and covered Bill.

"The fire's nice, Mr. Masters. I didn't know how to make one. I found the wood but didn't have anything to light it with. Guess I'm not much use out here," she said. "I've been so cold since I got here, even with this blanket. I didn't know what I was going to do, and then you guys show up out of the blue. I probably shouldn't have come out here, but I—"

"It's not hard to make a fire once you get the hang of it—and if you have dry wood, it's easy." Tom didn't know what else to say.

Joanie looked hesitantly at Bill and cleared her throat. "Bill . . . I'm really—"

"Joanie, forgive me, but we need to make a plan to get you both back to the inn. Can you table your discussion for a few minutes?"

Without waiting for Joanie's reply, Tom continued. "I've thought it over. I think Steve and I should walk back to the inn and get help."

Joanie jerked her head in Tom's direction. "What? Leave us here alone? That's crazy—"

He held up his hand at her tirade. "Hold on a minute. Hear me out, okay? I've tried the walkie-talkie a couple of times, but all I get is static. I estimate it will take the two of us about two hours there and two hours back *if* we push hard and *if* there's no complications."

He turned to Bill. "I don't think we can carry you that far in the dark. And we have to gather supplies, call the doc, and get him to come with us—and maybe a deputy or two. This is going to take time. What do you think, Steve? Are you game?"

"Yeah. So we're looking at getting back practically in the middle of the night, right?"

"Maybe early morning. It's iffy whether or not we should try to navigate in the middle of the night—it's not like Bill's injury is life threatening."

Joanie pressed her lips together in a tight line and drifted over to the fire, turning a stiff back to them. Tom knew she was angry, but he didn't care.

Bill spoke up. "I think you're right. I'd hold you up and maybe get us into trouble, with both of you trying to carry me." He looked pointedly at Joanie. "And we can't chance it with her. We need more help."

She turned to face them then, eyes narrowed, arms crossed in a weak show of defiance.

"Come on, sweetheart. We'd be safer here, waiting together for them to get back. We'll be fine, don't you think?"

Joanie dropped her arms, defeated, and drilled Tom with a sideways look. "But hurry, okay? I mean, I want to see my mom." Her voice quivered.

"We will, Joanie. We will," Tom said. "And you'll be with your mom soon. I promise."

Tom stood, put his hat and gloves on, and pulled his light out of his pack—a large one with a bright LED bulb. "Steve, got your flashlight?"

Steve pulled his out of his pocket, but the battery was dead. "I guess we'll have to share."

Bill reached into his pocket. "Take mine. Joanie has one, and we have the firelight. And mine's a real one, not like your wimpy wannabe one."

Steve took it from him. "Are you sure we can do this in five hours, Tom?"

"Yep, and it'll be easier going than what we just did. Except it'll be dark. You know the way, remember—you walked it before."

"Yeah, I know the way. I remember some rough parts though. We'll need to be careful."

Tom faced Joanie. "Okay, listen up. Keep the fire going. Don't let it go out. And don't go outside. Stay buttoned up in here. Take care of Bill—your main mission. He needs to be warm, and he needs water and plenty of blankets. And in case you hadn't noticed, there's no running water here. Do you have enough?"

"Yeah, found that out. I brought two water bottles with me, and one's still full."

"Good. Try not to drink it completely down in case we're delayed for any reason."

"Okay."

"And this is important. I told you before not to go outside, but you're going to have to open the door in order to get snow for Bill's ankle. Before we leave, I'm going to pack some snow in that metal bucket out on the porch. Every half hour, open the door a crack and reach to your right—I'll leave it right next to the front door so you won't have to go all the way out. Pack it on that ankle to keep the swelling down. It'll help with the pain, too."

"Yes, sir, I will. Hurry back, okay?"

"As fast as we can. You good, Bill?"

"We're good."

Tom hesitated, then drew his .44 and handed it to Bill. "You might need this. Better to be safe than sorry."

"Hey, you guys are the ones going out there. You keep it. We have a locked door."

"Don't worry. I've still got the Marlin here, strapped to my back. And if that was a bear Joanie heard, that door won't stop it, especially if it's hungry or has cubs. Black bears are plentiful in this area, but they're usually hibernating. So I'm not that worried. On the other hand, except for this storm, it's been a mild winter, and that means one might be awake and foraging for food. If so, a well-placed bullet from my friend there in your hand will slow it down considerably. Still remember how to shoot, Marine?"

Bill hefted the six-and-a-half-inch barreled weapon in his hand. "Yeah, it's coming back to me," he said with a grin. Always liked a Taurus. This isn't a factory grip, is it?"

"No, I changed it out some time ago—needed a bigger one."

"Nice." Bill shot a look at Joanie, whose eyes were like saucers. "This ought to do it. Hope I don't have to use it."

Tom nodded. "I hope not too. Here's some extra rounds." He handed Bill two six-round speed loaders. "Keep those nearby."

"Yessir." He put both loaders in his jacket pocket.

Tom laid his hands gently on Joanie's shoulders. "Remember, stay inside the cabin with the door locked, except for getting snow for Bill's ankle. Look out the window and take a minute to listen before opening the door. All you have to do is take a plastic cup—there should be some in the cupboard over there—reach out and around, fill it with snow, and bring it in fast. You shouldn't even have to step outside. Okay? Any questions?"

Joanie looked at Bill, who shook his head. "Guess not."

She followed Tom and Steve to the door.

After packing the large metal bucket with snow, they set off on the path back to the inn, the glow from their flashlights bouncing off the snow. After a few yards, they swung back around, blinding her with the beams.

"Get back inside and stay there," Tom yelled.

She obeyed, dropping the old metal latch in place.

Chapter 58

J oanie watched from the window until their flashlight beams disappeared into the trees.

Turning, she stared at Bill for a moment, then plopped down onto a chair on the other side of the fireplace.

Desperate to break the awkward silence, she blurted out the first thing that entered her head. "Don't you think your leg should be elevated? If it's sprained like Mr. Masters said, then we should elevate it."

Bill raised an eyebrow.

"I learned that in my survival course last year—remember? I took it as an elective."

"I don't remember that."

Joanie rose and surveyed the room. "Yeah, why would you? You were out on the golf course, trying to impress somebody." She turned away from the stricken look on his face. "Never mind. It's not important now."

An old three-legged stool stood in a corner, piled high with yellowed, dusty newspapers. She pushed them to the floor, coughing as dust billowed around her, then carried the stool and placed it in front of Bill. Joanie picked up his leg as she'd been taught—by his pant leg—and settled his ankle on the stool.

He winced as his foot flopped to the right.

Hurrying to the pile of blankets, she grabbed the cleanest one, also spying a flowered quilt for herself. She folded the smaller blanket in half, then in half again, and placed it under Bill's foot.

"Take off your belt please."

He frowned, not moving.

"Please? In case you didn't notice, I'm trying to help."

He shrugged and unbuckled it, pulled it through the loops, then handed it to her.

Joanie wrapped the blanket around Bill's lower leg, using the belt to cinch it, running it under the stool and up over his lower leg to hold the makeshift splint in place.

"There, is that better?" she asked. "I'll get some snow in a few minutes."

"Much. Thank you, Joanie. I'm impressed, more than I was on whatever golf course you mentioned."

Feeling her face flush, she stepped over to the window and peered into the darkness. Seeing and hearing nothing, she sat down again, pulling the colorful quilt over herself. It was small—smaller than a full-size blanket—and lavender, with tiny pink flowers and yellow bumblebees scattered over it. Joanie thought it must have been on a child's bed at one time. She searched the small, one-room cabin. There was no other evidence there'd ever been a child here. So how'd the blanket get here? And why?

She glanced at Bill. His eyes downturned at the corners, and the fingers of his left hand picked at the frayed blanket spread over him. She hated the oppressive silence, like a black cloud filling the space between them.

This was awkward. It was her fault he was sad. It was her fault he was hurt. But she didn't care about him—this man she didn't know.

Joanie didn't know how to penetrate the deepening silence between them, so she kept still, at least enjoying the warmth from the fire.

"I'm sorry, you know."

She looked away, unable to stop the crash of emotions in her chest. She didn't want to do this right now. She wanted to be left alone.

"You know that, right?"

She clenched her fists under the blanket. "No, I don't know that, Bill. How can I know that? And what difference would a 'sorry' make now? Tell me that, Bill."

She saw him flinch, but so what? She wanted him to know she wouldn't call him Dad anymore—that name belonged to someone she'd never know. He and Mom had both seen to that.

"Does saying sorry now somehow make it all go away? What's the point?"

"Your mother always wanted you to know the truth. I was the one who wanted it kept secret."

Joanie felt the heat rise from under her collar, setting her cheeks on fire. A vein throbbed in her neck. Refusing to look at him, she spat out the words. "Don't even talk to me about her. She's as bad as you. No, worse—she's my *real* mom, and she still lied to me my whole life."

Bill fell silent. Joanie stole another glance at him, saw his lips moving.

So now he talks to himself?

She looked at the floor, disgusted.

It was their fault. Fourteen years—was she supposed to ignore it, pretend it didn't happen? Why did grown-ups think they could get away with this crap?

Her thoughts flew in dizzying circles, first accusing, then excusing herself. The vision of Samantha's perfect blond curls rose in her mind—her mother sheltering her in her arms, her father standing next to her, his large hand cupping her small head. Every muscle taut, Joanie tried to eradicate the vision. Even they weren't Samantha's *real* parents, but at least they'd cared enough to tell their children the truth.

"Joanie, your mother and I, this weekend, we've realized we were so wrong. We've kept things from you that you should have known, things important for a young girl to—"

Joanie turned on him then, the battle in her mind bursting into the room like a shoulder-fired rocket. "No! You don't get to do that."

"But—"

"So what now?" she demanded. "You feel better? I'm happy for you. Okay, now I know your dirty little secret, yours and Mom's. Has anything changed between us? No. Except I don't have to call you Dad anymore." Her voice broke, and she despised herself for it. She bunched the quilt up under her chin and stared into the fire, then back at him.

Bill frowned and sat up straighter. "Would you stop long enough to hear me out for once?"

She squeezed her eyes shut and heard him clear his throat, his chair creaking as he shifted.

"Look, nothing I can say will make up for what we did. We both know that. Your mother is brokenhearted over this—but it was *my* fault. I convinced her that no one needed to know, that it would be easier that way."

Her eyes flew open. "Easier? For who?"

He leaned his head back against the chair cushion. "For me, of course. It wasn't your mother's choice. I not only persuaded her, I threatened to leave her if she didn't go along with it."

Joanie thrust her chin up at his words. She couldn't think of a retort harsh enough.

"I even made her swear her family to secrecy that she'd even been married before. No one was ever to mention it."

The enormity of his confession, how he'd used her mother to lie to her and the rest of the family, took her breath away. Fury exploded in her mind again. "Geez, Bill! Aren't you one of those honest-and-loyal, never-leave-a-brother-behind marines? *You* told me that. But I guess it's okay to leave a wife behind, to lie?"

He didn't turn away from her anger—his tormented face reddened in the heat of the fire.

Gratified to see tears sliding down his face, she lifted her chin in rebellion. "You're a hypocrite. You don't fool me anymore."

She fired the final missile at him. "I bet Mom's got you figured out too. We don't need you anymore. So don't feel obligated to us from here on out, okay? You can go ahead and leave us behind if it's easier for you. You can go and do . . . whatever it is you do when you're supposed to be at home, being a husband and a father."

He cried in earnest now, not covering his face.

She sat unmoved. He deserved it. She hoped Mom gave him the boot when they got home. Home? What was that? Home was gone. There was no home anymore. She guessed it died in Iraq, with . . .

Joanie gathered the quilt to her chest, listening to his sobs. She'd never seen a man cry before, and it seemed wrong somehow. Men's hearts shouldn't have tears in them. They should be stronger than any hurt. But then again, what did she know about men—other than they lied well? She gave him a side glance.

He looked small and weak. But she refused to waste sympathy on him. He deserved what he was getting.

She tried to dismiss him from her mind, but then he shifted under his blanket and spoke, his voice low and gravelly.

"Michael John Briggs."

Chapter 59

J oanie's head flew up.

"Wh . . . what? What did you say?" She hated that her words ended in a pathetic squeak.

He turned his face toward her. "Michael John Briggs. That's your father's name. And he was the best friend I ever had."

Her eyes burned with tears as she choked out the words. "No, I don't want to hear this—just be quiet."

Shut up! her mind screamed at him. She clapped her hands over her ears, but Bill raised his voice.

"You need to hear this as much as I need to say it."

She kept her hands over her ears, curling in a fetal position in the oversized chair, almost completely hidden by the quilt.

"Michael and I grew up together. We knew each other since fourth grade. That's when he and his parents moved to the small town in Iowa where I lived. They moved in across the street. The first time I met him was when he got into a fight with the block bully, Jake, from up the street."

She took her hands away from her ears and sat up. He waited, clearly in no hurry to continue unless she asked him to.

"What were they fighting about?" she finally asked, her voice flat.

He smiled. "About your mother."

She sniffed in disdain. "Mom? You mean they were fighting over her? How . . . juvenile. But it figures. That's all men ever want to do."

"No, not *over* her. Your mom lived three doors up from Michael's house. Jake lived at the end of the street, in the biggest house on the block. He was two grades ahead of us. He and his friends picked on everyone, and no one had ever challenged them before. Your mom was his target that day, and boy, was it entertaining—"

Her brow wrinkled. "Entertaining? You would say that—"

He waved a hand at her and chuckled. "No. Didn't mean it that way. I meant that I'd never seen Jake get what he had coming, but I sure saw it that day. He was built like a midget linebacker, taller and stronger than any sixth grader I'd ever seen. Your mom was only six at the time. Michael and I were both ten. Michael wasn't huge then, but he was mad, and he was strong and fast."

"What happened?"

He lifted his eyebrows. "You really want to know?"

"Wouldn't ask if I didn't."

"Michael came out of his house—they'd moved in a day and a half before—and saw Jake out on the sidewalk pushing Susan, calling her names, taunting her with threats of what he'd do to her if—"

"If what?"

"Not sure. Maybe if she ratted him out. Anyway, she was crying. I watched from our front window. Jake had knocked me around some, so there was no way I was going out there."

He glanced at her, his cheeks burning, then flicked his gaze away. "I should've though," he whispered. "Anyway, Michael came out of his door and shot down the sidewalk like a heat-seeking missile. He didn't even stop when he got close to Jake. He plowed into him and knocked him ten feet, right over the curb and into the street. I don't think Jake even knew what hit him. I'd never seen anything like it. He'd always been the king of the playground—all the kids stayed out of his way at recess. He had a small gang of sorts, wannabe tough guys who followed him around."

Joanie visualized the scene. She'd known boys like that, following the leader like lemmings. "Did . . . did Michael beat him up?"

"Nope. By that time, I'd gone out to our front porch to watch, so I heard what they said. Michael got up and stood over him, kicking him in the back—not hard—but enough to get his attention. He told Jake he was done, as of that moment, and no more of that junk would ever happen again. Michael said he'd be watching, and if Jake got out of line even once, he'd be back—with his dad. I'd gotten one glimpse of Michael's dad when they were unloading the moving van. Your grandfather wasn't one I'd like to tussle with, and I'm a big guy. At least six foot five and built like a bulldozer. Believe me, Jake lay there and took it. First time I ever saw *that* before."

She gulped at the word *grandfather* and lifted her hands over her eyes, fingers shaky. She wiped the back of her hand across her face.

"Yes, your grandfather. I'm so sorry you never knew him. He passed away when Michael and I were overseas. All the time we were growing up, I never heard him say a cross word to anyone. Kindest man I ever knew. And your dad was a chip off that old block."

Joanie squeezed her eyes shut. "What happened next? To Mom, I mean."

"Michael went over to her and asked if she was okay. By then Jake had gotten up and limped home."

"And *was* Jake done being a bully?"

"Yep. Never had another problem after that, in the neighborhood or at school. Jake and his parents moved away a year or so later."

Joanie felt the heat of the fire on her face. There were so many questions she wanted to ask. Like, what was it like the day her mother and father fell in love? How did he propose to her? Did they run away together or get married in a church? The questions stuck in her throat though, and she couldn't ask them.

"I think your mother fell in love with him that very day. She used to follow him around the neighborhood like a puppy whenever she got the chance, but he didn't seem to mind. Michael was the gentlest soul I ever met, and the bravest. That's who your father was."

She scrunched down in her chair, head lowered to her chest, and wrapped her arms around herself.

"Tell me more."

He told story after story of their childhood. She pictured him in her mind—the man who'd married her mother, fathered her, and then went back to war. A brave man, a gentle husband, fierce warrior, loyal friend. A man she'd be proud to call her father. Joanie's heart broke at the misery of it, never knowing this man. She'd never even seen a picture of him, never knew he existed. Her brain hurt with the knowledge. Surely she'd aged twenty years in the last twenty minutes.

And she wept in frustration and anger, hearing the lies Bill and her mother had told their families. Stories that denied her the knowledge of her father, yet puffed Bill up like some kind of hero. He talked right through her tears, saying all the things she should have heard years ago. Finally, he stopped.

Now what? What was she supposed to do with this?

Joanie had always wanted to be like her dad—successful in business—but dad who? This man she was stuck with wasn't her flesh and blood, so where did that leave her? Exactly where she was before . . . adrift, alone, with no idea who she was.

"He saved my life more than once, including the day he died," Bill said, once again diverting her angry thoughts. "D'ya want to hear?"

"Might as well."

"Once when we were in high school, tenth grade as I recall. As usual, I was showing off. We were on our bikes, racing down the street. I was watching him instead of where I was going. He saw the car ahead, racing through the stop sign, and he rammed my bike, taking us both to the curb before we got to the intersection. We ended up almost going through a plate-glass window. Instead, our bikes hit the curb and we went flying. I never even saw the car."

"Were you hurt?"

"Not much. A few scratches and a bruise on my shin where my leg hit the handlebars. But my bike was pretty much totaled. Frame bent, spokes broken. And as usual, I was oblivious to the danger I'd been in. I got mad at Michael and tried to hit him—until old Mr. Stephens from the corner grocery store ran out and grabbed my arm from behind. He about ripped my arm out of my shoulder and told me to behave myself, that I should be shaking Michael's hand instead of hitting him." His face darkened in shame. "I was a fool even back then."

Joanie saw it and knew it for what it was. Bill hated to admit personal weakness or wrongdoing. He was much better at pointing it out in others.

But one thing bothered her—she was more like him than she cared to admit. Her face heated at the sudden knowledge. But it wasn't enough to let him off the hook. Not nearly enough.

Joanie stood and drifted to the window, her back to him. She saw nothing outside but the dim outline of the pines against the black sky.

She turned back into the room and saw him peer at her out of sad eyes.

His expression rankled her. "What? Am I supposed to say something here? Like, 'That's okay, Bill'? Am I supposed to tell you it was a long time ago and it doesn't matter now?"

"I don't expect—"

She pushed hair out of her face and rubbed her eyes. "Here's a news flash for you. It *wasn't* a long time ago. It was yesterday, it's today, and it'll be tomorrow. It's been every day for fourteen years, and nothing you can say will erase that. Nothing will make it go away. And your stories about when you were a kid prove one thing—that you've always been the way you are now and you'll never change."

Chapter 60

Joanie expected Bill to be angry and yell at her.

Instead, he sat unmoving, his face so dejected she almost felt sorry for him. Almost.

He sat up straighter. "There's more—more that I need to say to you. You're right. Some of what you say is right, but the part about not changing is dead wrong. I'll tell you about that some time."

"Telling doesn't mean anything. Showing does."

His mouth turned up in a weak smile. "Wise girl."

She stepped closer to the fire and turned her back to it. Her imagination worked overtime, hearing noises outside when there weren't any. Looking at her watch, she was surprised to see that more than two hours had passed, and wondered how long they'd be stuck here.

Joanie knew she was stalling, but she didn't know if she wanted to hear more. Did and didn't. So she stared at the dusty floorboards.

"Do you want to hear more? If you want me to stop, I will. It won't change much between us, but I want you to know who your father was. It won't be the same as knowing him, but it might help.

And . . . I believe understanding what kind of man he was will help you to know who you are. D'ya know what I mean?"

"I guess." She lifted her shoulders, trying to seem disinterested, then huddled back down under her blanket, face covered. "Proceed."

"We graduated together. I got better grades, but people liked him more. I envied that. I guess my career as a salesman was my attempt to be liked. As long as I had a product to sell and could wine and dine my customers, I thought I was popular. But Michael cared about people. I . . . I guess I don't."

Joanie flipped the blanket off her head and peeked out. "Why don't you? Care about people, I mean?"

"Don't know. Just self-centered, I guess. But I can honestly say I cared about your father. As I said before, he was the best friend I ever had. My parents both worked. I didn't have any brothers or sisters, so I was always on my own and always felt pretty much alone."

She stared at him, then ducked under the quilt again, wishing the darkness would swallow her and save her from the pain of her next words.

"Huh. Kinda like me."

"Wasn't all bad, especially after Michael's family moved in. We had a freedom back then that kids—you and your friends—don't know anything about. Michael and I did everything together, without much supervision. And when we graduated, it seemed natural to enlist together."

She poked her head out of the blanket again, smoothing it around her like a cocoon. "Why'd you wanna go and do that anyway? Go to war, I mean? Didn't your parents care?"

He spread his hands and grinned. "It seemed like another adventure at the time. And no, they didn't object. I think my parents were glad I'd decided on something worthwhile that wouldn't cost them an arm and a leg and would get me out of the house. I do remember Michael's mother crying when she heard. But we were eighteen and didn't need their permission."

"*Was* it an adventure?"

Bill's eyes darkened, like the shadow of a bad dream drifted through his mind.

"Yeah, but not the kind we'd expected. All that hero stuff is mostly fiction. War means no sleep, bad food, and your buddies dying."

"I hate war. I don't understand why we always have to be in wars, killing people. I guess it's a man thing—you don't feel like you are one unless you win."

"You might be about half right. But the ones who hate war the most are the warriors who go fight them, men *and* women. We'd rather have been at home with our families—your father most of all. He couldn't bear to leave your mother."

"So were they, like, dating or something when you left?"

"Not dating, and not *something* either. They were married."

"Married? So young?"

"Yep. We enlisted but didn't leave for boot camp for about six months. At the end of that six months, your mom and Michael eloped without saying a word to anyone. They were gone over-night. And boy, did that cause a to-do in their families for a little while. Both their mothers had wanted a big church wedding. But they'd made up their minds, and it was done. Your mom had one argument with your grandmother. I remember it vividly because I was there—I'd been invited to dinner at their house the night before we headed out. Your mom and dad had returned the day before, sporting their wedding rings. During dinner, things heated up and came to a head between Susan and her mother."

"Mom? I thought she and her mother always got along. At least that's what she tells me."

"Remember, she was still a kid, but she loved your father. Any-way, it went back and forth between the two of them, right there at the table in front of your father and me. We didn't say a word. And neither did your grandfather. Then Susan threw her fork down and stood up. She said something like, 'It's done, Mom. If you can't live with it, fine. But he's my husband now, and you'd best get used to it if you want to see us at all. And anyway, didn't you and Dad elope? Seems like I heard that story from someone in the family. What about that?'"

After that you could have heard a feather drop at the table. Then her dad reached over and patted your grandmother's hand and told her to leave Susan alone."

"Mom sounds like she could hold her own back then—a real scrapper. Am I right?"

"Yes she could. There were a few more times that I remember too, from when we were in high school."

"She doesn't act like that now. She's a mouse, hardly speaking up for herself. At least that's how she is with you."

She saw his fists knot up as he stared at the fire.

"Yeah, she's different now. Also my fault."

Joanie fell silent, thinking she'd like to know this other Susan, the one whom her father had loved when they were just a few years older than Joanie was now.

"Why do you do that? Beat her down like that?"

"I promised your father I'd take care of her."

"This is taking care of her?"

She knew she was making this harder on him than she should. But she couldn't stop.

"No, it's not. But it's the only way I knew to do. Joanie, your mother and I have made some amends this weekend, and we've agreed to try again."

Joanie looked away. "I'll believe it when I see it."

"When it came to Michael, she was a warrior. The day we left for boot camp, she made me promise, in no uncertain terms, to bring him back to her." His face reddened and crinkled up. He whispered into the firelight. "Guess I failed again . . ."

Joanie turned over in her mind the picture Bill had painted of her father, this man who had spilled his blood on a faraway battle-field, the same blood that ran in her veins. Her anger at her parents still simmered, but curiosity now blazed in full force.

"So . . . so if you and . . . and"—she still couldn't bring herself to say *Dad*—"if you and Michael were in Iraq, then how did he . . . how did I . . ."

"How did you come on the scene?"

"Yeah, I guess that's what I mean."

"Michael came home for a week's leave when his father died. You were conceived during that time. It wasn't long after he came back to our squad that he was killed. Three or four weeks maybe."

Joanie's heart squeezed, like she was trying to jam her feelings into a small box—one she could hide away on a shelf somewhere.

"How did my father die? Were you there?" The question popped out before she could stop it.

"Are you sure—"

"Yes, I'm sure. We've come this far. We might as well finish it. I can handle it."

His eyes drilled into hers. "Yes, I believe you can."

He looked away. "We argued that day over who would drive the truck in the convoy. He lost the argument, so I drove. I pushed him and pushed him to let me drive, so he did. The roadside bomb blew the passenger side of the truck all to hell, and Michael with it."

She cringed. "You blame yourself."

"Of course I do."

"But—"

"If I'd given in and let him win this one argument, just once, he'd be alive today. Don't ya get it? You would've grown up with him . . . with him instead of me. I promised your mother I'd bring him back . . . but . . . not in a box."

She winced and wrapped her arms around her middle, rocking back and forth.

"I always have to win. Even with my best friend. It got your father killed."

She turned that over in her mind. "Hmm—guess we're not so different in the arrogance department, are we?"

"Joanie, I'm sorry that—"

"It was the bomb that killed Michael, not you."

She was unprepared for his reaction.

Chapter 61

Bill broke down and wept openly, hands to his head, yanking his hair like he was pulling noxious weeds.

The sound cracked something inside Joanie. She peered through the crack and saw him with different eyes. The day she'd lost her father—a man she'd never known existed—he'd lost his best friend.

As the firelight died down, so did his weeping. Finally, he heaved a great sigh and rubbed his face with the sleeve of his sweatshirt.

Joanie tried not to stare, but couldn't resist and braved a peek at him. He looked back at her, but she couldn't hold his gaze and turned her face to the warmth of the fire.

"Bet you've never seen a grown man cry like a baby, have you? Sorry if I made you uncomfortable. I'm surprised you're still sitting here."

"And where would I go? Not that this is so bad. At least I'm not alone . . . and . . . and I found out some stuff."

She sat up. "Hey, the fire's going out. I'd better get some wood and stir it up a little."

She busied herself bringing logs from the wood box and some kindling, poking at the fire until she had it blazing again.

"You really know how to get a fire going, don't you?" he asked.

"I bet you're not just talking about *this* fire, are you?" she teased. "I took a class once in how to be a smart-aleck kid and drive your parents crazy. Passed with flying colors."

Before she sat down again, she checked his ankle. "Need some more snow?"

"Not yet," he replied. "I want to tell you something else."

Dropping into her chair, she steeled herself, hoping he wouldn't go into more detail about her father's death.

He waited until she gave him a reluctant nod.

"Michael and I talked about a lot of things when we were in Iraq. But there were two subjects he talked about the most—Jesus and your mother."

Joanie ground her teeth and closed her eyes. She didn't want to hear the God stuff.

"All he could think about was getting back home to her. And there's something else too."

"What?"

"He wanted children. He dreamed of holding Susan's baby in his arms. He talked about having lots of children—both of them wanted a large family. They had everything planned out. After he got home, they'd both work for five years, then your mother would quit and start having babies."

"Bill, I—" Joanie couldn't force the words past the lump in her throat. She swallowed hard. Unable to breathe, she felt like she was drowning, the dark water flowing over her head. She flailed, trying to get back to solid ground—anywhere where life made sense again.

His voice pressed on relentlessly. "He wanted *you*—even though he never got the chance to know you, didn't even know he was a father. Still, he lived for the moment he would see your face."

Joanie grabbed at the first rock that presented itself and pulled herself out of the dark, swirling water.

She threw the rock. "And you wouldn't even adopt me."

His face crumpled.

He leaned over in his chair like he was trying to fold himself up as small as he could. No sound came from him. He buried his face in the blanket covering his legs, hands gripping the arms of the chair.

Joanie looked away. But she was glad she'd said it and didn't care how much it hurt him. Didn't care that her mother . . .

Without warning, a sob escaped her lips. She bent double, covering her face with her hands, and wailed her sorrow into the firelit room. Her heart railed at the heavens, every tear an indictment against a God who would allow such tragedy, such mindless grief, such injustice.

She spent herself, her grief lying in shards around the filthy cabin floor. She sat up again, eyes dull, head pounding, to find Bill once more staring at her, obviously more to say on his mind.

His eyes never left hers as he continued. "As much as he talked about your mom and their life together, there's someone else he talked about more. Michael loved Jesus with his whole heart. He used to say that's why he became a soldier—the people in Iraq we went to protect needed Jesus too. He wanted to give them one more day to meet Jesus. That's what he used to say. And something else—"

"Don't even go there with me. I don't want anything to do with a God who lets my father die . . . instead of . . . instead of—"

His gaze pierced hers. "Instead of me? Is that what you were going to say?"

"Yeah. That's what I meant. You should have died instead of my father. And I must be some kind of screwed-up kid to say that . . ." Joanie dropped her face to her hands.

"No, you're not screwed up. Remember, you said it was the bomb that killed him, not me. You were right. You're a victim of that bomb too, and so is your mother. It blew Michael right into heaven, but at the same time, it blew your family apart."

She stared at him, unable to look away. "Do you really believe my dad's in heaven?"

"No doubt in my mind. Do you want to hear what his last words to me were?"

"I . . . I guess."

"He always talked to me about Jesus, but I was like you—I didn't want to hear it, and mostly I blew him off. I didn't think I needed religion or church. But your dad was never discouraged, never gave up talking to me about it, or to anyone else, for that matter. He used to say, 'It's not religion I'm talkin' about, Mr. Bill—it's a relationship. And I'm not even talking about going to church. I'm talking about *being* the church.'"

"Huh?"

He chuckled. "Yeah, that's what I used to say. But not anymore."

"What do you mean?"

Instead of answering her question, he asked her again, "Are you sure you want to hear his last words?"

"Yes."

"All right. He said, 'Take care of Susan for me.' And then, right before he died, he said, 'Believe in Jesus, Bill . . . Believe in Jesus and follow him.'" Bill stopped, choking on his next words.

"And after that day, I turned my back so completely on God that even Susan noticed. It wasn't only the war that changed me— it was the day I held your father as he died. I vowed I'd take care of Susan, but also something else. I vowed that I'd never have anything to do with Michael's God—the one who let me win the argument, the one who knew right where that bomb was, the one who knew Michael would be sitting in the passenger seat."

Joanie's eyes filled with tears again.

"I didn't blame the enemy, or the bomb, or even myself. I blamed God. That's what we do when life gets ugly."

Yeah, I know about ugly.

Joanie didn't think she'd be able to come to terms with this God, but she did have a question burning inside her. "What did you mean, 'but not anymore'?"

He took a deep breath before answering. "Last night, before we knew you'd . . . left . . . your mother and I both decided to follow Jesus."

She had no idea what that meant. Follow Jesus? What did that even look like?

"Joanie, you don't have to say anything. I know you have a lot to process, and your mother and I have hurt you beyond reason, way beyond what any kid deserves, but we wanted you to know. And we also want you to have something."

"What?"

He leaned up in his chair and reached into his jacket pocket, but as he did so, his foot shifted and the stool fell over with a thud. Letting out a yell, he leaned forward and tried to pick up his leg by grabbing the belt wrapped around it.

Joanie threw the quilt off and sprang to his side. "Oh my gosh, that must have hurt. Here, let me help you." She gently righted the stool and repositioned his ankle.

"I'd better get some more snow on that—I completely forgot."

She stepped into the kitchen and found a large plastic mug in the cupboard.

"It'll only take a minute," she said, noting the sweat on his brow.

Forgetting to look out the window first, she unbolted the door. It creaked noisily as she opened it and swung the flashlight around quickly. Then she reached out, digging the cup into the snow-filled bucket.

Hearing what sounded like a faint grunt, she jerked the flashlight left. A pair of beady eyes stared back like twin headlights.

Joanie jumped to her feet, a scream trapped in her throat. She heard the scrape of claws on the wood porch and smelled a pungent odor. Sickening, like rotten fish. The small eyes fixed on her at knee level, then swiftly rose until they hung two feet above her head.

She froze, unable to move or make a sound.

Then the creature moved again, and she saw the outline of the massive head.

A bear!

 # Chapter 62

"Joanie? What is it?" Bill sat up and saw her frozen silhouette in the doorway.

He heard a grunt, then a clicking sound from the porch. For one terrifying instant, the hot desert swamped his consciousness. He heard the rumble of the truck, saw Michael's farm-boy grin next to him, heard the blast and Michael's scream as he blew out the passenger door.

"Michael!" His guttural yell filled the cabin. He jumped to his feet, gun stretched out in front of him.

But it was Joanie who'd screamed. She slammed the door so hard that it swung back open and crashed against the wall. She backed into the room and tripped over her own feet, sprawling on the floor between Bill and the doorway. The desert fled, chased out by Joanie's whimper.

She reached out and clutched his boot.

He shoved the gun into his pocket. Oblivious of the pain in his lower leg, he bent forward and grabbed her sweatshirt by the hood, hauling her away from the door. With one hand, he thrust her behind him.

"Get back and stay back."

She scrabbled behind his chair and cowered there.

Jerking the gun out of his pocket, he whirled around to face the bear.

The creature roared, then slammed its forelegs to the porch, rattling the windows and cracking boards under its feet.

Bill took one swift step forward. Holding the gun at waist level, he grabbed the door and slammed it shut, dropping the iron latch in place.

Joanie's voice squeaked behind him. "Bill? What do we do?"

"Keep quiet, okay? Maybe it'll go away if it thinks we're not in here."

"It already knows—"

"Shh—"

The bear stomped again. Then they heard a noise like fingernails on a chalkboard—the bear raking its claws from the top of the door down. Then a sound like a battering ram against the heavy board door. The latch gave, and the door swung open again, crashing against the wall.

Bill remembered what Tom had told him about bears. He grabbed the flashlight from where Joanie had dropped it. Shining it into the beast's eyes, he yelled, waving his arms and trying to make himself bigger. It backed away a step or two, lowered its head, and wagged it back and forth, huffing and pawing the porch. It never took its eyes from Bill, like red laser beams boring into his own.

This wasn't working.

Joanie moaned, attracting the bear's attention.

It rose to its hind legs—from just a few feet away it looked like a mountain—and now Bill could see it was a male.

He judged it to be five feet or more. Why was it out there? No hump, so not a grizzly. Why wasn't it asleep in its den somewhere—

The bear dropped to all fours and filled the cabin with its roar—a cross between a scream and a growl. Bill had never heard anything like it before. Adrenaline shot through his body as the bear launched itself toward the doorway.

Joanie screamed.

The bear roared back as it tried to squeeze its hulk into the cabin.

Bill aimed the .44 at the bear's head and fired, then pointed the weapon at its chest and pulled the trigger smoothly two more times, the blasts in the small room deafening. The two in its chest hit cleanly. The one to its head sliced through an ear.

The bear dropped, its body thudding to the porch, its head landing inside the doorway. The massive paws jerked and gouged the porch as blood spread under the body.

Bill looked back and met Joanie's eyes, a shaky smile on his face. "I think I got it—"

Her eyes widened, and she shrieked. "Dad, look out. It's getting up—"

He spun around.

The bear had its front feet under itself, its hot, red eyes fastened on him. It roared again, obliterating Joanie's scream.

Staring down the beast's throat from a mere two feet away, Bill gagged at the smell of rotten flesh. He saw bits of the bear's last meal sticking to its massive incisors.

Bill didn't hesitate a second longer. He limped one step closer and sent two rounds into its mouth and one between its eyes, then reached into his pocket for the speed loader Tom had given him. Standing on his good leg, he opened the chamber and dumped the spent casings, then reloaded. The bear didn't move again, but Bill waited, gun aimed at its head. He heard Joanie get to her feet behind him and motioned her to stay where she was.

The back of the beast's head had blown apart. Blood and tissue seeped over the floorboards of the porch and leaked through the cracks onto the ground below. He stepped cautiously over the bear and poked his head outside. Not seeing or hearing anything, he stepped back into the room and shoved the bear's head out of the doorway, shutting and engaging the splintered latch as best he could.

Joanie stood across the room, eyes like two saucers in her ghost-white face.

Bill stumbled to his chair and sat down, groaning in pain.

Joanie lurched around the chair and dropped to her knees in front of Bill, then leaned forward and grabbed him around the waist. She clung to him, shaking like an aspen leaf in the wind.

Chapter 63

"Are you okay?" She threw a backward glance at the door. "Is it dead?"

"Yes, I'm fine, honey. And yes, it's dead," he said, stroking her hair. He tried to pry her arms away, but she had an iron grip on him.

"You saved my life, Dad. You saved my life—"

"Are *you* all right?" Bill asked, hand on her chin, tipping her face up.

"Yeah, scared, that's all. I've never seen a bear up close except at the zoo. Weren't you scared? Even a little?"

"Of course I was. But I was scared for you, honey. I had a gun and you didn't."

She stared at the dark stain on the floor. "It was so big. They don't look so big in a zoo."

"No, I guess they don't. It was probably scrounging for food or something, although I'd think it should be hibernating this time of year. Now that I think of it, though, Tom did say that sometimes they wake up and hunt for food. But we weren't cooking anything, and I didn't notice a garbage can around. Did you?"

"When we were here before, we went all around the place and I didn't see one." Her round eyes grew wider. "Are you saying the bear smelled us and wanted to eat us? Maybe there's more—"

"Bears don't usually *want* to eat people. Mostly they're scared of us. But something brought him here. And it's a male, of that I'm sure. Females don't get so big."

"Is it a grizzly?"

"No, don't think so. No hump, and grizzlies are bigger still than this bear. Although it seems big enough. I wonder if it's what they call a cinnamon black bear. Tom told me there are a few around here—they almost look like a small grizzly."

"But what if there's another—"

He laid a finger over her lips. "Don't worry. If there *were* any more out there, they're long gone now. They wouldn't stick around after all that screaming and shooting. And I have more ammo. We'll be all right. I promise."

Joanie rotated and faced the fire but remained at his feet, with her head pillowed on his legs. She reached and pulled the quilt off her chair and spread it over herself.

"What was that back there, when you yelled—you said 'Michael.' Your face looked funny and—"

"Never mind that now. It's . . . something that happens sometimes. I've never talked to you about it because you're too young—you don't need to know."

"Really, Dad? Too young? After today? I've heard of PTSD, you know. I watch the news sometimes and read books. And I've heard some pretty bad stuff already, ya know?"

Bill reached down and smoothed her hair away from her face and patted her cheek.

"I don't have those episodes very much anymore, but when that bear made that clicking noise with its mouth, all of a sudden I was back in Iraq—on the day your father died."

Joanie faced him and knelt in front of his chair again. She reached up and gripped his wrists.

"I think I've misjudged you, Bill . . . I mean, Dad—"

Bill waved his hand, silencing her.

"But—"

He leaned over and cupped her face with both hands.

"Now let's get one thing straight. You do not have to call me Dad because I shot a bear, okay? You know now who your real dad was, so I won't take offense."

Joanie pulled Bill's hands from around her face and laid them in his lap, covering them with her own. Something loosened in her chest, something familiar and rock hard, and it was good to feel it float away, like the lightest of feathers.

Say it. Now. The thought traveled eighteen inches from her head to her heart.

"Here's what I think. Michael was my father, yes, and I'm proud to think of him as my father. But he never got the chance to be my *dad*. Being a dad is different than being a father. You've been my dad for fourteen years, and . . . and . . . I don't want that to stop. Dad."

Bill laid his hands on her shoulders. "I don't deserve that. But I do make you this one promise. From here on out, I *will* be your dad in every sense of the word. I'll always tell you the truth and take care of you, and I promise to be there for you and your mom. Deal?"

She thought her heart would burst. "Deal."

Bill stared at her a moment, then reached into his zippered jacket pocket and drew out two items. He studied one for a moment, then handed it to Joanie.

"Here's what I was going to give you before that darned bear showed up. I never go anywhere without these. They're reminders."

She gazed at the old photo in her hand, wide eyed. "Is this . . . is this—"

"That's me on the right and your father on the left, the day we shipped out to Iraq. We were a few years older than you are right now."

Childish wonder filled her voice. "I look like him. I look like my father."

He tenderly smoothed wisps of hair away from her cheek. "I've always thought so."

Bill watched her as she ran a finger over Michael's face, as if inspecting every square inch of it, her eyes glued to the face of the man who'd loved her mother so long ago, the man who'd longed to hold his child even though he never knew she existed.

Pain and regret crashed through Bill's chest as she touched his eyes—blue like hers. She ran her thumb over his hair, scraggly under the cap he always wore low over his forehead. She traced his square face and strong chin. He and Bill stood side by side, one arm across each other's shoulders, their other arms raised in youthful triumph, their expressions daring anyone to separate them.

Her voice was gravelly with emotion. "He has kind eyes. And my hair's the same color as his—when I don't mess around coloring it."

Bill waited for her to process this first sight of her father.

"I can't believe how much I'm like him," she said, her voice breaking. "I always wondered why I didn't look much like you or Mom. I thought maybe it was a generational throwback thing or something. Like maybe I look more like my great-great-somebody from the eighteen hundreds."

"You do resemble your mother a little, especially when you're mad."

Joanie giggled, sweet music to his ears. "And I guess you see that face the most, huh?"

He shrugged diplomatically. "Maybe. But you're right. You look more like Michael than you do her."

"Who took the picture?"

"Your mother. She was crying while she took it, as I recall. It was so hard for them to say goodbye to each other."

Joanie put the picture to her lips. "Thank you. Can I keep this?"

"Of course. That's why I grabbed it from my bag when we started the search for you. I was determined to give it to you. That's why I knew we would find you. I wasn't about to break another promise to your mother."

He held out his hand again and dropped something hard and cold into Joanie's.

"And you can keep these too."

"His dog tags?" She shook her head. "No, you keep them, Dad. You were his friend."

"And you're his daughter. There's one thing you need to learn. When I make up my mind, I don't go back on it. I've made up my mind on this. Michael would want *you* to have them. Maybe he's even watching us now."

Her eyes glistened as she slipped the chain over her neck.

"Thanks, Dad. I mean it. I . . . I know I've been a jerk—"

"I was a jerk first, way before you were even born."

She fingered the dog tags around her neck and focused on the photograph again.

Such wasted time . . . all these years. Why had he done it? He could kick himself.

"Dad?"

"Yes?"

"Aren't there any other pictures of him? That I can have?"

He had anticipated that question and was hoping she wouldn't ask. He took a deep breath. "No, there aren't. I was stupid back then. I insisted your mom get rid of every picture of him after we were married. This is the only one left. It's been in my wallet since that day—I could never part with it—and I kept the tags in the safe. I never travel anywhere without them. They remind me of . . . of the promise I made to him—the one to take care of your mother. I'm so sorry, Joanie." His heart broke at the expression on her face. One more failure.

It was his own arrogance that had led them all the way from that day to this. If only he'd listened to someone besides himself, had considered someone other than himself . . .

Joanie was quiet for a moment, pressing the picture to her heart and swallowing hard.

"It's okay. I have this one. And I'm never going to let it out of my sight. But I have another question."

"What's that?"

"What about my dad's family? You said his mom and dad—my grandparents—died, but didn't anyone else in the family know that Mom and Dad were married, that she was pregnant?"

"There wasn't anyone else. Your mom's family was small, her sister and one aunt somewhere—she didn't even know her. I think your aunt Aimee asked about it once—the timing, I guess—but you know she's so self-centered, it was easy for your mom to make something up. It wasn't that hard to keep everything secret, especially since we moved around a bit before we settled in Sand Point. And Michael was an only child."

She seemed satisfied with that, like she'd finally gotten all her questions answered.

"Do you think the others will be back soon?"

He knew she was trying to get off the emotional roller coaster they'd been on. It was clear to him that she'd had about all she could take. Glancing at his watch, he couldn't believe how much time had slipped by.

"I expect so."

"I hope they don't run into any more bears." She clutched the quilt to her chin.

"Probably not. But if they do, it'll have to face Tom and that rifle of his, and that's one man I wouldn't want to tangle with in the woods on a dark night, even if I were a bear."

He chucked her under the chin. "Let's not worry about it, okay? There's nothing we can do except wait, and there's no sense borrowing trouble."

Joanie stilled her hands in her lap. "That's what Mom always used to say when I was younger, the part about not borrowing trouble. Still does sometimes. She said her grandmother used to say that each day has enough trouble of its own."

"Wise women, especially your mom. I guess we should both listen to her, huh?" he said with a smirk.

"Do you need some more snow on your ankle? I could get some, but that bear—" She started to get up.

Bill stayed her with a hand on her arm. "No, honey, I don't need any snow. They'll be back soon, I'm sure."

Joanie settled back down at his feet, wrapped in the quilt.

He kept his face pointed at the window. He didn't want her to see the anxiety he knew must be etched there.

Her head dropped, her chin settled into the quilt, and she closed her eyes.

It seemed like only a few minutes had passed when Bill jerked awake. By his watch, though, a couple of hours had gone by. What had awakened him? Then he knew. A step sounded on the porch, then a grunt.

Joanie jerked upright at his feet.

"What is it?"

He silenced her with a hand over her mouth as he drew the .44 again.

# Chapter 64

Joanie, the lavender quilt wrapped over her coat, didn't think she'd be able to take one more step when they trudged over the rise and saw the bridge at the back of the inn. After the last fright, thinking another bear had found its way to the cabin, then hearing Tom's voice hollering through the door, she knew she was done.

She leaned over Bill's litter and grasped his shoulder. "We're here, Dad."

As they approached the back side of the inn and began the trek across the bridge, Susan burst out the back door.

She charged forward and enveloped Joanie in a tight hug, crying and laughing at the same time. "Joanie! Oh, Joanie! I was so worried. Are you okay, honey?" She stepped back, wiping tears away, inspecting her daughter from head to toe.

"Mom, I'm fine. It's Dad who's hurt." She stepped to the side, trying to avoid another hug from her mother and the tide of emotion that came with it.

Susan bent to hug him, almost tumbling him out of the litter.

"Here, ma'am, let's get him inside. He needs a comfortable chair by the fire and some food," Dr. Mason said.

"Thank you so much for helping my husband and daughter. And you too, officers," she said to the two deputies who'd accompanied the rescue team. "I can't thank you all enough."

Dr. Mason took her arm. "Ma'am, I'm glad I was available when Tom called. And glad we've got phone service now." He helped Susan and Joanie across the bridge, walking just behind the deputies, who carried Bill between them.

After settling Bill in the living room, the elderly doctor redressed the wound on his forehead. After one more inspection of his ankle, he stood and pronounced himself satisfied.

"Keep him warm, hydrated, and fed. Give him Tylenol for pain, some ibuprofen for the swelling, and let him rest. He should be fine in a day or two. And, Bill, stay off that ankle for at least a week. Ice it every couple of hours," he instructed. "And don't forget to have it checked out by your own physician when you get back home."

Tom's gaze swiveled toward the stairs. "Oh, here you are, Barb. We have some old crutches around here, don't we? You know, from your sprained knee a few years back?"

Barb didn't answer. She'd stopped at the bottom of the stairs, gaze locked on Joanie—then walked over and fingered the blanket. "Can I have it?"

"Of course." Joanie unwrapped herself and handed it over, wondering at the mist clouding Barb's eyes.

Barb brought it to her face and breathed deeply, then held it out to Tom. "Remember this, honey?"

Tom's gaze zeroed in on the blanket. He took it from her, stroking a tiny bumblebee. "Remember how she thought the bees would sting her and we had to convince her they weren't real?"

"She called it her buzzy blankie."

Joanie watched, confusion wrinkled between her eyes. "Who? Who are you talking about?"

Tom inhaled and exhaled slowly before he answered. "Our daughter, Katie, who died when she was two. Leukemia—"

He turned his back, shoulders heaving.

Barb took Joanie's hand in hers. "Her blanket kept you warm at the cabin?"

"Yes, ma'am, it did. But I didn't know . . . I had no idea—"

"It's okay, honey. I . . . I'm glad she came to your rescue. Or at least her blanket did."

Tom came to Barb's side then and put his arm tight around her shoulders. He kissed her cheek and whispered, "Crutches?"

She slid the backs of her hands across her eyes. "Yes, I know right where they are. I'll get them for you." She folded the blanket, leaving it on the table, and went out. Coming back with the crutches, she placed them where Bill could reach them.

Dr. Mason eyed them. "Make sure you adjust them for his height—they look like a midget used them before, they're so short." He glanced at Barb. "Sorry, ma'am. Didn't mean to belittle you."

Tom chuckled. "Nice pun, Doc."

The doctor scratched his head, joined in the laughter, then eyed Joanie. "And you, young lady, no more solo hiking trips for you."

"Yes, sir. And thank you for helping my dad." She reached to shake his hand.

He took it gently, covering it with his other hand.

Then, face scarlet, she withdrew it. Glancing around in the sudden silence, she saw everyone staring at her like she was a stranger.

"Hey, I'm only trying to be nice. Is that against the law or something?"

Tom smirked at her. "Not here, it's not. Nice is what we do around here."

"Okay, I'd better get along now," Dr. Mason said, closing his bag and grabbing his coat.

"Thanks again, Doc," Tom said. "Come spring we'll have to scout out that new fishing place I was telling you about the other day."

"You got it. Okay, folks, I hope you have a safe trip back to your homes. Take care, and it was nice meeting you," Dr. Mason said, with handshakes all around.

"And you, ma'am," he said to Susan. "I assume you'll be doing the driving? I don't think your husband should be—"

"Oh, I'm sure I can—"

Joanie waved an arm, seeing an opportunity. "I could drive—"

Bill picked up the crutch and poked the back of her leg. "Oh, sure you could, Joanie. There is the small problem of being under-age and no license yet. No, I'll—"

Susan's voice rose above the din. "Yes, I will do the driving."

Dr. Mason pointed at Bill. "Good. Don't let him talk you out of it. Doctor's orders."

Tom and Barb saw him out the back door, then came back into the room with the coffeepot and cups.

"There's still some breakfast casserole left from this morning." She looked at Bill and Joanie. "Would you two like some?" She didn't have to ask twice.

"No," she said as Bill started to rise. "I'll bring it out here. You stay right where you are."

Susan moved over to sit close to Joanie. They sat side by side on the sofa, Susan clearly unwilling to let her daughter out of her sight.

Barb came back with breakfast on a tray, followed by the Elliotts, who'd decided to stay out of the way by cleaning up after breakfast. Stevie tried to jump and grab a plate.

"You already ate, little man," Steve said, catching him by the nape of the neck. "This is for the ones who haven't eaten yet."

"Aww, Dad, I'm still hungry—"

"There's still plenty if he wants some," Barb said.

"Okay, Stevie, but wait until the others have been served. Deal?"

Stevie nodded and sat down to wait, fidgeting. Finally, he was given a plate and dug in as if he hadn't already had a huge breakfast.

After they'd eaten their fill, Tom cleared his throat loudly. "So

I was wondering. I didn't ask you about it while we were walking back, seein' as how you both looked a bit stressed and kind of out of it."

"Ask about what?" Bill answered, mouth full.

"What's the story about the bear on the cabin porch, hmmm? You know, the one that was so big and so dead it took me, both deputies, and the good doctor to drag the smelly thing away? *That* story. Must be an interesting one."

He looked from Bill to Joanie, then back at Bill.

Neither one said a word—just grinned at each other.

Chapter 65

Barb stared down the length of the table. "Bear? On the cabin porch? What are you talking about?"

Tom shrugged, thinking Barb sounded a bit hysterical. "Calm down. I'm just saying what we saw."

"Dang—sounds like I missed an adventure," Steve exclaimed.

Susan looked at Joanie, fear in her eyes. "Joanie, what's this? A bear?"

Bill grinned at Joanie. "It was nothing. No one got hurt. Really, it was no big deal. You tell 'em, honey."

"Mom, he was a true hero. I've never seen anything like it—well, maybe on TV. This huge bear was trying to break into the cabin. It was right in front of me when I tried to get snow out of the bucket for . . . oh, never mind that part. It was the biggest bear I've ever seen. Way bigger than the ones at the zoo. I was so scared, I couldn't move. Then he ran over, on his bad ankle even, and pulled me back and shot it right in the chest and head. And then shot him some more." She paused. "It was really messy too."

Stevie squeaked in awe, staring at Bill. "Cool!" He jumped to his feet and ran to Steve. "Daddy, can we go see it?" He tugged on Steve's sleeve. "I wanna see the bear—"

Steve laughed. "Uh . . . that would be a no. Go sit down."

"Aww, Daddy—" He trudged back around the table and plopped down. "Daddy—"

Sally took him by the chin and put a finger over his lips. "Hush."

"Oh, Joanie, you could've been killed—" Susan lifted the knuckles of one hand to her mouth.

Joanie leaned over and put her arm around her mother. "It's okay. Dad was there."

Tom stared at Joanie, frowning. *Hmm . . . something's changed.*

Bill took the last bite of casserole and sipped his coffee. "The only thing we couldn't figure out is why the bear was there to begin with. Shouldn't it have been hibernating?"

Tom drummed his fingers on the table. "Hmm, ordinarily, yes. But with the mild winter we've had—until this weekend—if he woke up, he was probably hungry. And you know what I noticed when we first got back to the cabin this morning?"

"What?"

"Pieces of bloody gauze on the porch, and also back by the trees where we fetched up after you did your bowling ball thing down the hill. That bear was rootin' around for food, then followed the blood trail right to your front door."

Bill looked thunderstruck. He gestured at Steve. "So we invited the bear to come and get us?"

"Pretty much. I should've picked them up before we left you and Joanie." Tom shook his head. "I screwed up."

"Don't leave me out," Steve said. "Guess I'm guilty, too. I dropped at least a couple."

Susan scooted her chair closer to Joanie and took her hand. "Honey, Bill and I have a lot to tell you."

Tom tensed, waiting for Joanie's sarcasm to emerge. He watched her face for signs of her well-developed teenage aversion to matters of the heart. He was pleasantly surprised.

"Mom, he told me a lot. Really, it's okay. You don't have to say

anything," Joanie replied. "We don't have to talk about it now. And
. . . I'd rather not." She tried to withdraw her hand.

Susan kept a firm grasp. "No, Joanie, we do. I'm so sorry we
lied to you. Forgive us?"

The question hung between them. Joanie turned away from her
mother and gazed out the window at the morning sun in the cloudless
sky, the snow gleaming with a million pinpoints of sparkling lights.

Storm's gone.

She slowly took the picture out of her pocket and stared at it
for a moment, then slipped her hand inside the neck of her shirt.
The dog tags glinted in the sunlight streaming in the window.

Susan's eyes—round as saucers—strayed to Bill's.

He smiled and nodded at her.

No one made a sound while Joanie contemplated the picture
and slid her thumb over her father's name on the tags. She looked
up at her mother then, tears glistening in her eyes.

She gulped. "I'm sorry you lost him. That . . . *we* lost him."

Susan's face contorted with anguish.

"And I'm so sorry never to have known my father," she continued. "Bill told me about him, about you and Michael when
you were young—oh, so many things I needed to know. I wish I'd
grown up with you and him. I can't pretend that it doesn't hurt—it
does—that you didn't tell me." Her voice broke then. She didn't
want to hurt her mother again, but the hardness needed to be said
out loud.

"There'll always be hurt there, I think."

Susan lost it then, anguished sobs stopping the conversation.

Joanie didn't touch her, didn't reach out to comfort her this
time. She stared at her plate, wondering what to say.

She felt her mother's hand glide over her arm. It was what she
needed. She grabbed Susan and clung to her for a long moment.

Joanie drew back and met Bill's gaze.

"Mom," she said, keeping her eyes on Bill, "Michael was my father, and I'm proud of him, for who he was, for his bravery. But as I told Bill last night, even though Michael was my father, Bill is my dad. And I'm . . . I'm . . . proud of him too. Of both of them."

Joanie looked back at Susan. "Maybe if you tell me more about you and him, like when you were kids . . . maybe"—her eyes strayed back to Bill—"if I know my father, I'll be able to figure myself out."

Susan nodded. "Yes, I'd like that too, honey."

Joanie clenched her hands in front of her. "I'm sorry for the way I've acted. You and Dad didn't deserve what I've been dishing out since—oh, I don't know—since forever. I don't know how long it will take for me to not be such a dweeb anymore, but can *you* forgive *me*?"

"Oh, honey, of course I can. Already have." Susan gave Joanie a tender kiss on the forehead.

Joanie pulled away, a frown deepening. She surveyed each one around the table in turn.

"And the rest of you too. I don't know why you put up with me."

Tom leaned forward. "What choice did we have, young lady?" His voice was tender though.

She gave him a small smile. "None, I guess."

"Forgiveness isn't an option with us." He lifted his eyes to Barb's. "It's the way we live—or try to."

Joanie stiffened, then sat back in her chair.

"I'm . . . I'm not sure about all this God stuff, ya know?" She sent a sidelong glance to Susan. "I hope you're not gonna get all religious on me or anything. I don't think I'm ready for that."

Joanie expected admonishment but was saved from it when Stevie piped up. "That's okay. God's ready for you!"

Joanie relaxed as everyone burst into laughter.

"What? Why's everybody laughing?" Stevie demanded, a frown wrinkled between his eyes.

Steve leaned over and cupped his son's small face. "It's okay, son. You said exactly the right thing."

Chapter 66

To om stood at the bottom of the stairs the next morning, a large suitcase in each hand. "Susan," he yelled. "Is that everything? Can I carry anything else down for you?"

Why did women have to pack so much when they traveled? Bill only had one bag to Susan's two.

"There's one more up here that I can't quite manage on the stairs, if you wouldn't mind."

Correction. Three bags.

He dropped the two pieces of luggage where he stood and headed up the stairs again, only to meet Joanie coming down with said suitcase, an oversized garment bag she could barely hang on to as she struggled to keep her backpack from slipping off her shoulders.

"Here, let me get that for you." He took the heavy bag from her.

"Thanks, Mr. Masters. I guess I can't manage it after all."

She cast a glance back at her mother. "Mom, do you need help with anything else?"

"No—oh, did you double-check your bathroom? I didn't."

"On it." She spun a U-turn on the stairs, almost wiping Tom out with her backpack as it swung around. Laughing, they steadied each other to keep from tumbling down the stairs.

"Mr. Masters! I'm sorry—that could've been bad."

"Yeah, we don't need any more injuries, do we?" He held his hand out. "Ladies first."

He stood aside, and she started back up the stairs.

Tom continued on down, then had to maneuver around Barb coming up the stairs.

"Wow. I think we need a traffic light on the stairway."

"You might be right. I'm just gonna go see if they need any more help." She squeezed by.

Tom reached the bottom with no more mishaps and entered the living room, loaded down with the three bags.

After setting the luggage by the door, Tom perched on the sofa near Bill. "How's the ankle this morning?"

"A little sore, but Susan gave me some Tylenol and it's working now. It'll be fine."

Tom rose and threw another log into the woodstove. He poked the fire until it blazed, cranked the fan up a notch, then sank into his recliner and picked up his coffee cup.

"Sure glad the power's back on. We were just about out of generator gas." He glanced out the window. "Quite a weekend, huh, Bill?"

"I'd say so. Not what we expected, that's for sure. We should've been getting on a plane to come back home after a wild weekend in Las Vegas. But here I sit—sprained ankle, recovering from a bear attack, no slot money in my wallet, and . . . and . . ." Bill paused. His face crinkled up in a slow smile.

"And the best gift I could ever receive," he finished in a husky voice. "Las Vegas has nothin' on this place."

"*That* we can agree on—"

"Wouldn't trade this weekend for anything."

"Neither would I, my friend."

Shrieking laughter erupted overhead.

Tom looked up. "Wonder what they're up to now."

Bill grinned. "Maybe it's best we don't know."

"You've got that right."

"I'd like to say—"

Tom held up a finger at a sudden commotion. "Hold that thought."

Taking the stairs two at a time and missing the last step, Stevie landed in a giggling heap at the bottom.

Joanie stepped down behind him and bent to give him a hand up.

He clutched a small device. "Can I really keep it?"

She roughed his hair. "I said you could, didn't I?"

"Keep what, Stevie?"

He held it out to his father. "This game."

Steve took it from him, turning it over in his hands.

"Please, Daddy? Can I?"

"It's my old tablet, Mr. Elliott. I brought it along this weekend to . . . anyway, is it okay if he keeps it? All it has on it is some kids' games—no music or anything else. And you can wipe it if you want and put some parental controls on it."

"Are you sure you don't want it, Joanie? Seeing as how your other one—"

"No, I don't need it. I'm thinking about getting a part-time job and earning the money to buy myself a new one."

"Hey, that sounds like a plan, young lady."

He looked at Stevie, hopping first on one foot, then another. "For now I'll put it in my bag, and we'll look it over when we get home. Joanie," he added, "that's generous of you."

Sally stepped forward then and gave Joanie a hug. She whispered something in her ear that made Joanie's face turn beet red.

The Elliotts shook hands and hugged all around. Tom helped Steve carry their bags out to their car.

Sally hung behind, arm around Barb.

Barb squeezed her hand and noted Sally's relaxed posture. "Did you hear anything more about your mom?"

"Yes. I forgot to tell you. She's improving and may get to go home instead of to Spokane. The doctor said he would wait until we arrive before making any decisions."

Barb blew out a breath and smiled wide at her new friend. "Oh, what a relief that must be for you."

"It is. And listen to this. Steve called the store, and they've arranged for him to take another week off. He didn't even argue— well, maybe a little—but that right there's a miracle."

Hearing a loud guffaw in the driveway, they both looked out the screen door and watched Steve shake Tom's hand.

"Steve really admires Tom. He said he kind of reminds him of his dad. This sounds funny now, but I'm so glad we got stranded here." Sally gave Barb another hug. "I'd better go."

"You must come back and see us," Barb said. "It's a whole different kind of fun without the ice storms."

"We've already decided we want to, and we have your email address and phone number. We'll contact you in the spring."

"Don't wait too long. We fill up fast. But you'll be on our priority list—you can be sure of that."

Sally shook Bill's hand and hugged Susan.

"Okay, kiddos, Daddy's waiting. Goodbye, Susan. Goodbye, Bill." She faced Joanie. "And Joanie, you take care of your parents, okay?"

"I sure will. Bye, and . . . it was nice to meet you—*Sally*."

Sally grinned at her, waved, and continued down the front steps, a firm grip on Stevie's collar.

Samantha stepped to Joanie's side, shyly putting her arms around Joanie's waist.

"I'm glad we're friends now, Joanie. I hope we see you again."

"Yeah, me too, twerp." Joanie's voice was gruff, but she softened it with a smile. "You behave yourself, okay? And remember, you have my email address. Ask your mom if we can write to each other. Someone needs to keep an eye on you."

Barb had to marshal herself to keep from giggling out loud at the difference in the two girls. *Thank you, God. You never do anything by halves . . .*

Samantha laughed and ran to the door, then shot a look over her shoulder. "Hey, I need to keep an eye on you too." She marched down the steps, letting the screen door bang behind her.

Barb grinned at Joanie and lifted her shoulders, then followed Samantha out the door.

# Chapter 67

Joanie watched them pull out, thinking how nice it would be to have a little sister. Maybe. "Twerp," she said under her breath.

"You're going to miss her?" Bill asked.

"Right. Miss that little brat?" Yeah, she'd miss her, Joanie thought, sitting next to Bill.

"You sure about that?" He took her hand and tucked it under his arm.

She shrugged. "Maybe a little. Never had a sister before."

"Do you want one? She kinda reminds me of . . . you when you were her age."

"Aww, Dad, come on. Let's not go too far with the sentimental stuff, okay?"

"What sentimental stuff?" Susan asked, coming in from the kitchen with two steaming cups of coffee. She handed one to Bill. "Hmm? What sentimental stuff?"

"Never mind, Mom. He's teasing me."

Susan looked from one to the other. "I see I'm going to have problems with you two." Her mouth lifted in a sly grin. "But it's good to see you holding hands."

Joanie pulled back and removed her hand from Bill's. "Yeah, don't expect it all the time." She put the sarcasm back in her voice.

"You don't fool me, young lady," Susan said with a smile.

Barb entered from the front porch and eyed the heap of luggage by the front door.

"Are you anxious to get on the road? Or do you want to stay longer?"

"I'd like to stay for a little while," Bill answered, "just until the roads dry up a bit."

Susan added her agreement. "Yeah. I'm driving, and I'd feel safer if we waited."

"That's what I was thinking. Tell you what—it's almost eleven now. What if I rustle up an early lunch before you leave? Susan," she added as Tom stomped back up the porch steps, "do you and Joanie want to help? I think we have stuff for tacos. I'm a little tired of leftovers."

"Sure, we'll help. Come on, Joanie. You can chop vegetables for us," Susan said.

"You sure you trust me with a knife? No—don't answer that." Joanie skipped through the kitchen door, barely escaping the playful flick of Susan's finger.

# Chapter 68

"What are they doing? Food again?" Tom asked, closing the door and hanging up his coat.

"Yeah. We're going to leave after lunch when the roads are better, so of course your lovely wife is going to feed us again."

Tom chuckled. "I think I'll go get another cup of coffee. Be right back."

He ambled through the kitchen door, poured some coffee, stopping to give Barb a peck on the cheek. Susan and Joanie bantered with each other as they worked side by side chopping vegetables and shredding cheese.

"Tacos?" Tom asked.

"Yep."

"Good. I'm a little tired of leftovers."

Tom took the coffee carafe with him and set it on the dining room table.

Bill inhaled the aroma from his cup. "Barb should open a coffee shop. She'd probably make a killing."

"You got that right. I don't know how I got so lucky."

"A certain marine would tell me it's not about luck—no such thing."

Tom smiled as he settled in his chair again. "Right again, Soldier." He paused, then added, "I was thinking—let's do a quick debrief about this weekend. I'd like to hear what you think, to continue our conversation from before."

Bill sipped his coffee, avoiding Tom's direct gaze.

"Most times, truth repeated to someone else sticks better."

Bill ran his fingers through his hair, then stroked his chin.

Tom waited, noting the quiver in Bill's hand.

Bill set his cup down, lining it up on the coaster. "I didn't tell you this yet, but I had a short flashback at the cabin when that bear showed up."

Tom sat forward, alert. "You did? What happened?"

"It—the bear—made this weird sound. I'd never heard it before, sort of like—"

"—Clicking?"

"Yeah, that's it."

"I've heard that," Tom said with a grin. "My gramma used to make that sound, too, when she was about ready to wallop on me."

"Joanie was petrified. She stood there, right in its path. I had to do something. I had to save Michael . . . I mean, Joanie." He stopped and set his cup down, hand now shaking badly.

"Go on, Bill. Say it."

"All of a sudden, I was back in the truck with Michael, and we were laughing. Then he was . . . he was . . . gone—blown out the window to the side of the road. Even his seat was gone—the whole side of the cab was blown up. And I heard him screaming. Then I realized. It was Joanie. If she hadn't screamed, maybe Joanie would have been—"

Bill stopped talking and shifted in his seat to meet Tom's eyes. The bright sunlight streaming through the window fell on Bill's face, a stark contrast to the shadow of pain etched there.

Tom lifted his chin and leaned forward. "But she wasn't."

"I couldn't save Michael. If I could go back in time—"

"You can't. Neither can I, or Mack would be alive today. But that's not what happened, for either of us."

Bill looked down at his hands. When he spoke again, Tom sensed another presence. One who listened to Bill pour out his grief.

"I've always had to do things my own way. I've been stubborn and willful, and that's partly what got Michael killed. I told Joanie last night—at the cabin—that I always have to win no matter what. That kind of character trait works well in the world of marketing and sales, but not so much in life."

"Yes. Go on."

"I took advantage of Susan. I rushed her into marriage. I made all the decisions for her, because that's the kind of jerk I am . . . was. I didn't consider her feelings. I didn't consider that she might need some time to grieve for Michael. I decided we needed to move on, and fast."

"Why do you think you did that to her?"

The words rushed out. "Because *I* didn't want to grieve, so I decided she didn't need to either. That's the imbecile I am—"

"Were," Tom interjected. "Why do you think you didn't want to grieve?"

"Because grieving is for sissies."

"And now? What do you think now?"

"That grieving is hard work—it's not for weaklings."

Tom chuckled. "I like the way you think, and in my book, you're exactly right."

They sat in silence, listening to the banter between the women in the kitchen.

"I'll tell you what *I've* learned from this weekend," Tom said. "Do you want to hear?"

"Of course. Enough about me already."

"As you know, Barb and I had a plan for this weekend that didn't include you and the Elliotts. Sorry, but it didn't. Instead, my nephew and his family had to cancel their trip and you guys showed up—and look what happened. God worked on all of us. I think he had to do some work in me before I was in any shape to be used by him in anyone else's life. His plans are always best. And now I think I need to redouble my resolve to help my nephew."

Bill didn't answer right away, clearly deep in thought. Then he looked up, a twinkle in his eyes. "I've got an idea. Maybe a really good idea."

"Oh yeah, what's that?"

"I'm going to a company sales conference in April."

"Okay—"

"Where did you say your nephew—Bob, is it?—lives?"

"In California."

"But exactly where in California?"

"Southern California—Tustin."

"Hmm. I know where that is. It's pretty close to Anaheim, where the conference is—about ten miles down I-5. We're going to be at one of the Disneyland hotels. I haven't told Susan yet, but I've decided to take her and Joanie along with me and make it a little vacation. A real one—you know, where I schmooze with the fam instead of with the blood-sucking clients."

Tom stared at him, a smile playing around the edges of his mouth. "Okay, sounds good. What are you thinking? Come on, give it up."

"I'm thinking I might like to get to know Bob. The conference is only two days. I'm planning to put in for two or three weeks off—I've got vacation time coming—and I might as well use my seniority and position as top salesman two years running to get it. I'll wrap up at the conference, spend some time with Susan and Joanie at Disneyland, and maybe—if he goes for it—look up Bob and his family and introduce myself. What do you think?"

Tom grinned. "I think it sounds like a real master plan—and not only is it a great idea, it's worth some serious prayer between now and April, don't you think?"

"Yep. Have you ever been there. To Tustin, I mean?"

"No, but I do know it's been designated as a Purple Heart city, with quite a network of services for veterans, including a Point Man Outpost. I've researched it. You'll find quite a lot of resources to share with Bob, right in his own area. I'm pretty sure he knows about all of it, but coming from you, a man nearer his own age and with some of the same experiences in the Middle East—I think you, rather than the old man here, might be able to connect with him."

"Old man, my eye. I couldn't keep up with you on that mountain, and I won't forget that."

After making their tacos assembly line fashion, the two families gathered around the table to share their meal. Tom looked around the table at his new friends. Instead of asking the blessing himself as he usually would, he asked Bill to pray.

Bill hesitated, then plunged in. "God, we thank you for this weekend, for keeping us all safe in the storm, and especially for keeping Joanie and me from harm. Thank you for Tom and Barb. Please keep the Elliotts safe as they travel, and us, too, as we head out. I pray that you will bring us all back together someday, in your time." He paused and looked up to find Tom gazing at him with tears in his eyes. Bill gave him a nod and finished his prayer. "And, God, may your plan for me next April be executed, and may the mission be fully accomplished the way you intend. Amen."

As soon as he raised his head, Susan blurted out, "What are you talking about—next April?"

"Yeah, Dad, what mission?"

"Umm . . . we—Tom and I—have something to tell you ladies," he said nervously.

"What?" Barb demanded, matching Susan's tone. "Tom, what's this about?"

Tom threw back his head and laughed, grabbing Barb's hand. "Honey, you're gonna love this. Tell 'em, Bill."

Chapter 69

After waving goodbye to the Brown family, Tom and Barb walked up the driveway arm in arm.

Tom stopped and tilted his head up at the cloudless sky. "Honey, are you thinking what I'm thinking?"

"Maybe. Tell me."

"This was truly the *Master's* Inn this weekend, wasn't it?"

Barb stroked his cheek. "Yes, it was. That's exactly what I was thinking."

"I'm humbled at what happened. I'm praying now, and we should continue to, that Bill and Bob can really connect."

"And don't forget about Joanie. She's so close to making a decision to follow Jesus. Susan and I were talking about it, and she's going to try to get Joanie involved in the little church near them. She said they have quite a thriving youth ministry. And the great thing is that Bill is all in on that." She tipped her face up to his. "Maybe us, too? Start going to church again?"

He smoothed her hair back from her forehead and kissed her.

"Yeah, us too. And Bill promised to keep in touch by email about the trip to California. I can't wait to see what God will do. It'll be another chapter in the story of the Master's Inn, don't you think?"

Barb nodded and squeezed his arm. "Come on, old man. I'm getting cold. How about some hot chocolate and—"

"Cookies?"

Barb answered him by stooping and forming a snowball, then taking quick aim. He backed up, turned, and ran for dear life, laughing all the way, Barb right behind him. After pelting each other, they ran toward the front steps.

Tom stopped and picked up the angel that had been knocked off the post. He brushed a hand tenderly across her face where it'd been chipped.

"I'll get busy and fix this tomorrow."

She stroked the angel's head, her fingers finding Tom's.

They locked eyes, and her wondered gaze drew him all the way back to their beginning, back to a time when they were full of joy and hope and love. After the badness of the war.

And Katie.

Barb looked down, and there she was, playing at their feet in the warm, late-spring sunshine, giggling as a bug climbed up her arm.

Father, what . . .

"Auntie Maggie, look! A pretty bug—"

Then Barb heard that calm, gentle voice from her growing-up years. "Ah, sweetie, you're just as pretty. It's called a ladybug." And Maggie—dressed in her favorite jeans and white tee—picked Katie up and kissed her on the nose. Then she set her back down on the lawn and walked around the corner of the inn and out of sight.

Barb, thunderstruck at her sister's sudden appearance, hurried after her. But rounding the corner, she saw nothing but the shed and the mountains in the distance.

She stood motionless, sniffing the air. Maggie's favorite rose petal scent wafted on the warm breeze.

Barb retraced her steps back to Tom's side. He took her arm

and stared at his feet, where Katie had tenderly placed the ladybug on a leaf. It sat, gently folding and unfolding its wings.

Then Katie jumped up and raced across the yard on stubby legs, begging Tom to give chase, her blond curls waving in the breeze. The last time Barb had seen those beautiful locks, they lay in wisps on her tiny pillow—the last of them in Barb's lap the day she'd gone away. Her shrill, high-toned laughter floated across the rich green grass. And she was barefoot, her toes wiggling. Katie had always hated shoes and socks, the whole two years of her life.

Barb watched incredulously.

This was a scene out of her life. This day actually happened, back before. Before they left, first Maggie, then Katie.

How can this be?

She didn't know, but she didn't want it to end.

"Dada, come and get me!"

Tom looked down at Barb—a smile playing around her lips as she watched Katie.

He lifted his head again and let go of Barb's arm, taking a long step.

"Here I come, Kate! You better run, 'cause you're gonna get tickled when I catch you!"

But he stopped in his tracks and stared, uncomprehending.

What are you giving us, Father?

Katie had somehow grown taller, willowy, and she was wearing a lady's dress, pale blue with a wide belt at the slim waist. Her graceful hand held a wide-brimmed white hat in place in the light breeze. She'd always liked to wear hats, playing dress-up with Barb's.

She bent over and plucked a tulip bloom and stuck it in the colorful band circling the hat.

She grinned at them, her broad smile spreading the freckles on her cheeks, as when she'd been young. Her feet were still bare under her long, slender legs.

Their beloved Katie pirouetted across the grass toward them on her tiptoes, skirt swinging, her fingertips to the sun.

And watching, barely noticeable behind her, his face cracked in a huge smile, was a tall, slender young man in marine dress uniform, purple heart dangling around his neck. Mack stared steadily at Tom, raising his hand in a slow salute. After his right hand snapped back to his side, his brown eyes twinkled with mischief, and he faded away like a mirage in the desert.

"Oh, Tom, did you see?" Barb's question came from far away, her voice young with wonder.

Tom couldn't drag the words from his heart to his mouth.

Enough, Father. I can't take any more . . .

Katie waved and called to them, her grown woman's voice like the low-toned smoothness of a concert cello—words which bypassed the ears and went straight to the soul.

"I'm fine, Daddy. Don't worry, Mama. We'll be together again."

Tom clutched Barb's hand. "Kate—"

"Tom, look. Oh, dear God, look—"

Katie had turned and reached up, a look of supreme joy adorning her face—such a smile as never seen in the shadowlands. Tom barely saw the thin gleaming outline of a massive hand holding hers. Then she shimmered in the sunlight and lifted off the grassy carpet. Her silken dress swirled around her legs. Katie drifted across the road, over the mountains, and finally disappeared like a shooting star.

Tom waited, hoping for another glimpse of her, but he knew it was over . . . for now.

He came back to the moment, squeezed Barb's fingers, and winked, a tear sliding out the corner of his eye and down his weathered cheek.

"She'll be back."

"I know."

Then Tom scooted away from her and ran up the steps—Barb right behind him—shrieking with laughter.

She tried to elbow her way into the doorway before Tom could squeeze through, but he won—and headed straight for the cookies.

As she swung the door shut, taking one last look at the snow-covered mountains in the distance and the twin angels keeping guard on the front steps—she heard the clink of the cookie jar lid and Tom's soft laughter. And in her heart, she heard Katie's soft giggle echo back.

Doesn't get any better than this.

But it will someday, baby girl. Some bright day.

THE END

PREVIOUS BOOKS BY DEB GORMAN

https://debggorman.com

Encountering Jesus amid our flawed lives, we discover He is bigger than our rebellion, our tragedies, and our confusion.

This devotional plunges you into the lives of twelve biblical characters who are mentioned briefly, almost parenthetically, as the stories of well-known players are told. Several of these obscure individuals aren't even named. But God included them in His Word for a reason, and the reason is us. Author Deb Gorman puts flesh on the bones of these shadow people, to name them, to fill in the canvas of their lives so spiritual truths can be extracted.

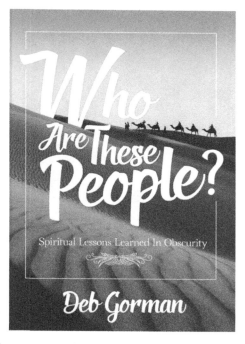

So get ready to meet these personalities in a new way. And the next time you're tempted to think your life is insignificant, that God can't use such a flawed, mistake-ridden person such as yourself, remember: these twelve people probably thought the same, and here you are reading their stories and learning powerful lessons from their encounters with God. God created you to impact others, and that is definitely not insignificant!

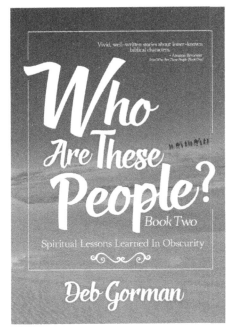

The path of your life will change each time you hold fast to your faith.

This book is about choices. If there is one thing universal in the human experience, it's that we make choices every day. Our choices range from determining how much we'll spend for a cup of coffee to whom we'll spend the rest of our lives with, but only one choice determines where we'll spend eternity.

This devotional immerses you into the lives of six Biblical characters whom God brought to the sharp point of radical decisions—decisions that would change the course of their earthly existences. We might think these six people have nothing to do with us in our century of instant communication, driverless cars, and computers mounted on our wrists, but the earth is old, and humankind hasn't changed. The choices we make each day still determine the next moment, the next year, the next millennium and have far-reaching consequences for the next generation. God included these characters in His Word for a reason, and the reason is us.

Have you ever confronted a fork in the road of life and paused, wondering which way to go? Or maybe you took the path that seemed most logical, without much thought.

Perhaps the new direction was the correct one … but perhaps not. What do you do if you travel the wrong path?

Read the stories of thirteen people from the Bible who stood at the fork and made a choice. See where their journeys took them.

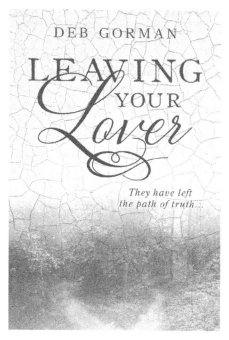

Pause at the fork in your own road and make the right decision, not just for the here and now but for future generations—your children, grandchildren, and generations beyond, doomed to suffer the consequences of a wrong choice and who scream silently at you to go back.

And if you discover you're on the wrong road, don't believe the lie that you can't turn back.

For the first terror-filled step into the great divide will lay out a cross-shaped bridge before you, stained with holy blood—the sure road that will lead you back to the beginning, where you will find grace to start again.

Deb contributed to this Chicken Soup for the Soul anthology, which includes 101 inspirational, compassionate, and empowering stories to help you cope with loss, regain your strength, and find joy in life again.

Losing a loved one is hard. It doesn't matter who it is—it creates a hole in your life.

I lost my only sister to suicide in 1989, and that hole in my heart and in my family is still there.

With these 101 stories, including a short story about my sister, you'll find people just like you who have loved and lost and have learned how to live, love, and even laugh again.